SWEET SENSATION

Rance's eyes glittered with mischief. "You allow my valet to call you Amanda? I hope you don't have designs on him. The man is spoken for."

"Maggie, I know."

"Well, well, you two have been busy exchanging confidences, I see," he said. She detected a touch of disapproval, or was it uneasiness in his voice? "What else did he tell you?"

Amanda shrugged. "Nothing significant," she said. "Did you truly enjoy the ride?"

"As much as this!" He burst into a deep laugh, snatching Amanda into his arms. A frightening shiver ran down her spine as his strong arms held her captive against his hard body. Her face was pressed into the rough cloth of the country jacket near his shoulder. Her heart hammered. She became heady with the overwhelming masculinity surrounding her.

His hands wandered over her back and stroked her neck sensuously beneath her hair. When his arms tightened around her waist, strange sensations darted up her spine. He nuzzled his face into her hair, and his lips grazed her forehead, moving toward her mouth. . . .

AN UNCONVENTIONAL MISS

Alice Holden

Zebra Books
Kensington Publishing Corp.
http://www.zebrabooks.com

ZEBRA BOOKS are published by

Kensington Publishing Corp.
850 Third Avenue
New York, NY 10022

First Printing: April, 1997
10 9 8 7 6 5 4 3 2 1

Printed in the United States of America

Chapter 1

"Good . . . good . . . good."

Amanda Lofton rose up slightly in her saddle and craned her neck in the direction of the overlook from which the staccato kudos emanated. But the dense spring leaves on the oaks and beeches in the intervening spinney obstructed her view.

Earlier that day in her father's office she had checked the estate's daily work sheet which he habitually drew up at the close of the previous day. None of the workmen, she recalled, were scheduled in the vicinity of the overlook.

Hunching over her roan's mane, she whispered, "Easy, Nancy," into the horse's twitching ear and stroked the mare's neck. Her brown riding boots peeped from beneath her cord riding skirt as she slid neatly to the turf her father's sheep had cropped into a tufted mat. Here and there, new growth popped through the parched grass. She dropped the reins. The mare lowered her head and chomped at the meager pickings.

Amanda moved to the rim of the thicket and cocked her head, on the alert for a further utterance from the disembodied voice. A newborn lamb seeking the comfort of its mother bleated in the next meadow. In the distance, rooks cawed, and near her foot a bee buzzed over the pink bloom on a single clover. Her motionless vigil was soon rewarded with "Aye, that's perfect, lad" delivered in a lilt she associated with an Irish brogue.

Determined to get a glimpse of the intruder and his mute companion, she crept forward gingerly on the narrow path she herself had worn through the spinney's tangled undergrowth over a year's time. She paused in her snail-paced progress, perplexed by the grunts and groans and sporadic thwacks that reached her attuned ears. The intruders were not Gypsies, for whoever heard of an Irish Gypsy? They could be poachers, but poachers would be more circumspect, she was sure. Better, though, to err on the side of caution than plunge unheeding into danger.

As she tiptoed along the crude path, she turtled her neck at each inadvertent crack of a twig beneath her boots. Before she reached the end of the path where the trail opened onto the overlook, she veered into the scrub of box and junipers that spread around the ash and whitebream. Crouching, she parted two beech saplings and peered out onto the freshly scythed plateau. The apprehension within her eased, but her eyes widened at the theater before her.

An exceptionally tall young man, his blond hair cut fashionably short, stood toe-to-toe with a muscular man of medium height with a thatch of flaming red hair and a freckled face. The blond had a face and form she knew would draw female heads whenever he entered a room. Amanda guessed the voice that had revealed the men's presence, however, belonged to the redhead.

Both men wore buff pantaloons strapped beneath short boots and were naked to the waist. Their arms were thrust forward, underside up with their hands balled into fists. Although she had never witnessed a mill, she recognized the fistic stance from drawings of fighters she had seen. The men were pugilists, or at least engaged in pugilism at the moment.

"Execution is everything, lad; don't be flinging your

arms. Jab, Terry, jab." With those words, the redhead, who was around thirty, a few years older than his companion, verified her supposition that he was her mysterious speaker.

With precise flicks he foiled the tall man's attempts to strike him. Amanda's eyes were riveted on the cross fire between them. Without warning, the taller man's long arm shot forward with a lightning thrust to the Irishman's shoulder, sending his opponent toppling backward. Vainly the redhead flailed the air to regain his balance before he sat down hard on the grass.

The blond's handsome mouth stretched into a triumphant grin. He offered a helping hand, which was readily accepted, and yanked the smaller man to his feet. The Irishman rubbed the sting from his shoulder and smiled as though he were proud of his opponent.

"Ah, Brian, me boy," the blond mocked in a broad mimicry of the Irishman's brogue, "as you say, execution is everything!"

His deep, pleasant, cultured voice came through the feigned accent. He was obviously gentry and indisputably a stranger, for Amanda knew everyone in the neighborhood, at least by sight. Never would she have overlooked such a dashing specimen.

No longer wary of the intruders, she stretched up from her cramped position, flexed her legs, and massaged the back of her neck.

When her gaze returned to the overlook, the tall man had draped his arm around the Irishman's shoulders. He spoke in a muted tone, which Amanda strained unsuccessfully to hear. The redhead nodded in response to the confidence.

The two men wordlessly resumed their fighting stance and began halfheartedly jabbing at each other with inept taps. The Irishman bounced backward. The blond danced after him in unhurried pursuit. They moved steadily toward the spot in the spinney where Amanda was hidden. She crunched down as the boxers came abreast of her. The blond let out a fierce war whoop and hurled himself into the brambles. Her heart leapt with fright as he grabbed her roughly about the waist and tossed her onto the overlook. She flew through the air, shrieking, and landed with a thud at the Irishman's feet, her heart beating wildly.

"Saints preserve us! It's a female," the redhead cried. He dropped to one knee beside Amanda's sprawled form, his Gaelic face a picture of grave concern.

"Are you hurt, lass?" he asked in a shaken voice.

"I'm in one piece," Amanda grumbled, rising on her elbows and regaining her breath. "No thanks to you!" She rounded on the blond man. The Irishman clucked solicitously and assisted her gently into a sitting position.

"Damme, woman, what the deuce were you doing spying on us?" The tall man glared down at her from his great height.

"Spying? I was not!" Amanda huffed. "And watch your language, sir, in the presence of a lady," she said saucily, dusting off the sleeves of her blue woolen jacket.

The blond's compressed lips quirked at the pert retort. The dread that had sprung into his breast and resulted in his accusatory outburst lest he had inflicted damage on her slender form, melted. He took her in with the sweeping appraisal of an interested man. Her casual attire, he noted, was as superbly tailored and fitted as his own London clothes. The polished boots were unexceptionable, created, if not by Hoby, then a booter equal to him. The snow-white frilled shirt beneath her jacket added a distinctly feminine touch. Hatless, she was running a slender hand through the warm brown hair that hung in ringlets just to her shoulders. She was eighteen or nineteen, he judged, but no beauty, certainly not a *belle idéal*, but she had an indefinable magnetism.

"What the deuce do you mean, manhandling me like that?" Amanda complained, forgetting her own admonition against improper language. She shaded her eyes against the bright sun with her hand and squinted up at him.

"What were you doing in the bushes?" he countered

mildly, apparently assigning the blame to her by implication for his precipitous action. He bent toward her, cupped her slim shoulders, and easily set her on her feet.

When his powerful hands dropped from Amanda's shoulders, she reeled a little. She was aware of his bare chest and the heady aura of maleness as he stepped back, quirked a brow, and waited for her reply.

"When I rode my horse into the high meadow beyond the spinney there"—she indicated the place with a toss of her head—"I heard your friend's voice, and not knowing what sort of interloper I would find, I proceeded with care. You are trespassing, you know. This is my father's land."

"Your father's?" he said. "I beg to differ, madam. Lord Woods owns this property, and I know for a fact he is not your father."

"The beech there marks the boundary between Willowwoods and Rook Manor," Amanda informed him authoritatively with a flourish of her hands toward the smooth-barked tree. "Everything this side of it belongs to Daniel Lofton, my father."

A dawning broke over the young man's face as her identity flashed across his mind. "I stand corrected," he acquiesced to her surprise.

Six months ago his half brother Leonard urged him to consider this same young woman, sight unseen, as a bride of convenience to alleviate his financial straits. He had a vague recollection Leonard had mentioned settling a dispute with Lofton when the merchant purchased the abandoned Rook Manor property two years before. He barely listened to Leonard when his brother suggested he marry Amanda Lofton, for the idea of marriage was unappealing to him. He had yet to meet a woman, rich or poor, who could not be replaced by another in his bed or in his heart. Leonard's dangling Miss Lofton's munificent dowry and lucrative inheritance before him left him cold.

Cutting into his retrospection, Amanda inquired in a stagy tone, "And what business, may I ask, do you have in this neighborhood?"

"You might say I am working for Lord Woods," he answered, amused by her imperious manner, which did not suit her and came over as playacting.

Her intelligent eyes narrowed suspiciously. The haughtiness dropped away. "You must take me for a flat. You're of the gentry, if your speech is an indication. Should your pockets be to let, you would not be hiring yourself out. More likely you would find a wealthy friend or a rich relation and rely on his hospitality."

He blushed at the near hit. Much as he disliked the situation, he was at Willowwoods on Leonard's sufferance, for his boyhood home had passed to his brother on his father's death.

"Nevertheless, Miss Lofton, I have fallen on hard times and my valet here and I have been reduced to beggary," he claimed with deliberate exaggeration.

"Valet?" Amanda questioned. What sort of valet was allowed the liberties she had seen here today and called his master by his given name?

Before she could put into words her skepticism, the Irishman said, "Brian McGonigal, Miss Lofton, at your service." His green eyes danced. "Mr. Straughn's valet," he verified.

"Straughn!" she cried, recognizing the family name of the owner of Willowwoods. "Then you are a connection of Lord Woods's."

"Alas, a poor relation, dependent for the moment on his largess as you have so aptly guessed."

She wondered if he was gammoning her. "I haven't heard anything about this," she said.

"Ah, you know the family?" he asked. "They keep you informed about their business?"

"Well, not exactly, but Freddie gossips a lot. He's the Viscount Willows, Lord Woods's heir," she explained, brushing back a stray wisp of hair from her forehead.

"I know," Straughn said blandly, being well acquainted with his sixteen-year-old nephew.

"Freddie and Albert, who is the brother of my bosom

bow, Josie Castleberry, are friends. This puts me in Freddie's company on numerous occasions. He gossips and I listen, to my shame," she said without a hint of repentance in her voice. "I could have spoken hastily, however. You may well be staying with the family."

"I assure you I am," he answered. Amanda looked off into the distance thoughtfully just then and missed the telltale glimmer of mirth that touched his eyes.

Perhaps this handsome Straughn was some *distant* cousin. He did not resemble his lordship and Freddie, who were both dark-haired and short of stature. She turned back to face him and held his deep blue eyes with hers. They reminded her of the sea near Bristol on a summer's day. She studied the color with bold fascination until she became aware his mouth quivered with merriment. Her eyes lowered. She gave herself a mental shake, disliking her inability to control the warm blush she felt coloring her cheeks.

To regain her poise, she glanced deliberately over his blond head at a blackbird. She followed the rooks line of flight down into the valley to a willow tree beside the brook at the bottom of the hill. At the same time, she decided to say no more about Freddie.

Amanda diverted the conversation by turning to the Irishman. "That was a boxing match you were engaged in, wasn't it, Mr. McGonigal?" she asked.

"Aye, in a manner of speaking."

"Other than being winded, neither of you seems to be adversely affected," Amanda noted. "I had been told boxing is a violent sport."

"Professional pugilism is. We were sparring," Straughn put in. "Pretend fighting."

"It could be likened to a game of chess. We try to parry each other's moves, albeit physically," Brian McGonigal explained.

Straughn continued. "A mill, however, involves brutal attacks that end when one bruiser is knocked senseless. Not a fitting sport for a woman to observe." He glanced down at his bare chest, belatedly aware of his state of undress before a young woman. "I fear we've forgotten our manners, Miss Lofton, standing here conversing with you underclothed as we are."

He scooped up a towel from the ground where he had tossed it earlier. Amanda's eyes tracked the linen cloth over the male neck, arms, and chest as he wiped the gleaming perspiration from his body. His golden hair riffled in the path of the towel.

The back of Amanda's neck tingled, and a vibration slipped deliciously down her spine. Neither his chest nor his shoulders were particularly broad. His muscles did not ripple as did the muscles of the heroes she had read about in popular novels. But there was a wonderful hardness, a whipcord strength, to his slim, wiry body. She had seen barechested sailors loading and unloading her father's ships and never felt this disturbing sensation in her breast. Her eyes ran down the tight breeches and over the muscular leanness of his thighs and legs. She winced when the quiver hit the pit of her stomach.

Straughn tossed the towel to Brian McGonigal and reached for his white shirt which was draped over the bushes next to his valet's. He twirled his index finger in the air, motioning Amanda to turn her back. When she faced him again, recovered from her sudden unexplained breathlessness, both men had tucked their shirts into their pantaloons and donned their wool jackets.

"You say you left your horse in the meadow beyond the spinney?" Straughn asked.

"Yes." Without warning, Amanda placed her pinkie fingers into the corners of her mouth and whistled shrilly. The two men's astonished eyes locked together and their chests heaved as they erupted into simultaneous laughter. Straughn slapped his thighs and his valet doubled over. Amanda's beaming face volleyed from one to the other, pleased with what she took as their appreciation of her dubious talent.

The horse came crashing over the rough path, exploded from the spinney onto the overlook, and stopped at Amanda's side. Nancy nickered and nudged her mistress's chest, tottering Amanda backward.

"Where did you learn to whistle like that?" Straughn sputtered.

"Pretty fair, is it not?" Amanda proclaimed with high spirits. Josie always clapped her hands over her ears and frowned disapprovingly when she whistled, and Papa flew into the boughs at her talent, but here was an appreciative audience.

"The first mate on one of my father's ships, the *Ellen*, taught me when I was about twelve."

Straughn mopped his face with the large handkerchief he had pulled from his jacket pocket while the Irishman knuckled his eyes. It took the men a minute or two to regain their composure. Amanda, meanwhile, basked in her notoriety.

Straughn, more himself now, picked up the dangling reins and stroked the mare's forelock affectionately. "She's a beauty," he declared. "Brian." He motioned to the Irishman. "Brian's father raises Irish hunters, Miss Lofton."

The Irishman approached the mare and ran his hand over a fetlock. "She appears to be a sweet goer," he commented on the long-legged look of the mare. He stepped back and judged the horse with an experienced eye.

"A proper highbred. Prime stock."

"All my father's cattle are," Amanda stated proudly. She unbuttoned her coat and lifted the floral enameled timepiece that hung from a gold chain about her neck.

"Oh, dear," she fretted, "I promised I would be from home no more than half an hour, just sufficient time to remove the cobwebs after having totaled the accounts all morning. I can't receive the curate dressed like this," she wailed, looking down at her riding skirt, "and Papa will be blue-deviled if he has to entertain Mr. Whitaker." She was reminding herself aloud more than imparting information to her listeners, who were, nevertheless, able to piece together her dilemma from the sketchy references.

Straughn moved to assist her into her sidesaddle. Before

he reached her, she slipped her foot into the stirrup and pulled herself into the saddle.

"Do you . . . ah . . . spar here often?" she asked as if searching for the appropriate word.

"Now and then, when it doesn't interfere with our duties at Willowwoods," he responded with an affable smile. She did not believe this Viking reincarnation was employed by Lord Woods. He had the poise of an aristocrat in the best sense. If he was in dun territory as he claimed, his pride had not suffered from his lowered status to judge from his ramrod bearing. He could be smoking her, Amanda decided. Terry was not a name she had heard associated with the Straughns, but he might well be a poor relation, as he claimed. But whoever he was, a strong desire to see him again overcame her. A staggering difference existed between this blond giant and the curate, her latest admirer. Certainly Mr. Straughn was far superior to the callow youths without charm who had tried to steal chaste kisses from her when she lived in Bristol. Amanda burst out laughing. She was quite mad about Mr. Straughn, a complete stranger, and it had all happened in a matter of minutes! His left eyebrow lifted quizzically. She shook her head, dimpling. "Nothing," she claimed, but gave him a soft look. "Besides, you wouldn't believe me," she said. She wiggled her fingers at him, touched the horse's flank with her heel, and rode off.

"In heaven's sweet name, Terry, she's the very lass your brother would have you take to wife," Brian gasped when Amanda disappeared into the trees.

Straughn nodded, dropped to the grass where the overlook began its gentle slope into the valley, and supported his tall frame on his elbows. His eyes swept his brother's fields across from the willow-lined brook at the bottom of the hill that marked the southern boundary of Rook Manor. He had forgotten the name Lofton in the six months since his father's death, when Leonard first proposed he consider the wealthy merchant's daughter for a bride. Had someone mentioned the name to him, he would have been hard put to recall where he had heard it. Only because she appeared at the point where the two properties marched together had his memory been jarred.

Brian joined Straughn on the grass. The Irishman crossed his extended legs at the ankles, leaned back on his elbows, and glanced at his friend sideways.

"I'd not blame you if you had second thoughts about matrimony and all that money after seeing her," Brian teased. "Sure an' you'd have to be a dead man not to have your heart turn when she looks at you with those big brown eyes!"

"Don't let Maggie hear you waxing romantic about Miss Lofton, or she'll take a frying pan to your head." Straughn smiled. Brian had hit upon the elusive quality that made Miss Lofton a charmer. Her enormous, expressive brown eyes made all ordinary eyes insipid and colorless. They drew him to her like a magnet.

"Of course, that whistling. Would a proper lass do such a thing? Surely her mother doesn't know," Brian said.

"She has only her father if I remember Leonard's words correctly. I fear I did not pay close attention at the time. She is a hoyden, no doubt, and too free-spoken for a female," Straughn said. "But"—his voice shifted into a devilish mode—"the promise of seeing those amazing eyes smoldering with passion is far from repulsive."

"Marry her, lad!" Brian cried impulsively. " 'Tis a far smoother row to hoe you'll be having than we have planned."

"And what of you and Maggie?" Straughn asked without serious intent.

"You could hire me as your valet in truth and pay me an exorbitant wage until I have accumulated a fortune," Brian jested.

"You shan't wheedle me into placing my neck into a marriage noose simply to accommodate you." Straughn laughed, but he wished he had the means to fulfill the Irishman's facetious request. One or two of his friends among the gentry had stood solidly by him when his father's will became common knowledge. Most distanced themselves, fearing he would tap them for a loan he would never be able to repay. Never had he given them cause to make such an assumption, and their attitude galled him. He could trust Brian. Their present collaboration for their mutual benefit formed a bond between them that transcended class.

"I think, Brian," Straughn said, breaking the silence, "we'll forge ahead with our original enterprise, see it to fruition, and forget this marriage nonsense." He snapped off a blade of grass, tucked it between his teeth, flipped it about with his tongue, and gazed into the friendly clouds overhead. "But why not a dalliance?" he said aloud as Amanda Lofton's image again wandered lazily into his mind. "The chit has an unrestrained manner that is amusing and bodes an easy conquest."

He was tired of pretending he couldn't see through the obvious drawing-room tricks, the affected sweet modesty London beauties learned at an early age. His flirts, on the other hand, seemed jaded. The environs of Willowwoods had nothing fresh to offer, since he had known all of the eligible females in the neighborhood his entire life.

"Yes, Amanda Lofton will do nicely as a bit of a diversion."

Brian had seen too many women with the same liquid look not to know Terry was already more than halfway home with Miss Lofton, but he had more important things on his mind than Terry's conquests. "What kind of a wager should we put down, lad?" he asked.

Straughn sat up and hugged his knees. "Well, we have a sizable sum put together with the money you brought from Ireland, the little we won on the Derby, and the proceeds from the things of value I sold. I think a quarter of it on this first fight."

"Done," Brian agreed, for a fourth of the total matched the amount in pounds he had figured in his head.

The two men sealed the decision with a handshake, more from custom than the need for a physical sign to reaffirm their bargain. Brian, too, had long before taken his friend's measure and trusted him implicitly.

Chapter 2

Amanda handled the ribbons of the snappy curricle with the skill and ease of the experienced driver. Her friend Josie Castleberry was perched on the box beside her. Josie's eyes stayed on the backs of the showy pair of chestnuts hitched to the yellow carriage as the mares trotted smartly up the one main street of the small village. The apothecary who lounged in the doorway of the chemist's shop during a lull in customers watched the horses admiringly.

Amanda's eyes lit on Bluebell, a mare from Lord Woods's stable. The horse plodded around the corner at the end of the street with a tall rider aboard. She drew in her breath at the sight of the blond young man whose awkwardly hunched-up knees reached to the top of the saddle. His face was every bit as divine as the image that had whirled in her brain since the previous day. A rush of compassion filled her, for he looked embarrassingly clumsy on Bluebell. Had his legs been dangling free of the stirrups, his boots would have scraped the ground. His comic appearance evoked a sadness in her, for he belonged on a stallion of size.

She nudged Josie. "Look there, the man on Freddie

Straughn's horse. Isn't he good-looking? I met him at the overlook yesterday. He is a Straughn too, some poor relation of Lord Woods's."

"My goodness' sakes, I don't believe my eyes!" Josie's small hand flew to her mouth, covering a giggle. "Mandy, he's no poor relation . . . well, not the way you mean . . . he's Rance Straughn, the *Honorable Terrance Straughn,* Lord Wood's younger half brother."

Amanda's mouth primmed. "The liar," she muttered indignantly under her breath. He had hoaxed her. The despicable man and his valet must have had a jolly laugh at her expense after she departed the overlook the previous day.

She parked the natty vehicle in front of Cauthen's dry goods store. Her flashing eyes never left Rance Straughn. He rode the cob toward her and Josie at a mere walk, his head tilted down. He seemed lost in his own thoughts and unaware of his surroundings.

Amanda secured the reins, slid over the box, and jumped to the stone walk where Josie had already sprung down using the mounting block.

Two urchins rushed up to contract to watch the horses.

"Horace, Joshua, a ha'penny each," Amanda offered. The ten-year-olds were disappointed she did not dicker as usual before naming the fee they always agreed on. Miss Lofton seemed out of sorts and not in the mood for playful haggling.

Rance Straughn dismounted and moved to tether Bluebell at a ring post a few feet in front of the curricle. He looped the reins through the iron ring, lifted his eyes, and broke into a grin of unbridled delight. "Josie!" he shouted. He reached the startled girl with three long strides, grabbed her two small hands in his large ones, and pumped her arms up and down with delighted vigor. His curly-brimmed beaver slid off his head onto the walkway during the energetic encounter.

Giggling irrepressibly, Josie protested, "Unhand me, Rance, before you pull my arms off and jar me to pieces."

She smoothed her pink gown and adjusted her straw bonnet.

Amanda picked up Rance's hat and handed it to him with a fulminating glare.

He popped the beaver on his head and grimaced. "Miss Lofton, I apologize for yesterday. Please don't challenge me to a duel!" He flung his hands up to cover his face, pretending to fend off an attack.

"What good would that do? You would probably take flight rather than face me," she said acidly.

"Most assuredly. You are, no doubt, more proficient with pistols than I am. You see before you a very poor shot."

"Now, now, children." Josie jumped in, assuming the role of peacemaker. "All this talk of duels! I cannot bear to have my bosom bow and my childhood friend engage in an affair of honor. Forgive each other this minute!"

"I have no wish to be shot, even by so charming a lady. I capitulate." Rance laughed, raising his hands in surrender. "Miss Lofton? Am I forgiven?"

Amanda shrugged her shoulders. "I suppose. You and Josie have known each other since you were children?"

"Lud, yes, since she was in leading strings. The overlook where I met you yesterday once was our playground. We would roll down the hill and dangle our bare toes in the icy waters of the stream below."

"I cannot remember a time when our families were not close," Josie added. "Rance tugged my pigtails and called me 'little one.' I despised being the smallest for my age in the neighborhood, although I admit the appellation has lost its sting and no longer sounds pejorative."

"But, Josie, it has always been a sign of affection," Rance objected. "You have been a darling girl since you were a baby."

Josie glowed at the compliment.

Why hadn't Josie ever mentioned this handsome playmate? Amanda wondered. Could Josie have a secret *tendre* for Mr. Straughn?

"Won't you be seated, ladies . . . that is if you can spare a minute," Rance invited, indicating the wooden bench in front of the store. "I must make amends to Miss Lofton for quizzing her, although, in effect, I was being truthful."

Josie looked at Amanda for permission. She nodded her assent. The two young women settled on the narrow bench. Rance leaned his back against the split rail that separated the street from the walkway.

"Well, Mr. Straughn?" Amanda asked, primed to do battle.

"Josie will verify I am extremely light in the pocketbook at the present time, for it's no secret, Miss Lofton, my father made unwise investments. When he died a few months ago, my only inheritance was those worthless shares. At present I am staying with my brother Lord Woods. I help out where I can with the work of the estate, as does Mr. McGonigal, to compensate for our lodging and meals. So you see, although I hedged on my identity, I essentially did not misrepresent my position."

Josie coaxed, "There now, Mandy. That clears up the matter. Everything Rance said is true. You must forgive him!"

"Oh, gracious, I do! What a lot of fuss and pother over nothing." The glower vanished from her brown eyes.

Grins broke out all around. "You've resided at Rook Manor for a year now, Miss Lofton?"

"Yes, although Papa bought the estate two years ago; the renovation took a full year, with the grounds and all."

"You should see it, Rance. You would not believe the magnificence that was created from that ramshackle place," Josie interjected, tucking in a golden curl that had escaped from her bonnet.

Rance puckered his lips. "The gardens were running wild the last time I passed there. Mr. Lofton must have needed a host of workers to put it in order."

"He did," Amanda concurred. "To oversee the task, Papa employed a local gardener who followed a detailed sketch Papa found in an old desk in the office. He insisted the gardener hire villagers to clean up and replant. Townspeople are less resentful of an outsider if their pocketbooks benefit.'' She echoed her father's assessment.

Rance could not argue with the logic. Any newcomer to the neighborhood would be regarded with suspicion, but a rich merchant without a drop of blue blood would be doubly suspect. Given her background, he was surprised the Castleberrys embraced Miss Lofton. Her acceptance by Lady Ainsworth as a companion to Josie was a coup for the merchant's daughter.

''Elias Parkenhurt did the house,'' Amanda volunteered.

''Parkenhurst? Are you certain? I don't think it could be he,'' Rance argued. He knew the renowned architect had been retired five years now.

''Mr. Parkenhurst is Papa's friend!'' Amanda snapped. The temerity of the man to question her. ''I have met him many times!''

''I know for a fact Parkenhurst has accepted no commissions in recent years. He isn't likely to take on a project in the country—'' Rance's sentence was abruptly cut off.

''Well, he did!'' Amanda shot back. ''Papa wouldn't hire some rackety architect who would bungle the job. Daniel Lofton is a man of taste, Mr. Straughn, even if your ilk look down on him because he made his money in trade!''

Rance's face darkened. His shoulders squared noticeably. ''If you had allowed me to finish, Miss Lofton, I was about to say, ' . . . unless Mr. Parkenhurst indeed considered your father a cherished friend.' ''

Perturbed by Amanda's denunciation and attack on Rance, Josie scolded, ''Don't be so toplofty, Mandy. You take offense too quickly. Rance did not deserve your setdown.''

''I know! I know!'' Amanda admitted, sucking her breath between her teeth. ''You must find my manners excessively cow-handed, Mr. Straughn.''

''It doesn't signify, Miss Lofton,'' he said in a clipped tone, but his hard eyes mellowed with her ready apology. He had to credit her for owning up to her error. Every woman he knew would have flounced off to put him in the wrong or argued in circles to justify her snap judgment. Quickly he smiled his forgiveness.

Josie giggled in relief. "At all events, Rance, you are fortunate you have been spared the lecture on Grandpapa Lofton, who was a bootmaker—Amanda's morality tale to prove the superiority of the merchant class."

"I would like very much to hear about Grandpapa," Rance said only half in jest.

A pink blush washed Amanda's cheeks. She shook her head, but Josie wouldn't be stopped.

"Would you? Let's see, the story goes that Amanda's grandpapa began saving pennies the day Daniel Lofton, Amanda's papa, that is, was born to insure his son's education. Not only did he provide the finest schooling for Daniel, but on his twenty-first birthday he turned over the tidy sum of two thousand pounds to his son to help him make his way. According to Amanda, her grandfather, a lowly bootmaker, had more gumption than any titled gentlemen she has ever met or heard of. And the story of the shipping empire Daniel built from that modest sum is legend in Bristol shipping circles, a testament to his superior character."

Amanda, a splinter of an insuppressible smile at the corners of her mouth, corrected Josie dryly. "Papa was twenty when Grandpapa turned the money over to him, and it was five hundred, not two thousand pounds, but other than that, Josephine, you are accurate."

"She is not as pure as she would have you believe, Rance," Josie confided from behind her hand in a stage whisper with a conspiratorial wink. "Mrs. Lofton was Quality."

Rance chuckled. "While others chase titles, Miss Lofton eschews them." He tilted his hat back with a flick of his index finger into a rakish angle. Amanda's heart turned over at the roguishly charming gesture.

"I think Mr. Straughn must be quite bored with these

vignettes from my family tree, Josephine. Don't you have some ribbon to buy?"

"Yes, I must find some in green to match the fringe on my cashmere shawl," Josie said, rising from the bench. "I bid you adieu, Rance. Now that you are once again residing here, no doubt we shall be thrown into each other's company."

"No doubt, little one," Rance repeated. "By the way, Miss Lofton, your father's matched pair are admirable. You wouldn't know where he buys his cattle, would you?"

"Lucie and Lizzie are not Mr. Lofton's," Josie piped in. "The horses belong to Amanda. Her papa gifted her with the mares and that dandy curricle on her last birthday."

Rance whistled softly. His eyes held Amanda's for a second.

"I happened to be a good girl last year," Amanda drawled. Then she whirled around and trailed Josie toward the store, calling over her shoulder, "Papa bought the horses from a private dealer outside of Newmarket. Good day, Mr. Straughn."

Rance bowed with a "Miss Lofton" and followed Amanda's willowy form with his eyes. The navy wool spencer she wore against the April chill was a jacket worthy of a London Incomparable. Her tall-crowned bonnet, adorned with miniature violets, added just the right touch of frivolity to her outfit. Miss Lofton would pass muster by the most critical, style-conscious matron of the *ton.* He looked at the sleeve of his herringbone jacket. His own clothes were of high quality and would not cry for replacement anytime soon, fortunately, considering his present finances. At least for a while his appearance would not be an embarrassment.

"Oh, Miss Lofton," he called. She turned back toward him.

"Will you be at the assembly on Thursday?" Amanda nodded. "Save a dance for me?" She paused for half a second, nodded again with a faint pleased smile on her lips, and passed through the door into Cauthen's.

He watched her through the window as she and Josie

fingered a spool of green ribbon. She was lively and outspoken and unpredictable . . . and desirable. Amanda would be ideal to relieve the social boredom of the country for the few months until he and Brian were in a position to leave Willowwoods for good.

He saluted Horace and Joshua, who sat on the curb, minding Amanda's team. The urchins tapped their foreheads in imitation of the grown-up. Rance strolled jauntily down the walk to the ironmonger's to complete Leonard's errand, whistling an Irish air Brian McGonigal had taught him.

When Amanda and Josie emerged from the dry goods store with their purchases, Amanda noted that Freddie Straughn's cob was gone from the hitching post. Mr. Straughn must have departed while she and Josie were examining the new fabrics that had just arrived. Mr. Cauthen had insisted on unrolling a portion of all ten bolts and describing the attributes of each piece of material in tedious detail.

Amanda tossed a full penny each to Horace and Joshua, who performed a concerted bow, aping Rance Straughn.

On the drive back to Ainsworth House, Amanda held Lucie and Lizzie to a slow trot.

"He's beautiful," she said dreamily to Josie.

"Rance Straughn beautiful?" Josie scoffed, not even pretending to misunderstand whom she meant. "Gad, Mandy, you've lost your wits. He's a giraffe!"

Amanda was relieved. She knew Josie well enough to be certain she had no *tendre* for Mr. Straughn, secret or otherwise.

"I am somewhat of a giraffe myself, *little one,*" she stressed, mimicking Rance.

Josie chuckled. "You are not too bad a giraffe. The top of my head does reach above your shoulder." She cast an oblique glance at her good friend.

Amanda had moved into Rook Manor just when she

herself had come from an unsuccessful London Season. Her father had gone on and on about wasted money and glared at her in disbelief that he, Lord Ainsworth, could have given birth to a rejected debutante. Amanda had been a balm to her pain and misery. Recalling their first encounter, Josie said, "You met Rance on the overlook too."

"Yes, in nearly the identical spot, next to the beech tree," Amanda confirmed.

Josie had never known anyone as unconventional as Amanda. She had been petrified when Lady Ainsworth had insisted on being introduced to her daughter's new friend. At times Amanda dispensed commonsense advice with the tact and wisdom of someone far beyond her years. However, it was the Amanda who could be outrageous and blurt out shocking, unwomanly ideas Josie feared introducing to her very proper mother.

"Amanda, you won't mention those books your father lets you read?" Josie had pleaded. Her nerves had dashed about in her stomach when her new friend smirked and said, "Maybe I won't."

"I would be locked in my room for a week on bread and water if Papa caught me reading them and severely chastised at even listening to a description of their contents."

"They are perfectly repectable volumes, dear Josephine, certain to enhance any drawing-room discussion" had been Amanda's unsatisfactory reply.

But on the appointed day Amanda arrived promptly at four in a chaise driven by a liveried coachman. She was the picture of propriety in her yellow sprigged-muslin gown with matching bonnet decorated with daisies and tied with a yellow ribbon.

Her unevasive answers to questions about her background impressed Lady Ainsworth. Moreover, Josie's mother was sentimentally affected by Amanda's fierce pride in her socially unacceptable merchant father.

"Now, there's a gel with manners and a fine sense of family loyalty you might well emulate, Josephine," she said to her astonished and relieved daughter. "We shall take up Miss Lofton and see she is properly introduced at the next assembly." Josie and Amanda had been inseparable ever since.

"Josie, that's true, is it, that Mr. Straughn has no money?"

"Oh, yes, Mandy. He wasn't bamming you. He had to dismiss his servants, all except his valet, and vacate his rooms in London. He kept Brian McGonigal on only because he treats him more as a friend than as a servant."

"Yes, I noticed theirs is an uncommon master-servant relationship. Did you know Brian McGonigal calls Mr. Straughn Terry? What's that all about?"

Josie shook her head. "As far as I know, Brian always addressed Rance as Mr. Straughn or sir. Rance's Christian name is Terrance. It could be a diminutive for that, but I never heard anyone use it before. He's always been Rance to us, never Terry."

Amanda feathered a curve with precision, earning Josie's silent admiration for her superb driving.

"I wonder how Mr. Straughn intends working himself out of the coil in which he finds himself," Amanda reflected.

Josie gave her a knowing look. "That's no mystery. He is seeking a rich woman to marry; Freddie told Albert as much. But it won't be easy now that he is as good as disinherited. Rance has a number of faults that would be overlooked in a wealthy man with a title, but won't be tolerated in a second son who is a pauper."

"What sort of faults?"

"Nothing many others don't have. He loves the gaming tables of St. James, winning more than he loses, I hear, but he gambles deep at times. For another, he was sent down from Cambridge and never reinstated. The offense must have been horrendously serious to warrant a permanent expulsion." Josie paused and said in a near whisper, "He has been known to keep company with women of disputable reputations."

"That is serious," Amanda jeered in mock horror. Young men of a certain age she had learned from servants' gossip and her own father's frankness were known to form liaisons with loose women. "Josie, Rance must be well into his twenties."

"He's twenty-four," she said.

"I would be more surprised if he never had a mistress. Wouldn't you?" Amanda asked with a twinkle in her eye, waiting for Josie's fair skin to blotch red.

Josie did not disappoint her. "I don't know. I never think about those things," she said, squirming in her seat.

"If Mr. Straughn is in want of a rich wife, I could buy him for myself." Amanda smirked. Josie's prudery always brought out the devil in Amanda.

"Whatever do you mean, Mandy?" Her blue eyes were suspicious.

"I have scads of pounds in my own name and will have more when I reach my twenty-first birthday in a little over two years. I haven't seen a finer piece of male merchandise than Mr. Straughn in my entire life. Did you notice how his tight breeches mold those athletic legs?"

"Amanda Lofton, what a thing to say! I for one do not look in that direction. If my mama knew you said shocking things like that, she would forbid me to associate with you!" The red returned to Josie's cheeks.

"Dear me, Josephine, I certainly hope you don't repeat our intimate conversations to your mama," Amanda said blandly.

"Of course I don't," Josie maintained. She pouted in silence for a time, flicking quick glances at her friend's grinning face. Amanda was teasing her again. Come to think of it, never once had Amanda followed through on a scandalous inclination. "You're not serious, are you? You wouldn't really propose to him?"

"No, ninny, I have more pride than that," she said. Josie visibly relaxed. "Besides, my father would never allow it. Mr. Straughn would have to ask Papa's permission to pay his addresses."

Amanda slowed her team and reined them in, stopping at the side of the road under an oak tree. Ainsworth House would come into view around the next bend.

She stared pensively into the distance. "Josie, is it madness to desire a man one has seen only twice for a matter of minutes? I cannot stop thinking about Mr. Straughn for longer than two minutes at a time. I am unable to breathe at the thought of never seeing him again."

"Goodness, Mandy, you really are taken with him. Just listen to yourself."

"I know. My brain cries for me to be sensible, but my heart yearns quite fiercely for him."

"Mama says love at first sight is twaddle. A solid marriage is one arranged by the parents, who know best." Josie's mouth drooped. "But, oh, Mandy, I do so want someone who I am head over heels for, not a man Mama selects."

Amanda reached over and patted Josie's hand, nodding in agreement. "Mr. Straughn asked me to put aside a dance for him at the assembly Thursday," she confided softly. "Josie, you have known him all your life. Is he so awful?"

"No! No! Rance is not mean, Amanda, not at all. But there are stories of women and gambling and Lord Woods did leave him without two pennies to rub together."

Amanda knew the last would be the most damning with Daniel Lofton. To her father, being without funds was a deadly sin in any man who showed an interest in her. Papa would never believe that Mr. Straughn was not after her money.

"Why can't I be attracted to a gentleman who will bring forth words of commendation from Papa, rather than condemnation?"

"I know, Mandy. Someone like Mr. Whitaker, for one," Josie suggested. "He has dangled after you for these six months with never a word of encouragement from you for his pains. Can't you like him? Your papa would surely approve of a churchman."

Amanda pulled a face. "I can like him, Josie dear, but I

shall never love the curate." Even Whitaker had exemplary manners. He honored her by standing up with her at every assembly for the two dances allowed an unengaged couple and sat out at least one other dance, bringing her punch and sweet cakes. But he bored her! Besides, Josie was wrong. Mr. Whitaker would not pass the money thing either.

"No, Josie, I cannot return Mr. Whitaker's affections."

Josie nodded sympathetically.

Amanda slackened the reins, clicked her tongue against her teeth, and set Lucie and Lizzie into motion. Within a minute the curricle wheels crunched as the vehicle rolled onto the gravel drivepath in front of Ainsworth House. Amanda pulled up neatly before the gray stone steps, the horses prancing to a smooth halt.

The front door of the house flew open and Lady Ainsworth came bustling out onto the portico. Her small, plump hands fluttered in the air. The blue ribbons on her white lace cap streamed behind her. She was no taller than her daughter, but while Josie had a perfect little figure, Lady Ainsworth was a dumpling. An unconcerned footman followed languidly in her wake.

"Amanda dear," she cried even before she was midway down the steps. "I am terribly sorry! They descended on me without warning. Not a letter, not a message, nothing! Just arrived this afternoon announcing their intention to visit for weeks! Lord Ainsworth is beside himself! He cannot tolerate his sister-in-law and calls the children barbarians. Barbarians!" Lady Ainsworth paused at the bottom of the steps, emitting rapid gasps as she clutched her chest.

The footman, quivering with restrained laughter, assisted Josie from the curricle. "Have Aunt Emma Castleberry and my cousins come for a visit, then?" Josie asked, wondering why her mother was apologizing to Amanda for that.

"But of course, Josephine, what have I been saying? Amanda, we shall not be able to accommodate you Thursday for the assembly."

Amanda's heart sank. She had long taken for granted the invitation to dinner, sharing the Castleberrys' carriage, and spending the night with Josie whenever there was a dance.

"Can you imagine, Emmanuel Castleberry had the effrontery to die and cast that woman adrift to prey on unsuspecting relatives with her unruly brood." Ordinarily Amanda would have found humor in Lady Ainsworth's ironically maligning her deceased brother-in-law, but a gloomy picture of Rance waiting in vain for her at the assembly clouded her sense of humor.

"But, Mama," Josie protested, "Amanda can share my bed for the one night. I shan't mind at all." A glimmer of hope welled up in Amanda's breast with Josie's offer, but was soon dashed.

"It won't do, Josephine. Your bed is needed for your cousin Felicia, who shall sleep with you, not just the one night, but for her stay. We can't take Amanda up in our carriage either. Even with the two boys sharing Samuel Coachman's box, the vehicle will be bursting with two grown girls, their mother, and us two. Our gowns will be crushed, hopelessly crushed!" Lady Ainsworth wrung her hands. "You do understand, dear Amanda?"

"Of course, my lady. It's of no consequence," Amanda assured her with a polite lie. Lady Ainsworth waved a grateful hand at Amanda, relieved she had settled the withdrawal of the standing invitation without unpleasantness. She picked up her skirt and slowly ascended the steps into the house, muttering to herself about uncouth relations.

When her mother was out of earshot, Josie said, "Amanda, I'm so sorry. How disappointing for you with Rance expecting you to be at the dance."

Amanda chewed the inside of her mouth. "There is only one possible solution, Josie. Papa."

Josie's expression brightened. "Do you think he would agree to take you?"

Amanda shrugged. "I can only ask."

Chapter 3

Rance poured a half glass of port from the crystal decanter Leonard slid across the Chippendale dining room table. Ernestine, Leonard's wife, paused behind Rance's chair, lightly resting her beringed fingers on his shoulders. He repulsed a powerful urge to shrug off his sister-in-law as she bent to his ear.

"The sooner you find a woman with a generous dowry, dear boy, the better it will be for you," she said, her tone haughty rather than helpful. "I shall prepare a list for your edification of wealthy Antidotes from last Season who did not manage to trap a man."

"Kind of you, my lady," Rance mumbled in a honeyed voice dripping with sarcasm. If Ernestine dared to present him with her abominable list, he would shred it into snippets and throw them in her face in a most ungentlemanly manner. She had already nearly ruined for him the excellent meal centered around a butter-tender leg of lamb. Her unctuous regard for his welfare had been an irritant throughout dinner, but thankfully she was, at last, leaving him and Leonard to their after-dinner port and removing her thin, angular form from his presence.

Leonard noted the byplay between his wife and half brother with a tight-lipped frown, his black eyes vexed. He ran a stubby hand over his dark hair which was graying at the temples. Ernestine's sermonizing during dinner had annoyed him more than usual, not that he disagreed with her criticism of his father's frittering away the family fortune. But he liked Rance and found no joy in gloating over the life of perpetual financial anxiety to which his brother had been sentenced. He was certain Rance, who was nobody's fool, had detected Ernestine's perverse delight when she commented on his hollow bequest with feigned sympathy. His wife was not an accomplished actress.

After she made a pretentiously regal exit from the room, Leonard said, "Pay no mind to Ernestine, Rance," in way of an apology for his wife's pettiness. Commenting on her presumptuous offer, he added, "Although were I you, I would not dismiss out of hand a marriage of convenience as a means of alleviating your difficulties."

Rance's eyes flickered warily. He swirled the red wine distractedly in his goblet. "I think we tilled this soil before, brother. I cannot imagine anyone of consequence turning over a heavily dowered daughter to me," he countered sardonically.

"What of the merchant's daughter I mentioned a while back? The one whose father bought Rook Manor. Have you considered her? There's an enormous fortune to be had there, for she's his only child."

"As a matter of fact, Josie Castleberry presented Miss Lofton to me this afternoon in the village," Rance said blandly, his face an inscrutable mask. The glow from the five-pronged candelabrum played on his short blond hair.

"Oh." To give himself time to repress his eagerness, Leonard examined the ash on the cigar he held in his hand and gazed up into the smoky haze that hung above the table.

Carefully, he asked, "What did you think of her?"

Rance shrugged noncommittally. "We were in one another's company only a matter of minutes."

"At least she's tall enough," Leonard pointed out with a nervous laugh. "I remember well how your mother held her sides when as a youth you complained you had to bend over double to dance with half the girls at the assembly and vowed you would never marry a petite woman."

Rance grinned wryly. Amanda was tall enough all right; moreover, she had managed to knock the desire for any recent female conquest clear out of his head. But he did not intend to share that tidbit with Leonard.

Rance made a tent with his fingers and pressed his hands to his chin. "What makes you think this wealthy merchant would be more lenient than the fathers of the *ton* and accept a pauper as a husband for his daughter?"

"Buying Rook Manor shows Lofton is vying for respectability," Leonard claimed, obliged to his brother for offering this opening to present his views. "He is a man of no consequence, willing to overlook a lot in a son-in-law if he is the son of an earl, even a younger son, and could bring a title into the family, even a minor one. You are after all the *Honorable* Terrance Straughn. The Straughn name alone carries a good deal of prestige with it."

Leonard's avidity was not propelled solely by an altruistic desire to see his younger brother well placed. The undeniable riches Rance would come into if he offered for Miss Lofton would benefit them both. Rance would be in a position to take over the payment of the monumental debts incurred by their late father.

Rance was conscious of his brother's motives, but puzzled at his persistence in pressing for this particular union.

"Frankly, Len, I would have thought you and Ernestine would be embarrassed to have me allied with a merchant. Your wife is not known for her democratic views on hobnobbing with social inferiors," Rance pointed out.

Leonard was quick to explain. "Lady Ainsworth accepted the chit as Josie's companion, I'm certain, on the strength of her mother's people. You may not know, Rance, but

Lofton's wife was Quality." He paused as though to give Rance time to digest the significance of his pronouncement. "Unfortunately, she was a bluestocking who disgraced herself by disobeying her father and marrying beneath her station. But birth counts for something. I would never suggest a complete misalliance for you. And your peers would understand, given all that money. The man is rich as Croesus. No one would ostracize you, if that's what you fear."

Rance absentmindedly swept the crumbs on the lace tablecloth into tiny piles. Leonard was not suggesting anything the vast majority of the gentry would not echo. An arranged marriage was an honorable expediency Rance himself had taken for granted all his adult life. For others. But when applied to himself, this aspect of the mores of his society was distasteful.

"I cannot see myself deliberately entering holy matrimony without feeling some passion for my bride. I'm afraid, Len, I am a hopeless romantic. A marriage to fatten my purse is out of the question for me."

A downward tug of Leonard's mouth heralded his disappointment. He had banked on Rance's good sense in ultimately acquiescing to a seemingly perfect solution. He became a bit desperate when he saw his labors had been unprofitable and plunged ahead imprudently, taking a different tact.

"Miss Lofton seems presentable enough, but with the brass her dowry alone would bring to you, you could set up a place in London and find your passions where you always have."

Fear that he had crossed the boundaries of propriety was plain on Leonard's face when his brother's head snapped up and the sea-blue eyes stared at him. Rance was amazed Leonard believed he would consider such an arrangement. Did his brother know so little about him? And Miss Lofton? Would she put up with her husband taking a mistress even before the marriage lines were dry?

He smiled behind his eyes. Even from the little he had seen of her, not likely!

To Leonard's relief, Rance broke into an easy grin. "It won't do. Sorry to disappoint you, Len."

Leonard drained his wineglass. He shrugged his shoulders in resignation, smiled his acceptance of defeat, and lifted the decanter toward Rance's goblet. He withdrew the decorative vessel when his brother raised a hand, refusing the refill.

"Of course, you can rack up here indefinitely. I want you always to consider Willowwoods your home, but I can't give you money. I have little cash," Leonard explained not for the first time. "Father left me with a pile of duns this high." His hand moved six inches above the table. "Even if the estate continues to show a profit, it could be a matter of years before I clear his dismal record."

For nearly a year before his death, Lord Woods had requested a substantial share of the profits from the estate, leaving Leonard with barely enough to pay his bills. Leonard still resented that a portion of the fruits of his own labors had gone to finance Rance's gentlemanly idleness.

Rance, as if reading his brother's thoughts, said, "You must know, Len, I had no idea. Papa never uttered a syllable that revealed he was in trouble. He had the draft for my allowance in my London bank by the fifth each month . . . never a late payment . . . never a word about cutting back.

"I wish Papa had told me," Rance said lamely. He had been plagued with guilt since the lawyer had laid out the sorry truth after probating Lord Woods's will. "In any case, Len, I shan't impose on you for long. But Brian and I will try to be of some use to you while we're here."

Leonard bristled at the mention of Brian McGonigal's name. At least he had scotched Rance's attempt to have McGonigal sleep in the family wing of the house. The Irishman was housed with the kitchen servants, where he belonged.

"I see you still fob him off as your valet."

Rance threw his head back and laughed heartily. "Leonard, Leonard, you doubt he's my valet!"

Leonard snorted, not joining in the laughter. Rance's befriending a low-class lout was not amusing. "I suppose he was the Irish cousin you were seen with at the Derby, since I know of no Gaelic relations on either side of your family." Rance gave him an infuriatingly enigmatic smirk, and Leonard knew there was no sense in berating the Irishman further.

He stubbed out his cigar. He could not force Rance into a marriage with Amanda Lofton, but sooner or later his brother would become disenchanted with his penurious existence. Rance would then abandon his romantic notions about marriage and look favorably on Ernestine's list.

"It's a shame you don't have some prospects from your mother's family. Your great-aunt Agnes passed on not long ago, didn't she?" Leonard asked, more to make conversation than from a real interest.

"Two months ago. You never met Aunt Agnes, Len, but my mother and I went often to the small cottage in Hertfordshire where she lived. She was a cantankerous old lady, but she was the only one who did not turn her back on Mama when my grandfather died. I found the old lady rather amusing these last years, for she had a rapier wit, and I rather enjoyed crossing verbal swords with her. I think she came to quite like me in the end, but the proceeds from the sale of her house and belongings were willed to a home for indigent women."

"If your mother had brought anything to the marriage, I would have given you that, Rance, as a just portion. But Margaret did not have a feather to fly with when our father married her," Leonard said. He had been seventeen at the time. His new stepmother had been left destitute when her father had died. Everything had been entailed and passed to a distant cousin.

"I know my mama had shallow pockets when she accepted Papa," Rance said. "She told me as much herself.

Mama was fortunate Aunt Agnes made a place for her and that Papa came along shortly after and married her."

"Father had many happy years with your mother before she died," Leonard conceded. In the beginning he suspected Margaret had not loved his father. Lord Woods was so much older. After Rance was born, she seemed to change. Leonard thought in the end she had come to care deeply for his father.

"Do you have any money?" Leonard asked bluntly.

With his hands hooked together behind his head, Rance pondered before answering. "A little, at the moment, from the sale of my horse and some jewelry." This was dangerous territory. Any discussion of his finances would force him to lie to Leonard. Better to say nothing. Should his brother become aware of his true relationship with Brian, he would explode with fervent indignation. He pushed back his chair and rose abruptly. "You will excuse me, Len? I fear the wine and fine meal have suddenly made me lethargic. I think I'll turn in early."

Leonard nodded, although he noted to himself Rance had barely touched his wine. "Why don't you look in on the assembly Thursday?" Leonard said. "One of Ernestine's wealthy Antidotes might be in attendance." He laughed to make his true sentiments seem a witticism.

"I plan to, brother," Rance said. Leonard's dark brows rose in surprise. His mouth pulled into a satisfied smile.

Rance did not bother to correct the inaccurate construction Leonard had obviously put on his intention to attend the dance. Better for his brother to remain in the dark about Amanda Lofton since marriage had nothing to do with this chase.

"Good night, Len," Rance said from the doorway. When he reached the staircase, he did not go up to the bedroom he had occupied since his boyhood, but crossed the foyer and continued down the hall. He opened a side door and stepped outside onto a wooden portico that overlooked Ernestine's garden.

Dusk had just faded into night. Rance inhaled the cool

country air deeply to clear his lungs of Leonard's cigar fumes. The sweet scent of honeysuckle pleased his nostrils. He leaned against a thick white column on the secluded porch. Willowwoods was quiet except for nature's agreeable night noises.

It was odd how deeply imprinted on his mind the image of Amanda Lofton had become in two brief meetings. He was certain he knew dozens of London lovelies who would put her in the shade. Yet, strangely, he could not bring to mind even one at the moment who eclipsed her. Although there was something radiant about her merely pretty face, it was her natural, unaffected behavior that appealed most to him. The women he knew often sounded as if they tried too hard to be pleasant. She had no such obstructive inhibitions.

Rance flexed his shoulders, yawned, and his drowsy eyes narrowed. An image of Amanda with her generous lips parted, and exceptional brown eyes ardent, caused a rush of desire in him. In his mind he had already conquered her, and she was succumbing to his passionate lovemaking. He brought himself up short, aware he had to be realistic. The dalliance must be a tidy arrangement that to a casual observer would be above reproach. After all, she was not some common creature or fancy-piece. He could take some liberties, but nothing that would impel him into an enforced marriage. He envisioned a mutually amenable short-lived fling on comfortable terms that would end without her making a serious claim on him. No impediment to his conquest existed, for he saw she had already taken a fancy to him. The chit wore her feelings in her eyes, he thought with a smug smile.

He stretched his arms high and yawned again. The sparring with Brian and the honest labor in his brother's employ left Rance each night with a good kind of tiredness. He was more fit than he had been for years. At times his London life now seemed a folly. But the country could be dull. Amanda Lofton would add just the right pinch of spice to give his sojourn a needed touch of diversity without jeopardizing his long-range plans.

Amanda had been turning over in her mind a dozen ways to broach the subject of the assembly. The cheery fire in the brick hearth gave both warmth and a cozy ambience to this favored eating place. She sat with her father at a small round table in the room referred to commonly in country homes as the breakfast parlor. The atmosphere was more conducive to family meals than the formal dining hall with its French furnishings and magnificent chandelier that had graced a chateau before the Revolution.

At forty-eight, Daniel Lofton's dark-brown hair was without a trace of gray. His eyes were the same lively brown as his daughter's. But his handsome countenance was marred by the lines of pain etched between his brows from the rheumatism that gave him sleepless nights. He shunned the laudanum that sent his brain into oblivion and depended for relief on the milder, less effective draughts his doctor prescribed.

Daniel had been watching Amanda fidget with her napkin since she finished her baked apple with clotted cream, the dessert that topped off the simple supper of mutton pie and oatcakes. He wondered what could be of such import that she would be wary of approaching him.

Breaking the silence, he commanded, "Out with it, Amanda. You shan't find me in a more receptive mood than now."

"Papa, will you escort me to the assembly on Thursday?" she asked, a nervous tremor betraying the depth of her emotions.

"Amanda, please, anything but that!" Daniel's slender fingers stroked his temples. He shifted his rheumatic leg, seeking a more comfortable position to ease the persistent pain. "I suppose this has to do with the onslaught of relations at Ainsworth House you were telling me about."

"Lady Ainsworth can't accommodate me, Papa, and I

do so want to attend the assembly. I know it's not your favorite place," Amanda conceded. Daniel rolled his brown eyes heavenward in response to his daughter's understatement.

"Surely, missing this one dance shan't ruin your life, Mandy." He detested the assembly, where he suspected that more than a few of his neighbors sneered "merchant" behind their hands. He had attended the dances only twice, long ago, when Lady Ainsworth had first taken Amanda under her wing. He had looked in on the proceedings to be certain his daughter was not being snubbed or some forward young buck was not taking liberties with her because of her supposedly inferior connections. His fears for her vanished when he observed the exemplary manner in which she was received. He decided society's acceptance of her was the result of Lady Ainsworth's protection. Though he had never openly been slighted, neither did he feel comfortable at an assembly, for he harbored the suspicion he was merely being tolerated. Once satisfied that Amanda was in good hands, he never appeared at a dance again.

"Papa, please! I can't go without an escort. There is no one else but you who can take me," Amanda pleaded. "Suggest a favor I can do to repay you. I'll agree to anything!"

"What is so important about this assembly that it can't be missed? Gracious, child, you haven't gone sweet on that curate who calls here and makes sheep's eyes at you?"

"No, Papa, I cannot warm to Mr. Whitaker's attentions," Amanda said.

"I can well understand it. The man appears to be a dull dog." The curate was a paradoxical combination of obsequiousness and priggery.

Relief flooded him that Amanda had rejected the smitten curate as a serious contender for her hand. Even his daughter's present allowance for fribbles would appear a fortune to Evan Whitaker in comparison to the churchman's own yearly stipend. Judging a potential suitor by the man's pocketbook might be unfair, but he knew no other certain method to keep fortune hunters at bay. He would have given a year of his life to secure a love match for Amanda as strong as had existed between his late wife, Ellen, and himself, and for a responsible son-in-law who could be trusted with the stewardship of his substantial holdings once he was gone. Amanda had been a sterling pupil in learning financial management, but the laws of England were not written to prevent a husband from squandering his wife's legacy. Even his substantial assets could be dissipated in record time by a loose-screw who played ducks and drakes with her inheritance. For proof, one needed look no further than his neighbor the Earl of Woods, who had died owing every moneylender in London.

"Papa, you could play loo with the other gentlemen in the card room. You know what enjoyment card playing gives you. The night would fly by," Amanda wheedled.

The idea of being trapped in an airless room at the assembly, enwreathed with a miasma of tobacco smoke for hours, was oppressive. Yet not too long ago Daniel's greatest pleasure had been a card game with his cronies that lasted until three or four in the morning in just such surroundings. But those were different men, the merchants of Bristol.

"Amanda, I can't agree. You shall have to wait until Lady Ainsworth's kin take flight and she once again is willing to chaperone you."

Amanda's spirits sank. The picture she carried in her mind of Rance Straughn and herself dancing together was evaporating into an airy hope never to be realized.

Daniel shifted in his chair and rubbed his knee.

"It's your leg, Papa, isn't it?" Amanda cried with melodramatic sympathy. "No wonder you denied me! I should have noticed your suffering. Dear, dear Papa, I am a selfish girl."

She jumped up, ran behind his chair, and flung her arms around his neck. "Of course we shan't go. You really should complain more. How can I know you are hurting if you insist on being stoic?"

Her outburst was not calculated but instinctive; yet it smacked of a long-standing ploy that had worked before in appealing to her father's guilt at refusing her a desire that was easily in his power to grant.

"Good gracious, Mandy, no need to make a Cheltenham tragedy out of my affliction. My leg is neither better nor worse than it's been for months. I shall take you to that infernal dance."

His own rapid acquiescence surprised Daniel. An instant before, he would have wagered a pony with all takers that nothing she said would induce him to promise to escort her to the dance. "Now let go of my neck or you'll throttle me!" he thundered, annoyed with himself for giving in too easily.

Amanda danced around the table. "Thank you, darling Papa. I love you, love you," she sang, and meant it.

"Such transports of delight," he muttered, but his lips traced a pleased smile. She was his life now that Ellen was gone. Of course, there was the pretty little widow in Bristol he had met a year before, but he wouldn't even consider remarrying until Amanda was settled.

"Come, Mandy, play the piano for me,' he invited, all crustiness faded. "We shall sing one of those risqué ditties the crewmen on our yacht taught you when you were seven or eight which used to send your mother into such a pet."

Amanda emitted a giggle, then turned sober, and gave her father a peck on the cheek. "Thank you, Papa . . . for giving in on the dance," she said softly, knowing what it had cost him.

"Certainly, Poppet." He pulled her arm through his, patted her hand, and led her to the music room for an hour of spirited singing at the pianoforte.

Chapter 4

During the intermission between the orchestra's first set of dances and the second set yet to come, Amanda stood conversing with Evan Whitaker and three of the Castleberry cousins. Ever since Rance's arrival nearly an hour before, Amanda's eyes had drifted across the assembly hall, watching him. Her heart had performed a funny little twist when she first caught sight of him in his formal finery. Whenever prudent, she followed his movements on the dance floor while she stood up with one young blade after another.

She noted each of the young women with whom he danced. But he seemed to be pinned to the opposite end of the dance floor and was selecting his dance partners from one or another of the tall young women in his immediate vicinity. If he maintained his current pace in choosing partners, the assembly would be over before he claimed the dance he had eagerly solicited from her in the village a few days earlier.

She laughed with the group around her at a witty trifle of gossip Felicia, the oldest Castleberry cousin, related. Caught up in the lively conversation, she momentarily neglected to track Rance Straughn's movements. So when he suddenly appeared beside her, she was nonplused to find him there.

Rance pushed past Evan Whitaker, nodding perfunctorily to the curate, whom he knew slightly.

"You look admirable this evening, my dear," Rance murmured into Amanda's ear. "I compliment you on your exquisite gown."

Evan Whitaker's pious eyes apprehended Rance's lingering gaze on Amanda's creamy bosoms above the décolletage of her rose silk dress. The clergyman's countenance darkened.

Amanda presented Rance to the three Castleberrys, Corrine, Felicia, and their brother, Stanley. Rance and the Castleberry cousins had just exchanged polite greetings, when Felicia nudged her sister. "Mama is beckoning to us."

The mother of the Castleberry "barbarians," who were actually rather handsome, fair-haired young people whose only crime was an outgoing nature, signaled her daughters from a green velvet sofa next to a Palladian window. She sat beside her sister-in-law, Lady Ainsworth.

Stanley Castleberry moved off with his sisters after reminding Amanda of her promise to dance the minuet with him later in the evening. Evan Whitaker moved closer to Amanda to safeguard her from Rance Straughn, who was rumored to be a rake.

"I've come to claim my dance, Miss Lofton," Rance said with a sweeping bow. "You haven't forgotten your promise to save a dance for me, have you?"

Evan Whitaker scowled. The young woman whom he had pursued for months gazed adoringly up at Mr. Straughn. She had never looked at *him* in such a breathless manner.

"Of course I haven't forgotten," she said to his sudden rival with a smile.

"Where did you and Mr. Straughn meet?" Evan blurted out. His normally cautious temperament flew away with the suspicion his courtship was in jeopardy and his undeclared love at risk.

"We met on my father's land when Mr. Straughn and his valet were boxing," Amanda said.

"Boxing?" Evan exploded, drawing censorious stares from several patrons for ignoring the socially dictated moderate tone appropriate to a ballroom. "You mean he and his valet were engaged in pugilism, and you watched?"

Rance stood with his hands clasped behind his back, an amused smirk about his lips and a twinkle in his sea-blue eyes. Amanda's brows rose into question marks at Evan's uncharacteristic loss of control. She could not recall ever having heard the curate raise his voice before.

"Oh, I see, Mr. Whitaker. You're shocked because Mr. Straughn and his valet were only partially clothed," she said unflappably.

Rance turned away, covering his mouth in a fit of coughing.

Amanda frowned at Evan's beet-red face. His apoplectic overreaction was uncalled for, even if he was a churchman. "You must realize, sir, I have been exposed numerous times since early childhood to bare-chested seamen on the Bristol docks."

Evan looked down his long nose at her disdainfully, but Amanda never learned his response to her dubious self-vindication. Just then the orchestra leader tapped his music stand to bring the small stringed orchestra to attention, and the floor came alive with ladies and gentlemen forming squares for the quadrille. Rance led Amanda to where three other couples waited for another pair to complete their set.

Evan, with arms folded, leaned against the wall, his sensibilities quite overset at the pernicious behavior of his fallen beloved. At this moment she was dancing with a suspected libertine. The two of them flirted outrageously, exchanging overly warm looks.

Could he, a curate, marry a woman who cared so little for her reputation that she would admit without a blush to having witnessed half-dressed men engaged in bare-knuckled brawling?

The orchestra's next selection would be a waltz, which he never danced, even though the board of governors of the assembly the previous year had deemed the continental import socially acceptable. Before the orchestra struck up the Viennese music, he would invite Miss Lofton to take refreshments with him as usual and make his feelings about her want of conduct known to her.

As the performers of the quadrille completed their final steps, Evan braced himself to swoop down on Miss Lofton as soon as the music stopped. Unknown to the curate, however, Rance was in the process of engaging Amanda for the upcoming waltz.

"But, Mr. Straughn," she demurred, "it would be unseemly for us to dance two dances one after the other."

"No one will notice, and should they, the offense will merit no more than a raised eyebrow or a mild scold from one of the dowagers." Amanda needed no further persuasion.

Evan was poised to dart to Amanda's side, when Lady Ainsworth's voice stopped him. "Mr. Whitaker," she called. Reluctantly, he moved to her side.

"Yes, my lady?" he asked more impatiently than politeness would allow, for he should have been making his way across the crowded floor to intercept Miss Lofton.

"I wish to make you known to Lord Ainsworth's sister-in-law, Mrs. Castleberry," the duchess said, dismissing his curtness without a thought. He managed to say all that was polite to Mrs. Castleberry and bowed to Josie, who sat perched on the edge of a mahogany side chair. The strains of the waltz drew his attention. He looked over his shoulder to see Amanda and Rance sailing past with buoyant unrestraint. He swept a cavalier's bow before Josie and impulsively pulled her to her feet with a mumbled invitation to dance.

* * *

Inwardly, Amanda was miffed whenever Evan Whitaker kept her captive during the first waltz. But she never showed her displeasure, for he was so obviously smitten with her that she could not find the backbone to refuse him. The chaperones seldom allowed more than two waltzes on a particular evening. Since the dance was Amanda's favorite, she would feel cheated if during the subsequent waltz her partner proved awkward and bungled the steps.

But tonight, even if Rance Straughn had proved to be an inept waltzer rather than the polished dancer that he was, she would have been in paradise, for she was in his arms.

Rance moved around the floor with grace and twirled her about with a fluid ease. She matched his exhilarating motions, following him with perfect synchronism. Like birds in flight they swooped and glided, their bodies moving as one.

"You are very good at this," Amanda said. Her voice had a breathy sound.

"The result of all the footwork when one learns to box. It makes a man light on his feet." His handsome mouth was set, but his blue eyes laughed merrily.

"More likely years of practice in the ballrooms of the *ton,*" she teased.

"Next you will accuse me of pursuing all things fashionable."

"Why, Mr. Straughn, I thought that the pursuit of the fashionable was indeed the sole occupation of the idle rich."

"Now, Miss Lofton, you know I am a poor man," he said, curling his lips in feigned sadness.

"Clown," she said under her breath. She gave him a wicked grin. "But you yourself confessed your distress is of a recent nature. When you were better situated, you must have spent an eternity mastering the fine points of cutting a dash in society."

"Spare me, my dear Miss Lofton. A gentleman of leisure who has pockets to let should be pitied, not chastised." He looked less like an object for pity than any person she was likely to meet. Amanda was certain he was a man who would never brood for long about his condition nor be brought permanently low by circumstances. Her heart quickened its pace when she knew she was in love with him.

"Have you ever been fathoms deep in love?" Her tilted face carried a bemused expression.

"Where did that unbeautiful thought come from?" Rance cringed without missing a step.

Amanda wrinkled a disapproving nose at his quelling remark, but she, too, wondered what caused her to ask the brazen question. Was she so dull-witted that she expected him to say "Yes, with you, my dear."

But she persisted. "Have you?"

He groaned. "Don't you know you are being impertinent?"

"Am I?" She could not believe her own audacity.

"Yes. One does not ask a gentleman questions of a personal nature on so short an acquaintance."

Her twinkling brown eyes challenged him. "Should I wait until we know each other better?"

"No," he said with intensity. "The question is inappropriate at any time. A man of honor does not gossip about former attachments."

Amanda smiled when she noticed a funny quirk dancing around his mouth as he battled to suppress a smile of his own and failed.

Rance wondered if she would ever say what he expected. She was guilelessly indifferent to the strictures of society. He found it one of her charms. He could not imagine anyone but a stiff-neck, like Whitaker, taking offense at her artless indiscretions. She may be shockingly forward, but he loved laughing with her over some bit of nonsense.

Rance manuevered her adroitly around a couple who

would have bumped into them had he and Amanda continued on their original path.

Amanda, encouraged by Rance's faltered reprimand, went on. "Josie often takes me to task for breaking the rules of polite society, but if I cross my heart and promise never to share your answer with anyone, will you confide in me?" She paused dramatically. "Have you ever been terribly in love?"

Rance raised a dubious brow. He appeared to be regarding her critically. She felt a little nervous. Had she gone over the line with her bad manners? She stared at him with stricken eyes, afraid he was disgusted with her.

Rance made a tutting noise and shook his head incredulously. "All right," he said at last, "I'll trust you with my secret."

Amanda's eyes widened, unable to believe she had worn him down so easily. But did she really want to hear him confess to being in love with someone? She suspected she would be quite jealous.

Rance stared into her eyes, brightened with excitement, and leaned nearer to her. He drank in the gentle fragrance of her hair and skin.

"I have not lost my heart irretrievably since I was five," he whispered. They shared a muted smile. Relief flew through Amanda at his facetious reply. He looked down at her and smiled his warm, attractive smile that caused her pulse to race in a ridiculous manner. She gave him back a smile of pure joy.

Their eyes locked, blue on brown. Her heart beat a wild tattoo against her chest, but she attempted to appear utterly calm.

"You dance beautifully too, my dear," Rance said, his voice a soft caress. He forced a tight rein on himself to vanquish the overpowering need to embrace her and taste her lips.

Unconcerned with anyone's critical opinion, their eyes remained locked. The naked desire he felt for her and she for him was there in their eyes for each to read.

Amanda willed the orchestra to play forever. She did not ever want to be released from Rance's arms. But all too soon the music stopped. Her breasts rose and fell with her quick breaths, and Rance gave her a warm hug so fleeting, no one around them noted the impropriety.

Earlier in the evening, Daniel had joined a foursome in the card room for a game of whist. After well over an hour's play, his leg cramped in the confined space beneath the card table. He relinquished his seat to a spectator eager to try his luck.

Bearing heavily on his cane, Daniel limped from the smoky card room, leaned on the jamb of the wide door to the ballroom, and worked the stiffness from his leg. Just then Amanda whirled past him, waltzing with a tall, good-looking young man, her radiant eyes locked onto her partner's. Daniel's heart leapt. Irrefutably, this blond giant was the reason Amanda had dragged him to the assembly that evening.

Daniel assessed the young man's formal jacket, snowy, frilled shirt, black satin breeches, striped silk hose, and fine leather pumps, and mentally calculated the cost of each tasteful, expensive item.

The well-to-do young man held Amanda properly with the exact light touch needed to guide her smoothly around the room and prevent a misstep. The two were completely absorbed in each other, a perpetual smile on each face. His daughter and her partner were the most graceful, as well as the handsomest, couple on the floor. A frisson of hope for Amanda's happiness coursed through Daniel's breast; and the Bristol widow, arrayed in a wedding dress, popped into his head.

Daniel shambled to Squire Samuels's side. The portly man was drinking a glass of fruit punch. Daniel suspected from the squire's obvious enjoyment of the drink that it had been liberally spiked with rum from a bottle stashed in the recesses of a deep pocket.

After proper greetings were exchanged, Daniel asked casually, "Squire, who is the young man dancing with my daughter?"

The squire surveyed the dance floor until he found Amanda and her partner. "That, sir, is the Honorable Terrance Straughn, the late Earl of Woods's younger son."

Daniel's optimism faded. "I gather the lad is the one who fared badly with his inheritance."

The squire cleared his throat, tugged Daniel's sleeve, and gave a quick jerk of his head toward the door. "Join me outside for a smoke, Lofton. I have some outstanding cigars from the West Indies. We can't talk free here."

Rance shepherded Amanda to two chairs that were hidden behind a trio of short but dense potted palms. The seats were not sought after, for the foliage successfully obliterated three quarters of the dance floor. The trees afforded a measure of privacy, but not enough to cover the cuddling of serious lovers. Amanda noted with satisfaction that the palms hid her and Rance from the eagle-eyed dowagers, whose occupation was to monitor the assembly for social improprieties.

Rance dabbed his flushed face with a clean white handkerchief.

"I enjoyed our dance greatly," he said.

Amanda snapped open an ivory fan. "As did I. I often sit out the first waltz with Mr. Whitaker. I fear I may have tweaked his nose, to say nothing of assulting his ideas of all that is proper."

"Is he a serious beau, then?"

Amanda laughed. "Hardly, just persistent."

With blatant desire Rance's eyes ran over Amanda's bosom, up her throat, and settled on her mouth. She moistened her lips with her tongue. His blond head moved closer and her breath quickened. "Straughn." A passing voice greeted Rance. Neither of them saw the encroacher, but Rance drew back.

"I'll fetch some fruit punch," he said.

Amanda fluttered the ivory fan with its whimsical Oriental scenes before her warm face and closed her eyes, imagining the near kiss. The moment had passed and would, regretfully, not be repeated that night. For a fleeting second, when his lips had come close, she had forgotten they were in a room filled with people. Had their lips connected, the results could have been disastrous. When she opened her eyes, Rance was approaching, juggling two glass cups.

Their conversation flowed easily and touched on this and that as they drank the lukewarm punch. He entertained her with vivid anecdotes of a grand tour he embarked on with a male companion when he was eighteen. Her comprehensive knowledge of European geography and history surprised him.

"You must have paid closer attention than most girls or had superior teachers at your school," he remarked.

"I never attended school. Both my mother, who died when I was fourteen, and my father actively participated in my education." She paused. "And you, Mr. Straughn, where were you educated? Oxford? Cambridge?" she asked. Too late, she remembered Josie's mentioning he had been sent down from Cambridge. She felt a twinge of guilt for allowing her tongue to run wild.

Rance studied the empty cup he cradled in his large hands. "Cambridge, but I never finished."

"Oh, neither did Mr. Coleridge . . . graduate from Cambridge, that is," she said, smoothing over her bad moment.

Rance straightened. "Ah, you are acquainted with Coleridge, the writer? 'It is an ancient Mariner/And he stoppeth one of three . . . '?"

"Yes, my mother attended literary salons. She sometimes took me with her. I met Mr. Coleridge there, but I was more fascinated with Lord Byron. He read excerpts from *Childe Harold* when it was first published. I had a mad crush on him and went to embarrassing lengths to insinuate myself into his conversations with other women, until my mother had to take me in hand and give me quite a shake."

Rance chuckled. "You were bold even then, I see."

"Bold?" she said with such a sweet expression of innocence, he almost believed her ingenuous mien.

"Bold," he reaffirmed, smiling.

"Perhaps," she owned up with a flutter of her fan.

"And tell me, did all this poetic absorption arouse the muse in you? Are you a poetess as well?"

"Oh, no, I haven't the fancy for successful verse. What writing I have done has been of a mundane nature. I wrote an essay describing the vendors I saw on a London street early in the morning, when my parents took me for a visit to the city. You know, the muffin man, and the milkmaid selling fresh milk from her cow, and the flower girl, and such. My mother read it to the literati and everyone clapped, but I know those learned people were being kind to the child thrust among them by a doting parent."

"If no one chronicled daily life, how would generations to come know how we lived in these times?" Rance said. "Your mother's friends probably recognized the merits of your effort."

She gave him a velvety look for his unexpected support, but he was leaning to the side to see better the portion of the dance floor open to his view. "If I'm not mistaken, Lady Ainsworth is bearing down on us."

"Oh, dear! Have we been talking together for more than one dance?" she cried.

Lady Ainsworth's censoring voice cut off any further exchange between them. "Amanda, my sister-in-law has belatedly pointed out to me that you have been in a tête-à-tête with Mr. Straughn for the last two dances. Have you no concern for your reputation? Conventions must be observed," she scolded. "And you, Rance, are no youth wet behind the ears. You are well aware of the rules, and, surely need no further blackening of your character."

Amanda's eyes widened at the insulting reprimand, but Rance laughed insouciantly, scratching behind his ear. "I apologize, my lady," he said, unruffled. "Believe me, I am innocent, in this case at least. I simply did not mind the time."

"Hummmph!" Her ladyship was clearly not convinced. "You are promised to Stanley for the next dance," she said, grasping Amanda's arm in a steel grip. Amanda tossed a doleful glance at Rance and handed him her empty punch cup before Lady Ainsworth hustled her off.

Amanda searched for Rance's blond head while she danced the minuet with Stanley, but he was nowhere in the room. Daniel signaled her discreetly from the edge of the dance floor, and she directed Stanley toward him at the completion of the minuet.

"I wish to go home now, Amanda," Daniel said after the young man withdrew. "Let us say our good nights to Lady Ainsworth."

Settled in the opulent carriage with Amanda beside him, Daniel tapped his cane on the roof of the coach, and William, his driver of twenty years, sprang the bays. The coach moved forward. Daniel snapped the carriage blind down, flung his hat and cane onto the opposite seat, and stretched out his afflicted leg. He pressed the back of his head against the magenta velvet squabs and closed his eyes.

Amanda's whole being was enveloped in a euphoria caused by, in her own words to Stanley Castleberry, ". . . the best dance I have ever attended." She could not see her father clearly in the shadowy interior of the coach, but was aware of the tension in him. He had seemed perturbed ever since she joined him after he signaled her while she danced with Stanley.

"Was it too bad, Papa?" she asked solicitously.

"Leave off, Amanda, please," he begged. "I do not care to listen to your rattle." The hard words were not spoken harshly, but floated on a resigned sigh.

Amanda settled into the opposite corner of the seat with a small pout and wrapped her rose velvet pelisse securely around her against the night's chill. She would not let

Papa's grumpiness sully her evening. She wanted to tuck this wondrous night into a secret place in her heart, where she could reach down and bring it out to relive whenever she was alone.

Beside her, Daniel had less agreeable meditations. He forced the unsettling random thoughts that chased about in his brain into a semblance of order. On the veranda at the back of the building that housed the assembly, Squire Samuels had unleashed the most damning evidence against the Honorable Terrance Straughn. The young man he had taken to be proper at first glance was far from acceptable as a suitor for Amanda. "The boy is heavy in the petticoat line." "Bets deep on card games." "Frequents the racecourses." "Sent down from Cambridge." His was the pattern of the wild London dandy.

The most telling evidence, however, was the squire's testimony that Leonard Straughn, the present Lord Woods, had confided to him that the sorely strapped younger Straughn was in the market for an heiress. Amanda's name had been bandied about as a possible candidate.

Well, the wastrel will not get a cent of my money, Daniel vowed, knotting his fists.

Amanda nudged Daniel's hat and cane on the opposite seat with the toe of her satin slipper. Her father emitted a sound that came out a cross between a grumble and a grunt. Her own joy overrode her guilt that the dance she had forced him to attend had left him morose. She planned, however, to thank him prettily for his sacrifice when she kissed him good night. But once inside the house, Daniel waved off her gratitude, mumbled an incoherent reply, and limped down the hall after Jeffries, the butler, to the drawing room, where a fire had been laid and a superior French brandy decanted.

Upstairs in her bedroom Amanda's abigail helped her to change from the rose silk gown into a lace-edged nightdress.

"You may go, Mary," Amanda said when the small, dark-haired maid had turned down the silken bedcovers and plumped the goose-feather pillow. Amanda was eager to be alone and give full attention to the visions of Mr. Straughn that played deliciously in her head.

"But your hair, Miss Amanda." Mary reached up to unpin a coiled knot.

"I will take it down." Amanda moved beyond the reach of the rosy-faced maid. "Go to your bed now."

Mary nodded, curtsied, and left the room, closing the door quietly behind her.

Amanda curled up in the big wing chair near the fireplace, where a brightly burning fire warded off the chill of the spring night. She covered her bare feet with the hem of her cotton nightgown. Daniel's strange demeanor flitted across her mind, but was pushed aside immediately for more deserving memories of the evening. She shut her eyes and hummed the Viennese tune the orchestra had been playing when she waltzed in Rance Straughn's arms. He liked her. He had singled her out for special attention. An indifferent swain did not stand up with a woman for two dances in a row, lead her to a secluded corner for a private conversation, and risk incurring the wrath of the eagle-eyed chaperones to spend some intimate moments with her.

Amanda hunched her shoulders and made a great show of shivering when she recalled the scene with Lady Ainsworth. She had felt a swift rush of fear when Josie's mother had approached them with a dreadful scowl on her face. How unmercifully she had scolded Mr. Straughn. But he had not been at all perturbed, and defused the bad moment with a cheerful reply, she thought with admiration.

Josie claimed Rance Straughn was kind. Amanda could not quarrel with her friend's assessment. She refused to credit the black marks against his name, certain they were just misunderstandings. Their conversation had been light, inconsequential, and exploratory. All that one would wish between nascent lovers, she thought happily.

Amanda uncurled herself and rose from the comfortable chair, lifted her nightgown to her knees, and executed a few carefree waltz steps from her fireside chair to the vanity table. Her shadow, taller than herself, danced breezily with her on the bedroom wall. She dropped down onto the crewel-embroidered seat of the cherrywood bench facing the mirror and toyed with the lid of the blue Grecian jar that held her hairpins. She plucked their mates from her elaborate coiffure, deposited them into the receptacle, and disentangled the knotted locks of her freed hair with her spread fingers.

A few days before, on the overlook, she first saw Mr. Straughn and learned that time had absolutely nothing to do with love. She had lost her heart in a second, although she had known little about him. The next day in front of Cauthen's she had a bad moment when Josie revealed his true identity. But Mr. Straughn redeemed himself after Amanda accused him of hoodwinking her. Tonight she had looked into his laughing blue eyes and knew she would never be the same again.

"Rance," she said aloud, testing the name on her tongue. She wanted him more than ever. He had aroused in her unfamiliar feelings of sensual awareness when he flagrantly devoured her with his eyes in full view of society.

Yet she knew instinctively that his emotions were not as seriously engaged as hers. Men were accomplished actors when it came to seductive flirtation. Although she had laid bare her true emotions, Rance had been far less sincere. He was not deliriously in love with her. But she was sure he liked her more than a little.

Amanda puffed out the candle and climbed into bed. For a long while she battled to force her eyelids open, reluctant to relinquish Rance Straughn's handsome face to a random dream.

When she next became aware, morning birds were singing in the oak tree beside her balcony.

Chapter 5

Forty minutes later Amanda sat alone in the breakfast parlor, Daniel having eaten earlier. The spring sunshine surged through the sheer jonquil curtains, flooding the room with cheerful morning light. She rotated a soft-boiled egg in its cup, dipped a spoon into the center of the egg, mixed the yolk and white, and lifted the spoon to her mouth.

The previous night she had pushed aside Daniel's peculiar behavior in favor of concentrating on examining Rance Straughn's attentions to her. This morning she turned over the possible reasons her father had plunged into a blue funk, but she could not come up with a plausible answer. His vile mood of the evening before nagged at her, nearly but not quite dwarfing her happiness at her success with Rance Straughn at the dance. Even after a night's sleep she remained certain Mr. Straughn liked her above the common. No man could have been so charmingly and conspicuously attentive and felt nothing for her.

Amanda nibbled on a piece of buttered toast. She would burst if she couldn't speak his name aloud to someone. Josie must be awake by now. After a dance, when Amanda spent the night at Ainsworth House, she and Josie would compare notes and talk into the early morning hours. But her father had rushed her away from the assembly without allowing her an opportunity even to bid her friend good night.

Amanda drained the last trace of her tea, made to pour more from the Spode teapot, decided against a refill, and replaced the pot on the trivet.

She stared down at her comfortable old riding skirt and scuffed, well-broken-in boots. She wasn't dressed properly for a morning call at Ainsworth House, but it would take too long to change and order a chaise. Besides, Willie, the stable boy, would already have saddled Nancy and brought the mare around for Amanda's morning ride. Lady Ainsworth slept until noon after an assembly, and Josie's father was in London, no doubt escaping the Castleberry "barbarians." She could sneak up to Josie's room without being seen by the cousins or their mother, who probably would not be about this early either after the late night. Unable to contain herself, Amanda threw down her napkin and pushed back her chair.

In a short time she was rapping the brass knocker on the door to Ainsworth House.

"You needn't announce me, Graves," she said to the senescent butler who admitted her, his dim eyes squinting unbelievingly at Amanda's casual attire, which he deemed fit only for working in the garden.

"I'll just skip up to Lady Josephine's room," Amanda said, running past him to the steps of the divided staircase. The old man shook his head, certain his weak eyes had deceived him. Miss Lofton was the sole of propriety when it came to dress. She would never arrive for a morning call in dishabille.

"Unthinkable, unthinkable," he muttered, convincing himself he had not seen what he knew he had.

Amanda knocked on Josie's bedroom door and entered on her friend's "Come!"

"Amanda," Josie squealed from her bed, where she was

enjoying her breakfast from a tray, "what are you doing here this time of the morning and dressed like that? Have you lost your wits? Suppose Mama should see you."

Amanda flopped down at the foot of the bed. "I just stopped by for a second on my morning ride. Anyway, your mother doesn't stir until after noon." She scanned the tray, lifted the silver lid from a covered dish, removed a muffin, and took a bite. "Did anything exciting happen with you last evening?"

Before Josie could answer, Amanda blurted out proudly, "Do you know I danced two dances in a row with Mr. Straughn and scandalized myself by sitting out two more with him?"

Josie giggled. "I know. I watched him exchanging torrid looks with you. Mama carped about your behavior, but most of her maledictions fell on poor Rance's head."

Amanda hunched her shoulders and grimaced. "Should I apologize, do you think?"

"I would leave it alone were I you. She is taking out some of her peevishness on Aunt Emma for not warning her sooner that you and Rance had your heads together behind the palms." Josie paused, and a sly smile curled onto her lips. "Amanda, I waltzed with Evan Whitaker."

"Mr. Whitaker? Josie, I don't believe you!" Amanda cried. "Why, the curate sits out every waltz." Her eyebrows arched as she observed Josie's smug little face. "Did he really waltz?"

"He did!" Josie fairly shouted. "I must warn you, Mandy. You are quite lowered in his eyes after having made such a cake of yourself with Rance."

"Indeed?" Amanda chuckled.

Josie nodded happily. "You remember how it was with you and Rance in front of Cauthen's the other day? It was the same for Evan and me, only stranger, for we have known each other an age and never realized we suited until last night. And I have you to thank, Mandy. I know he asked me to waltz to spite you. But he realized quickly how shallow you are, and how fine I am!'' she revealed with gleeful malice.

Amanda chortled. ''That's putting me in my place.'' How fickle her former swain!

Josie's pert little nose wriggled with pleasure. ''I told Mama that Evan wanted to call on me and she agreed. She says Evan's family can afford to help a younger son, so Papa can have no objection should I be able to bring him to the point.''

''Josie, you're in love,'' Amanda teased.

''I'm not exactly yet, but I do think I would make a much better parson's wife than you, Mandy.''

''That is a certainty,'' Amanda agreed, wiping her hands on Josie's napkin. ''That muffin was good. I should send our cook over to get the recipe.''

''What of you and Rance?'' Josie asked, indifferent to the merits of the muffin. ''Will he be courting you, do you think?''

The realities, which until that moment Amanda had been unwilling to permit to darken her rainbow, could not be concealed from Josie.

''We got on splendidly, but I fear Papa won't approve. I think, Josie, someone might have had Papa's ear at the dance last night,'' she guessed. ''Did you see him speaking to anyone who is known to gossip?''

''Gracious, Amanda, you know everyone does,'' she said. ''I thought I saw Mr. Lofton with Squire Samuels when Evan and I were waltzing.''

Amanda sighed. ''The squire could have been the one. I do hope I'm mistaken. Papa's leg could have been paining him, or he may have imagined an affront, which would be certain to put him in a foul mood. I feel responsible because I shamelessly cajoled him into escorting me to the dance against his will,'' she said, rising from the bed. ''Oh, well, if I'm at fault, Papa will admonish me soon enough. Where is Felicia?'' Amanda looked around the room.

''She went down to breakfast a while ago.''

''I'd better leave before she returns and begins an interrogation. Have you confided your feelings for Mr. Whitaker to her?''

"Heavens no, although naturally Mama won't be able to resist lording it over Aunt Emma that I have captured the interest of an eligible suitor. The whole house will soon know Mr. Whitaker has turned his attentions to me." Josie was clearly pleased with her new status.

Restraining Amanda with an outstretched hand, Josie endeavored to solace her friend. "Perhaps Mr. Lofton saw Rance and took no notice. He and the squire might have been discussing crop yields or something."

"Perhaps, but sooner or later Papa will know who Rance is, particularly if Rance calls on me, as I hope he will. Papa is like a horse with blinders that sees only in one direction. Mr. Straughn has no money; ergo, he must be a fortune hunter."

Josie said sheepishly, "There's no denying, though, Mandy, that Rance is looking to marry a rich woman. His sister-in-law has drawn up a list of eligibles who failed to bring a suitor up to scratch. Albert heard it from Freddie, and Freddie wouldn't make up unflattering stories about his own uncle."

"Just because Rance is in the market for a wealthy woman doesn't necessarily mean he is after my money if he courts me. He could be in love with me, you know, or terribly interested anyway."

"Oh, of course, Amanda," Josie rushed to say. "I did not mean to imply otherwise. He is probably genuinely attracted to you, but you're the one who insists your papa won't believe him."

Amanda bent down to touch cheeks with Josie. "I'd better go," she said, deflated. The visit to Josie, instead of uplifting her, had disheartened her.

Daniel shambled toward the library as Amanda burst through the front door. "Easy, Amanda," he scolded mildly. "Where did you ride?" he asked, balancing with both hands on a hickory walking stick.

"Over to see Josie."

"Dressed like that?" Daniel's mouth formed a stern line. "You have several armoires crammed with the latest fashions. Surely, you could have found something more appropriate. Wasn't Lady Ainsworth scandalized?"

"My lady was still in bed. After a dance she is never downstairs until at least one o'clock. Anyway, no one who really matters saw me."

Daniel shook his head. "You are bent on disgracing me," he said, but his voice lightened perceptively. "Do change into something more appropriate before lunch, however." The harsh line of his mouth molded into a smile as he looked down at his own disreputable house shoes. "Go," he said, motioning her away with one hand. Amanda grinned and fled up the stairs.

She felt easier after her encounter in the hall with Daniel. Perhaps his petulance of the previous night had not been about Mr. Straughn at all. She began to think she had overblown the severity of his pique.

After a pleasant lunch with Daniel, Amanda retired to her upstairs sitting room to write a letter to Sylvia Morrow, an old friend from her Bristol days. She tapped her pen against her teeth for inspiration while she gazed out the window that faced the drivepath from the village road. She leaned over the desk to see better the horse and rider who had just come into view around the bend in the carriageway. Her heart gave a funny little twist. The horse was unmistakably Bluebell, and the awkward rider could only be Rance Straughn.

Amanda watched Rance for a few seconds before she threw down the pen, sprinkling Miss Morrow's letter with unsightly black blotches. She dashed into the adjacent bedroom, plopped down onto the vanity chair, and began brushing her hair vigorously. She ran to the rosewood-framed cheval glass and smoothed the nearly invisible wrinkles from her lilac cotton gown. Should she change into the new blue dimity frock that had arrived from London last Monday? There wouldn't be time, for she did not want to keep him waiting. Facing the closed door with her hands clasped nervously in front of her, she anticipated Jeffries's knock and his announcement that her caller awaited her in the drawing room.

After several minutes passed without the butler summoning her, Amanda pulled open the door, moved into the upstairs hall, and peered over the mahogany rail. A man's beaver hat lay on the hall table. Descending the stairs, she caught the butler just before he vanished into the servants' wing.

"Did you just admit a tall young man with fair hair, Jeffries?" Amanda asked.

"Yes, Miss Amanda. He's in the library with Mr. Lofton."

Amanda thanked him, climbed to the top of the stairs, and sat where she could look down on the closed library door visible on the far right of the hall. She did not even try to guess what Rance had to say to her father, but a terrible hollow formed in the pit of her stomach.

Jeffries had taken Rance's engraved card into Daniel and within a minute had returned and ushered Rance into the library. The room had book-filled floor-to-ceiling shelves on two walls. The pleasant smell of ancient leather from the book bindings mixed with the odor of beeswax from the highly polished walnut library table and gentleman's desk.

Daniel Lofton sat in a burgundy leather easy chair, his right leg resting on a matching leather footstool. "You must excuse me, Mr. Straughn, for not rising, but I have a rheumatic knee that seems to have chosen this moment to act up."

Rance begged him to remain comfortable and approached Daniel to shake hands with the seated man.

Just as Rance proffered his hand, Daniel's eyes dropped to the papers in his lap that he had been reading before Rance entered, and he began shuffling them. When he raised his eyes to his visitor, Rance had withdrawn his hand and was standing before him, stiff and straight, a trace of irritation on his lips.

Rance glanced toward an inviting forest-green armchair, but his host did not invite him to sit down. An incipient doubt about the wisdom of this call crept into Rance's mind. Apparently he was to be kept standing as if he were an errant schoolboy. He straightened his shoulders and brought his tall frame into a military stance.

Daniel set aside his papers on a side table. "Now, Mr. Straughn, have we met before?" he asked.

"No, sir, we haven't. However, I believe you are acquainted with my half brother, Lord Woods."

"Ever so slightly, I'm afraid. We met, with our lawyers present, to iron out some long-standing boundary disputes when I purchased Rook Manor. I must admit the meetings were amicable, but I have never had the pleasure of being invited to Willowwoods." Daniel emitted a short, mirthless laugh. "But, of course, I am not such a boor that I would actually believe that as a man of trade those doors would be open to me."

Rance's mouth tightened and his body stiffened. Daniel Lofton was being deliberately rude. His brother had made a bad mistake in believing this man would be eager to receive a Straughn. Nevertheless, Rance decided to be courteous. It would have been poor taste to barge into the man's house to call on his daughter without making himself known to him. At that moment Rance wished he had introduced himself to Daniel Lofton at the dance and avoided the necessity of this more formal meeting.

"What is your business with me, Straughn?" Daniel asked, intentionally dropping the "Mr."

"Not business, sir. I am here to request your permission to call on Miss Lofton." Rance's voice was strong and firm despite his discomfort. He met Daniel's frosty brown eyes straight on.

"If my daughter wishes to receive you, I have no objections provided your intentions are not running toward a serious relationship," Daniel said. "Marriage, perhaps?"

"No, certainly not," Rance answered. "Not that Miss Lofton isn't a worthy young lady," he added quickly, not wanting to give the impression he found Amanda unacceptable. "We got on well together at the assembly. But marriage, no. In any case, I find myself in straightened circumstances and am not in a position to support a wife," he said honestly. Burning to quit the room and end the interview with this disagreeable man, Rance hurried on. "With your permission, I shall leave you to your work, then, sir, and see if Miss Lofton is available to receive me."

Daniel ignored Rance's bid to leave, rested his chin on his clasped hands, and stared with glacial eyes at his visitor. "Are you saying Lord Woods has not suggested a marriage to my well-dowered daughter as a means of solving your financial dilemma?"

Taken aback by the rude query, Rance felt trapped. He said, "That's not what you asked me." But he was aware his evasive answer was as good as an admission Leonard had put forth such a proposal.

Daniel did not bother to ask Rance to clarify his circumvention. He had the verification he sought.

"Your courtship is doomed to failure," he said sullenly.

Rance's eyes darkened. "Courtship? I thought I made myself clear on that. However, from your tone, sir, I see I am unwelcome in your house. In that case, we may consider the interview concluded." He made to leave, but checked himself when Daniel droned on.

"Amanda has a little money of her own. I once gave her five hundred pounds to invest in some cargo, and she made a few hundred pounds profit on the speculation. Since then, the money has been invested with a business firm in Bristol, but the income would hardly keep you in imported brandy for a year."

Rance shook his head. This visit had begun as a conventional social call. Now he was being rejected for an untendered marriage proposal. The man was clearly mad. "Marriage is not a consideration," Rance reiterated impatiently.

Disregarding his visitor's disclaimer, Daniel went on. "Should you think to elope with her, you might keep that figure in mind, for it is all you shall have."

Rance's brows beetled. The situation was ludicrous, but he stood rooted with perverse fascination, unable to break away from the unwarranted lecture by this ill-bred churl.

"You can expect not even an additional pound from me, but then, perhaps you are better heeled than I have been led to believe. How much money do you have?"

"Nearly two thousand," Rance blurted out, his mind muzzy from the inane situation. Too late, he wished he had told Lofton to go to hell.

"Far from what Amanda's accustomed to," Daniel continued, "but not an impossible income."

"No, no, Lofton, not income, cash," Rance corrected the older man as he began to regain his equilibrium.

"Damme, guineas, I suppose?"

"Pounds," Rance shot back, "as you damn well know! I'll wager you know my balance to the penny!"

Daniel shook his head and smirked maliciously. "No, I don't, as a matter of fact. I'm surprised you have that much. You could always pray I'll die, for then Amanda would inherit all, but I am still a relatively young man, and this damned leg aside, I am in excellent health. But should the worst happen, or from your view the best, and I should put my spoon in the wall prematurely within the next few months, you would be in luck. Amanda is capable of running the estate for a profit, if you were to keep your bungling hands out of the business."

Rance clenched and unclenched his fists. His anger rose. "That's enough of your charade, Lofton. You've made your point. During a brief sojourn here, I'm assisting my brother with the management of the estate. But I see I'd best forget any calls on Miss Lofton."

"You are involved in the overseeing of Willowwoods? What could you possibly contribute?" Daniel derided him.

Since Rance had been working with Leonard on the estate, he had begun to appreciate the labor that went into maintaining a productive property. He had been reading pamphlets on scientific farming and discussing his ideas with his brother. He got along with the tenants better than did Leonard. He was able to hold the dignity of his position as a Straughn and still show friendliness, while Leonard often played the lord of the manor with a certain heaviness toward the people who lived and labored on his land.

"More than you might think," Rance defended himself. "Riding here, I had the opportunity to survey Rook Manor, and I could see where some improvements could be made to benefit your own estate."

Daniel's eyes were ice. "You would dare advise me! Boy, have you ever earned a farthing that didn't depend on the turn of a card? When I was your age, I owned a four-masted sloop that called with a full load of cargo at Boston, Barbados, and Jamaica! And I was well on my way to outfitting a second ship. I fought and scratched to create a successful business in spite of the thieves and marauders of your class . . . like you . . . who tried to cheat me out of what was mine," he stormed, losing his composure. He tilted his head back, put a hand over his mouth, and closed his eyes for a second, regaining the self-control he prized. "Straughn, I don't believe for a moment that you would not like to get your hands on my daughter's money," Daniel said. "My fondest hope is that the truths I have instilled in her are so firmly in place that she will not be taken in by a handsome, aristocratic face with nothing to offer her but misery, for I cannot lock her up." He paused for a calming breath. "Amanda does not reach her majority for more than two years. She requires my permission to wed, and for all my talk of an elopement, I don't believe she would set off for Gretna Green with you. *Your* needs, on the other hand, are immediate. You cannot afford to wait for your bride of convenience. I strongly suggest you and your brother cast your lures elsewhere."

Rance fumed inwardly, but with great difficulty maintained his control. To protest he had not fallen in with Leonard's scheme to offer for this merchant's daughter would be futile. Lofton despised the aristocracy. Should England ever have an upheaval as France did in eighty-nine, Lofton would head the bourgeois who would lead Rance and his class to the guillotine.

"You know, Lofton, it's not that you have sullied your hands in trade that deems you unacceptable, but your unbearable arrogance and rag manners that separate you from the true gentlemen of England. Good day, sir." Rance turned on his heel, stormed from the room, and slammed the door to the library.

Daniel's lips curled into an unhandsome sneer. He felt a certain pride on being man enough to note the justice of Mr. Straughn's reprimand, but he resented it all the same.

On the staircase Amanda winced at the crack of the door. Rance snatched his hat from the table, and nearly bowled over the hapless butler who hurried before him to let him out. After he closed the door on Rance, Jeffries let out an undignified whoosh and trod back to the servants' wing.

Amanda, skirts raised, raced down the stairs and out the front door. "Mr. Straughn," she called. Rance was already on Bluebell's back, impatiently urging the lethargic mare forward. He reined in the horse and waited for Amanda to reach his side.

"Did he send you off with a flea in your ear?" she asked more lightly than she felt.

Rance smiled wanly in spite of himself. The anger died a full degree. "I had the last word," he bragged. "But we are not likely to share a friendly glass of port anytime soon."

Amanda scratched Bluebell's neck. "That bad. What did you want from him?"

"Nothing that warranted the set-down I received. Just to call on you. The rest you best ask him. Your father has a wicked tongue, Miss Lofton. I shall not cross the threshold of Rook Manor again if I outlive Methuselah's years."

Amanda taunted playfully, " 'Faint heart ne'er won fair lady' as Shakespeare said."

"No, you are wrong."

"About which? Faint heart or fair lady?"

"Neither. You are wrong about Shakespeare. It was Cervantes."

"Never!" Amanda objected.

"Sorry, some character—can't recall who—in Motteux's translation of *Don Quixote* uses it something like this: The adage says, 'Faint heart ne'er won fair lady.' "

"Well, there you are! He's quoting someone else. Spenser, maybe."

The incongruity of a literary argument after his dressing-down by Lofton struck Rance suddenly as being absurd.

"It doesn't matter. Call me fainthearted if you will, but I do not have the stomach to cross swords with an indignant father. I hope, Miss Lofton, my ill-advised visit to Mr. Lofton will have no repercussions for you."

She laughed. "What an ogre Daniel Lofton must seem to you. I have never seen that side of him. No fear that he will beat me, Mr. Straughn."

"That is reassuring. I would not want my folly to cause you pain in any way. I must be off now on my Rosinante."

"Don't insult Bluebell. You are hurting her feelings. Don Quixote's steed was a bag of bones." Amanda stroked Bluebell's white neck, whispering to the cob, "Don't listen to him, sweet girl, you are a beauty." The horse's ears twitched in response to her soft words.

Amanda patted the homely cob's nose. She looked up

at Rance, who, with an abstracted stare, was watching her antics.

"Couldn't your brother furnish you with a better mount?" she asked.

"He keeps only carriage and cart horses, some drays, and one decent rider of his own, but the stallion is off limits to me. Bluebell is Freddie's, but my nephew is ashamed of her. He begs for a new horse, but Leonard hasn't the funds now; so Freddie will have to make do with this hack or go without for a good while yet."

"What happened to your own horse? You surely had one."

"When you lack the ready, Miss Lofton, a horse is a luxury you cannot afford. I had to sell Kelly, my blood stallion."

"Kelly?" Amanda's lips quirked. "Very Irish."

Rance half grinned. "Brian McGonigal named him," he explained. "I could not afford to feed both myself and the horse. I suppose it was selfish of me, but I despise going hungry."

"Wise choice. I regret things didn't work out, Mr. Straughn, I think we might have dealt well together."

"Perhaps. But we shall never know, shall we?"

Their eyes met and held as they had at the dance the previous night, but there was no promise in his eyes now.

"Good day, Miss Lofton," Rance murmured, holding fast to the reins and touching the brim of his hat with his left hand. Amanda noticed one tanned finger was banded in white. He had worn a ring until recently on the hand. Another item sold to raise money.

She watched him urge the cob into a canter and did not turn back to the house until he was out of sight at the end of the lane. Papa had never forbidden her to receive a young man. Should he do so now, she could plead on Rance Straughn's behalf, but probably to no purpose. Mr. Straughn had made it clear he would never come to Rook Manor again. She could still run into him on the overlook and dance with him at the assembly, unless Papa specifically prohibited her from communicating with him. Such a restraint would be unbearable. She would remain mute as Josie had suggested when she asked her friend if she should apologize to Lady Ainsworth. Silence was safest when one faced an unreceptive parent. Let Papa be the first to mention Mr. Straughn, and she would react in her best interest when he did.

Chapter 6

A few days after his altercation with Rance Straughn, Daniel sat in the burgundy leather chair in his library. He nursed a tumbler of French brandy and stared unseeingly at the business papers resting in his lap, his thoughts on his daughter. He had prepared himself for her attempt to cajole him into permitting Straughn to call on her. But she never mentioned his name. He knew from a remark Jeffries let drop that she had been aware of Straughn's visit.

Her starry-eyed countenance when she waltzed with the young aristocrat had led Daniel to believe she welcomed the man's attentions. That coupled with Straughn's appearance the next day in his library solidified his first impression. But all the attentiveness must have been on Straughn's part. The young aristocrat was strapped and leeching off his brother, unable to earn enough to support himself. By his own admission he had a small reserve of two thousand pounds, pin money to a young buck with dissipating habits. In all likelihood, Straughn had seen the futility in pursuing Amanda and had gone on to greener pastures.

The fiery brandy slipped warmly down Daniel's throat. If Amanda had been interested in Straughn at all, it had been no more than a one-night flirtation. Since the assembly, she had cheerfully involved herself with the Castleberry cousins who had invaded Ainsworth House. His concern that Amanda had fallen prey to Straughn's charms was unfounded, Daniel decided. He congratulated himself on successfully running off the pinched aristocrat with the grasping hands. With a clear conscience he turned his attention to the cost estimate for the sawmill he was constructing for his tenants.

At the exact moment Daniel relegated Rance Straughn to the past, Amanda settled her back against a boulder and arranged the skirts of her fashionable riding outfit demurely about her legs. She looked up in time to witness Rance's soft left jab into Brian McGonigal's shoulder. The Irishman successfully deflected the following hard right punch to his chest. Rivulets of perspiration ran down the intense faces and disciplined bodies of the two boxers as they sparred in the warm spring sun.

"Time!" Rance called and the Irishman dropped his knotted fists. "Enough for today, Brian."

"You're through already?" Amanda cried, jumping to her feet. "I just got here."

"We're not doing this for your pleasure, Miss Lofton," Rance said with an ironical twitch to his lips. "Brian and I have been at this better than an hour."

She screwed up her nose and stuck her tongue out at him, her laughter commingling with his as he chortled at the childish antic.

As he toweled his chest, he gazed at her reflectively. For the second time since the ill-fated interview with her insufferable father, she was on the overlook, watching Brian and him spar. On the previous occasion he had hurried away with Brian after the training, exchanging only a few inconsequential words with her. That day he had looked back as he entered the path to Willowwoods to find her staring after him with a woebegone expression marring her usually sunny face. Inexplicably, he had experienced a tug at his heart and a fleeting urge to dash back to her and apologize for brushing her aside. But, plainly, his neglectful conduct had left her undaunted, for here she was again.

Rance reached for his white shirt draped over a bush. Amanda busied herself adjusting the cinch on Nancy's saddle, her back turned decorously to give Rance privacy. He buttoned the shirt and tucked the garment into his pantaloons and strolled over to her. He sat down on the boulder. Brian dropped onto the grass a discreet distance from Amanda and Rance, pretending an interest in the hill dotted with dandelions like so many golden guineas sprinkled over the landscape.

"Miss Lofton, I don't think you should be visiting me here," Rance said. "Your father does not approve of me, you know."

"He lets me make my own decisions," she declared with a defiant toss of her chin. Rance raised a skeptical brow.

"He does!" she asserted.

"Amanda . . . may I call you Amanda?" he asked. Her name on his lips had the sweet sound of an endearment.

"You may," she agreed with no hint in her voice of her inner pleasure.

"Amanda, I know for a fact Mr. Lofton would prefer you to cut me dead when we meet. Are you asking me to believe he has left the decision to you and not made it clear I am to be shunned at all cost?" He found it inconceivable, given his interview with Lofton, that the merchant had not forbidden his daughter to traffic with him.

"I can tell you with complete candor he has never spoken of you to me," she said. "And I'll have you know, he does not dictate my friends."

Rance rubbed his hands over his lips. His instincts told him she was playing a May game with him. Lofton, he was certain, would never sanction a friendship between him and his daughter at her discretion. But he would not allow himself to be cast in the role of watchdog. She was deuced appealing and had given him every sign of a willingness to carry on a dalliance.

When he spoke again, she knew she had won the day and would not have to persuade him further.

"Your Nancy is a sweet mare," he said, stroking the horse's nose. "She rides well?" he asked.

"Oh, yes! Would you care to try her?" she asked impulsively.

Rance laughed. "How? I haven't mastered a lady's saddle."

When Amanda was still a baby, Daniel acquired a small farm outside Bristol. It was there Amanda learned to ride. As a child, she envied the boys who were not constrained to using the unwieldy sidesaddle. One day when she was ten, she rode far from the house, stripped off the lady's saddle, hiked up her skirts, and tossed her bare legs over the back of her small mare. Being perfectly balanced on a horse was a revelation. The sidesaddle quickly seemed a ridiculous, unnatural contrivance. Over the years, at times, she secretly rode astride in the confines of the secluded farm. Only since Daniel had moved his stables to Rock Manor had she totally given up the practice.

"Can't you ride bareback?" she asked Rance.

"I haven't in years," he said, and shrugged. "All right." His spartan existence was wearing thin. It had been an age since he'd ridden a decent horse.

"You can take her out for a good, long jaunt, if you like," Amanda offered, eager to ingratiate herself with him. "She requires a light hand."

He nodded, accepting both the ride and the caution in one gesture. He removed Amanda's saddle, leaving the saddle blanket in place, and mounted the mare with the fluid motion of the skilled rider.

Nancy shied at the unexpected extra weight on her back, but Rance gentled her into accepting him. The horse under control, he cantered down the hill toward the brook and accelerated the mare into a gallop on the flat land beside the meandering stream.

He looks quite magnificent on Nancy, Amanda thought. His back was straight and proud. All the awkwardness he displayed when mounted on Bluebell was gone.

Brian broke through her thoughts. "Let's sit in the shade of the beech tree while we wait for Terry, Miss Lofton," he said. They strolled over to the large tree, unwittingly dispatching a handful of rooks. The blackbirds rose as a body and alighted in the willows beside the brook.

"Why do you call Mr. Straughn Terry, Mr. McGonigal, when everyone calls him Rance?" she asked when they were settled on the soft grass.

"And what should an Irishman call anyone christened Terrance, I ask you?" He laughed. "And it's Brian, miss," he added.

"Amanda," she reciprocated. "Have you known Mr. Straughn long?" Amanda wondered, running her finger over the head of a dandelion.

"Awhile. He saved me from drowning," the Irishman volunteered in his lilting brogue.

"Drowning?" Amanda burst out at the surprising statement.

"A bit of dark humor, lass. A trio of drunken louts who hated all Irishmen dunked me head into a horse trough. Terry happened to be passing by, and being the fair-minded lad that he is, took exception to the odds of three against one and jumped into the fray. While I spat foul water all over the gentlemen's Bond Street clothes, Terry decked all three in short order. 'Twas then I knew he had the makings of a fighter. Of course, the Honorable Terrance Straughn had the advantage; the lad was cold sober, and his opponents were foxed out of their heads. Then, too, I had softened them up for him, having gotten in me licks on all three before Terry got there." He chuckled merrily. "Glory be, had I been able to take them on one at a time, I never would have taken a bath."

Amanda smiled with him. "London is dangerous. A

friend of my father's was set upon in the city as well,'' she commiserated.

''Not London,'' Brian corrected Amanda. ''This was in Cambridge. Terry was attending university there at the time.''

''Goodness! I had never heard that Cambridge was dangerous,'' she said, wide-eyed. ''What were you doing there?''

''Searching for a neighbor lass from Ireland, I was.'' He paused. Her artlessness was perilous for a man bent on holding his tongue. ''But enough of that. That's the manner in which Terry and me met. I've been the lad's valet ever since.''

''A valet doesn't call his gentleman by a nickname,'' Amanda said, but pressed the point no further. Brian would not supply an answer to that particular enigma regardless of how firmly she prodded. ''I should like to hear more of the girl from Ireland,'' she said instead. ''Is she your sweetheart, Brian?''

''You are one for asking bold questions, lass,'' he said not unkindly. ''Maggie fled Ireland for misguided reasons. I finally found her, but not in Cambridge. She is in service as a kitchen maid to a family some twelve miles from here. An', yes, 'tis no secret, she's agreed to return to Ireland with me once I save enough for our passage and to buy a wee farm for us. I'd like to raise horses as me dad does.''

''You will never earn the needed sum as a valet to Mr. Straughn. In his circumstances, he can't possibly be paying you more than a pittance. Besides, even if he were paying you a fine wage and you were exceedingly frugal, it would take you years to amass the funds to buy a property and prime stock.''

Brian chuckled. ''How true, Miss Amanda.'' His twinkling emerald eyes sobered. ''God knows, till now I haven't been a lucky charm for Terry,'' he mumbled more to himself than to her.

''Why do you say that?''

"My conscience smarts from getting Terry dismissed from the university."

"How are you responsible?"

"The rowdies whose daylights he darkened were students like himself. The three cried rope on Terry to the university authorities, swearing our attack was unprovoked and we were drunk. Terry was sent down for a term, but rather than apologize to the gentlemen, his condition for reinstatement, he left school for good."

"What a miscarriage of justice!" Amanda cried. "Why, Rance is blamed even among his peers," she added indignantly, recalling Josie's words.

"That's his own doing. Refused to defend himself, he did. Stiff-necked pride. Not that the *ton* would be in sympathy, considering who I am. But his dad knew and supported him. The old Lord Woods was a fair man, for all he's maligned for making bad investments."

Brian's disclosure moved Amanda. Rance, as a victim of injustice, gained even greater status in her egalitarian mind. She vowed to enlighten Josie and put quit to the scurrilous insinuations about his expulsion from Cambridge. She mulled over Brian's words while she watched the object of her reflection in the distance galloping across Lord Woods's fallow fields on the opposite side of the brook. The spire of St. Catherine's Church was visible above the trees, the sole evidence of the village beyond a small verdant forest.

The distant horseman wheeled back toward the overlook, raced the fleet mare around a hedgerow, and reined in before a narrow stone bridge. Rance guided the mount over the span and spurred her up the hill. As he neared, Brian exclaimed, "Such a gleesome face! You'd think he was a schoolboy released unexpectedly from his lessons."

"Rance suffers from not having a quality animal to ride. I should miss Nancy terribly if I had to give her up, particularly if, as has happened to him, I had to make do with a hack," Amanda said.

Brian hopped to his feet and offered Amanda a hand up from the grass.

"She's a sweet goer indeed," Rance said after dismounting and leading the mare to where Amanda and Brian waited. "Lots of spirit, but terribly good manners." He pressed the horse's face with his own in a spontaneous sign of affection. "I forgot to ask you if she would jump for me. She seemed to want to when we came to the hedgerow, but I was afraid to chance pulling her up lame if I were misreading her intentions."

"She probably would have carried you over, but you best permit her to become accustomed to you on her back. You do weigh a bit more than I do, but after a few more times she'll know you."

"I won't ride her again, Amanda. I doubt your father would approve."

"Pish-posh!" Amanda rejected his objection with a wave of her hand. "I thought we were past that nonsense. The horse belongs to me. I decide who rides her. In any case, Papa has never interfered with my lending her out."

"And how many people have ridden her besides me?" Rance asked with a suspicious grin. "Not counting the grooms, of course."

Amanda giggled. "None," she admitted.

"I thought as much." Rance laughed.

Brian resaddled the horse for Amanda as she and Rance talked. He shaded his eyes to gauge the time from the position of the sun. Lord Woods would be annoyed that he was behind times again. *Let the man nag. I work hard enough for a room no bigger than a closet and two meals a day,* Brian thought. At least the Straughns did not stint on the food, but the prime advantage to the arrangement was that both Terry and he could keep their funds available for wagering.

"An' back to work I'll be returning now, Terry. Goodbye, Amanda," he said with a wave, and set off toward the Willowwoods stables.

"Bye, Brian," she answered, waving at his back.

Rance's eyes glittered with mischief. "You allow my valet to call you Amanda? I hope you don't have designs on him. The man is spoken for."

"Maggie, I know."

"Well, well, you two have been busy exchanging confidences, I see," he said. She detected a touch of disapproval, or was it uneasiness in his voice? "What else did he tell you?"

She shrugged. "Nothing significant," she said. "Did you truly enjoy the ride?"

"As much as this!" He burst into a deep laugh, snatching Amanda into his arms. A frightening shiver ran down her spine as his strong arms held her captive against his hard body. Her face was pressed into the rough cloth of the country jacket near his shoulder. Her heart hammered. She became heady with the overwhelming masculinity surrounding her.

His hands wandered over her back and stroked her neck sensuously beneath her hair. When his arms tightened around her waist, strange sensations darted up her spine, through her midsection, and over her breasts. He nuzzled his face into her hair. His lips grazed her forehead and moved toward her mouth. She remained rigid, her unbending arms at her sides. Rance held her away from him at arm's length and studied her face.

He dropped his hands and turned back to the horse, patting Nancy's flanks. "I hope I haven't overtaxed her," he said, his voice husky and strained. "I think you had best take her home now. She is lathered and requires a good rubdown."

When he first released her, Amanda had been afraid he might be angry, for he had been attempting to make love to her. He had disconcerted her when he seized her unexpectedly, causing her to rebuff him unintentionally by being as wooden and unyielding as a floorboard.

Their eyes met, and she was relieved that his sea-blue eyes were neutral and held not even a hint of affront.

Perhaps she had misread the whole episode. He had

probably just been delighted with his ride on Nancy and showed his appreciation with a brotherly hug.

Amanda knew she was consoling herself with nonsense. There was nothing fraternal about his caress. He was just too much of a gentleman to show he was sorely disappointed to find he had made advances to an unsophisticated twit.

"I should be getting back," she murmured. He lifted her into the saddle. She was unwilling to look at him and catch the scorn she believed reposed behind his eyes. Her face flushed with humiliation. Seeking to escape quickly, she pointed the mare toward the spinney path and spurred the horse foreward.

Rance turned in the opposite direction and walked briskly, mulling over what had occurred.

She was not being missish. What he had seen in her eyes was stark terror. Her startled brown eyes were a deer's caught in the lamplight. She was an innocent. He would wager a pony that Amanda Lofton had never even been thoroughly kissed. The bold talk and coquettish looks were a masquerade. This daughter of a permissive father and bluestocking mother was as inexperienced as Josie Castleberry. Lofton had claimed, "I can't lock her up." Damn his eyes! He *should* lock her up.

The righteous indignation of an injured party faded quickly. He had not been deceived when Amanda had pitched her folderol at him with a straight face. No father worth his salt would give a marriageable daughter carte blanche to choose her friends. Lofton allowed Amanda more freedom than would be given to the average girl, but after the inquistion he himself had been subjected to by the merchant, he knew Lofton had not given his daughter free rein to tarry with the Honorable Terrance Straughn. And Amanda was aware of her father's choler.

Rance let out a resigned sigh. The little fool had imposed herself on him and pursued him shamelessly, ignoring the peril of her father's displeasure. Unlike any sensible girl, Amanda would not be daunted by his ungentlemanly advances. Because she was inexperienced with worldly men, instead of prudently fleeing from him, she would invent some nitwitted excuse to justify his improper overtures.

Even harmless philandering had rules for an honorable man, which forebore forcing unwanted attentions on an innocent female. He needed to put paid to her soft-headness with a good tongue lashing and without mincing words.

Each memorized detail of Amanda's face assaulted Rance's brain. She was so appealing when she teased him with her wide-eyed, ingenuous stare that it never failed to put a smile in his heart.

Almost at the borning, he rebelled against his own resolution to give her a set-down. He could not bring himself to wound her with hurtful rebukes that would send her home in a flood of tears, despising him forever. Crushing Amanda's pride and trampling on her heart to repay her for withholding a few inconsequential kisses would brand him a cad. He wasn't some mewling schoolboy who was unable to accept reality and curb his base emotions. His dalliance with Amanda had crumbled. He had wanted to kiss her. Badly. But it was over. From then on when in her company he would pretend that the fizzled seduction had never occurred. He would be as proper as a priest and devote himself wholly to his boxing.

His enterprise with Brian was built more on expectation than certitude, but those qualms were waning. His pugilistic abilities had grown over the past weeks, and his awareness he was a smart fighter boosted his self-confidence. The venture he depended on to change his life and replenish his purse was still very much on course.

The stone stable came into view beyond a stand of oaks. Rance ran his hand carelessly through his fair hair. "The merchant should have kept his unconventional daughter under lock and key," he grumbled aloud. The next second he unleashed an irrational string of vindictive oaths at Daniel Lofton, then grimaced, feeling a bit foolish at what he saw as his own inanity, but admitted to himself that he felt considerably better for all of that.

Chapter 7

Amanda was awakened by brisk winds rattling the shutters. Moonlight fluttered where the flowered wallpaper met the white ceiling. Her hand found the tinderbox that was laid conveniently next to a candle. When the candle flared, her eyes sought the ormolu clock on the nearby table. It was nearly midnight. Amanda doused the candle and lay back on the goose-feather pillow.

For a week now, rain had kept her from the overlook. Before the bad weather had set in, she had seen Rance twice after the disaster in his arms. He had been . . . cordial would be the word, but he and Brian had left together after their sparring match without lingering for more than a minute or two to exchange a few words with her.

Doubtless he had meant to make love to her when he enveloped her in his arms that day, but she had instinctively starched up. Being a stranger to London society, she did not know how to go on in these situations. Rance was a sophisticate and must have thought her a peagoose. His conduct on examination still seemed more appropriate toward a light-o'-love to her, but the standards of the *ton,* she knew, were more daring than the plebian Bristol society with which she was familiar. In any case, she would not miscalculate again. Next time she would respond in kind to his passionate overtures—to a point. Amanda might be green in affairs of the heart, but her parents had never shielded her from reality, and she was aware of the price of surrendering her virtue without benefit of marriage.

She sighed heavily. The pandemonium Rance Straughn caused in her heart had to be love. Eventually, she hoped, he would come to admit he had deep feelings for her too. Once he declared his honorable intentions, she would convince her father to agree to their wedding, a task that would require a major effort on her part, but was not impossible.

The list of rejected heiresses that Lady Woods had drawn up for Rance, however, troubled her. She had to fix his interest before he decided to court a viable candidate from her ladyship's roster, she just had to.

Amanda swung her feet over the edge of the bed and groped for her slippers with her toes. She went to the fogged window and cleared a spot to see outside. Wind-driven clouds were scudding across the moonlit sky. By morning the wind would have sponged up the earth.

Fortunately, during the past week the activities at Ainsworth House had not been curtailed, and Amanda had been invited to participate, eliminating the necessity to remain housebound. Josie had given a soiree a week before to which Rance had been invited, but he had begged off because of a business trip to London. The soiree had lost most of its appeal for Amanda after that, but she had attended and watched with some amusement Evan Whitaker losing his head over Josie.

Freddie Straughn had joked that his uncle's trip with his valet to London was likely the business of waggery and merry frolicking rather than for serious purposes. At times Amanda longed to gag Freddie, but he possessed a wealth of information about the man she loved, so rather than give him the upbraiding he deserved, she encouraged his indiscreet disclosures with an insincere smile.

Amanda returned to her bed and slid between the soft cotton sheets. Yesterday, during a game of charades, Freddie had announced that his uncle was leaving town again in a few days. Amanda had feared that the rain would last and she might not see Rance for another unbearable week. She nuzzled her head into the soft pillow. The fine moon boded well for the morrow. The sun will shine, she prophesied optimistically, and Rance and Brian will be boxing on the overlook. Treasuring the prospect of seeing Rance again, she drifted into a contented slumber.

True to Amanda's prediction, the sun shone brightly as she rode into the high meadow the following afternoon. She slid off her horse and led Nancy over the path through the spinney onto the overlook. Her heart gave the funny little twist to which she was becoming accustomed. Rance was stretched out full-length on a huge flat boulder that she and Josie had nicknamed the sacrificial altar. His large hands cradled his head.

Amanda dropped the horse's reins and edged the few feet to where he reclined, his eyes closed, his handsome face tipped toward the warmth of the sun. His thick blond lashes fluttered, but he did not open his eyes as she studied his face. The urge to drop a kiss on his sensuous mouth welled in her, but instead she snapped a dead twig from a sapling and teased the stick down his aristocratic nose.

"Hello, Amanda," he drawled lazily without opening his eyes.

"How did you know it was me?"

"The lily-of-the-valley scent," he replied, opening his blue eyes a slit.

"It's white lilac," she corrected him.

"Is it? Actually, I peeked," he admitted, sitting up and smiling at her.

"Brian's not with you," she said, stating the obvious.

"The ground is too soggy. We worked out in the barn," he stated as he rubbed a spot of mud from his shiny calfskin riding boots. "I just came here to get away from Ernestine . . . well, the house," he amended sheepishly. He dared not admit even to himself that he had hoped to see Amanda.

When he lifted his head to face her, Rance noticed that the beams of sunlight put golden highlights into her warm brown tresses. She had her head cocked to one side fetchingly, a mischievous grin at his faux pas in naming Ernestine transposing her unexceptional mouth into an extraordinary handsomeness. The desire to touch her coursed through his body.

He jumped from the boulder and shoved his hands safely into his jacket pockets.

"The brook is rushing along from all the rain," Amanda observed, looking down toward the bottom of the hill where the brook's banks barely contained the normally docile stream.

"Let's take a closer look," he suggested. Releasing his hands from his pockets, he seized a slim wrist and pulled her down the hill.

Amanda tripped along beside him valiantly, racing to match his long strides, their boots raising a spray of water as they plunged through a hidden puddle in the meadow grass. Finally, unable to keep pace, she cried, "Wait, Rance. I can't gallop." He chuckled, threw his arm companionably about her shoulders, and moderated his stride. Nancy trotted past them and stopped on the bank of the brook to drink.

A long-ago storm had felled a great walnut, leaving tenacles of roots reaching into the air. The tree's branches spread onto the meadow grass. The old, withered leaves clung tenaciously to twigs, while the stripped trunk formed a rustic bench close to the banks of the stream, where dark green ferns studded the embankment.

Amanda tested the fallen trunk with the flat of her hand for dampness before sitting on the log. Rance rested one booted foot next to her and leaned forward, his crossed arms resting on his knee.

For a time the two silently watched the brook tumbling

and churning over the rocks with passing interest until a flock of rooks cawing raucously in a nearby willow caused Amanda to comment, "Rook Manor is well named, although I dislike the name and wanted Papa to change it, but he wouldn't."

"He likes it?" Rance asked with no real interest.

"Not particularly. He feared his neighbors would be affronted if he renamed the ancient house."

"What's that to them? It's his estate."

"You know well enough that every bit of reconstruction was scrutinized by your brother and Lord Ainsworth," she complained. "They are fortunate that Daniel Lofton has excellent taste. Not that it should matter to them; they haven't been near the house since it was completed."

"I suspect a lecture on the horrors of the gentry is forthcoming," Rance conjectured. "Mr. Lofton was at the assembly last time, and I don't recall anyone snubbing him," he added, decidely unsympathetic. "Your father didn't behave like a gentleman to me," he muttered.

"That's unfair, Rance, and you know it, considering the circumstances. Did you really think he would exchange his daughter for a title in the family?"

"I don't believe the question of a title ever came up." Rance scowled.

"Yes, but wasn't that what you thought would turn the trick?"

Rance suppressed a spasm of genuine anger at her unfounded accusation. "Is that what he said?" he asked.

"No, I've told you that he never mentions you. Your nephew Freddie fancies himself all the crack, sharing his little *on-dits* like some London dandy. He's told anyone who would listen that you are seeking a rich wife, and that my father would be thrilled to have a son-in-law with a title."

Freddie must have heard Leonard repeating the contention that an affluent merchant would be willing to disregard the misdeeds of a suitor to gain a title in the family. He would have to speak to young Viscount Willows about the impropriety of gossiping about one's own family. Rance had never accepted his brother's specious assertion, and that Leonard had misread Daniel Lofton badly Rance knew only too well. He couldn't blame Lofton for being incensed. But let Amanda think what she would. It no longer mattered.

Undeterred that Rance remained mum, Amanda went on. "You know that in this country, titles automatically bestow privileges. Being highborn allows a far greater latitude for behaving odiously. Rance, you can be as wild as you want. You can go gaming, drinking, and wenching and the world will shrug because you are the son of an earl. Papa has worked hard to accumulate his wealth, but because he is the son of a bootmaker, he is an outcast of society."

"You make too much of that, Amanda. I agree that in London, entry into the *ton* is impossible without a proper family background, but the *ton* is not all of London society. I have been to parties in the city where people recently in trade were invited."

"And mocked behind their backs. You yourself have passed Brian off as an Irish nobleman, I've heard. Is Brian not good enough to go with you to the Derby as Brian McGonigal?" she posed heatedly. Rance felt his ire rising, but except for a mild warning, he showed no sign that her thrust had found its mark.

"Amanda, don't bait me. You know what my answer is. But I can't change society single-handedly. Here in the country the rules get bent all the time, so perhaps Mr. Lofton should invite Lord and Lady Ainsworth to dinner along with Josie. I feel strongly they would accommodate your father for your sake."

"But do you know why they accept me?" Amanda did not wait for his reply. "Lady Ainsworth knows that my grandfather was Sir Quincy Bartlett; therefore, she overlooks what she considers the worst, and I consider the best part of me, being the daughter of the merchant Daniel Lofton. My father is the most decent man I know, while my maternal grandfather was an insufferable tyrant. Yet hypocritical society elevated Sir Quincy by virtue of a title above my papa because Papa earned his money by his own wits and labor."

Fueled by her harbored hurts, Amanda warmed to her subject. "After my mother died, my grandfather insisted I be turned over to him. Admirable, I bet you are thinking."

Rance's shoulders lifted slightly. "I must own, Amanda, I don't see any harm in Mr. Lofton placing you with relations who could introduce you to others of the aristocracy and give you a leg up in polite society. But I feel I am about to be shown my error," he disclosed with a sardonic grin.

"You are. My grandfather shunned my mother from the day she ran away and married my father. For my mother's sake, Papa tried to make peace with him even after I was born. But Sir Quincy would have nothing to do with us until Mama died. You believe Papa filled my head with Banbury tales, don't you? I can see it in your face."

Rance studied his boots. His mind had indeed been working along those lines. Daniel Lofton could easily advance himself in his daughter's eyes by maligning Sir Quincy.

Amanda leapt at his hesitation. "You're wrong. You see, Papa isn't the one who told me the worst. The sister of the woman who was my abigail at the time of my mother's death worked as a companion to Sir Quincy's unmarried daughter, Regina. She passed on to me that Sir Quincy berated Aunt Regina for not having convinced Papa to let me live with them. Sir Quincy's anger at Aunt Regina stemmed from his having lost the guineas he would have realized from—and these are his words—'taking in the mongrel child from that despicable union.' "

Rance winced at the crude invective.

Amanda, in high dudgeon, failed to catch his sympathetic cringe. She did not slow her tirade. "Sir Quincy had no intention of aiding me. My own grandfather bragged in his household for all the servants to hear that he expected to collect money from Daniel Lofton for the pleasure of mistreating me. So much for the honor of the Quality!"

Amanda stood and paced, glaring at Rance. She slapped her riding crop against her riding skirt.

"Are you thinking of beating my noble little hide with that thing?" he teased.

"It's a thought," she uttered.

He sat down on the log, and when she stalked within reach, he grabbed her arm and tugged her down beside him. The riding crop flew from her hand and landed at her feet. Amanda's heart thudded as she fell against Rance, steadying herself with her hands on his shoulders. His lips parted and his eyes narrowed as his blond head came down toward her face. She steeled herself for his certain kiss, but he straightened abruptly, causing her hands to fall away. Fiddling with a button on his jacket, he stared at his wet boots and cursed the inner angel who waved an admonishing finger at him and invoked his honor.

Rance disciplined his voice and said lightly, "Now that you are a shade calmer and are no longer armed, let's turn to more pleasant subjects. I wager that Nancy was your father's gift to you on your seventeenth birthday."

"Actually it was my sixteenth birthday," she said, bending over to retrieve the fallen riding crop, disappointed that he had drawn away from her.

"Gad!" he burst out, throwing his head back. "Mr. Lofton has superb taste in gifts! What will he give you when you turn twenty-one, Windsor Castle?"

"Probably," Amanda agreed facetiously, beginning to recover her aplomb. "I'm not given everything, Rance, and taught nothing about money. I have to do the accounts independent of Papa, and then he checks them. I know all the household expenses, and the profits and losses incurred in running the estate." Carried away, she bragged, "I could outfit a merchant ship and send her off to America and give the captain a list of what to bring on a return journey to England. Am I impressing you?"

"Yes, you are," Rance admitted. "Can you really do that?

Not the household accounts, I don't doubt that, but fill a manifest for a merchantman?"

"Wellll"—she dragged out the word—"not exactly without assistance, but I do understand a great deal about shipping."

"You little humbug. You had me going with that whisker." He chortled, giving her a brotherly hug, which was much less than she had hoped for.

She continued. "I did once earn a nice profit when my father gave me a lesson on how his trade worked. I bought English bone china and sent it on a trip to America and realized a handsome profit when the dishes were sold in Philadelphia."

She scuffed the damp grass with the toe of her boot. "You may sneer at Papa, Rance, for indulging me, but I do not see that your own father has done well by you. Lord Woods wasted his fortune and left you impoverished."

Rance's eyes snapped in a show of temper, but no retort passed his tense lips, for he could see a fairness to her rebuke. He had not been reticent in voicing his disapproval of Daniel Lofton. The truth from Amanda's lips stung, but to retaliate would perpetuate a quarrel he was not willing to commit himself to carrying on with her. Where he was going, titles, and how a man acquired his money did not matter, and arguing with her would be self-indulgent.

"True enough," Rance agreed mildly. Amanda glanced at him, perplexed, for she had been prepared to be chastened for the rash remarks about Lord Woods that she had rued as soon as the words had passed her lips.

Nancy shook her head and snorted restively, bored with standing around in her traces. Amanda rose from her seat on the log and ambled over to soothe the mare.

Rance, too, stood and stretched his long arms above his head. "I need to be on my way. Leonard, no doubt, has one last errand for me to carry out before dark. Since Freddie has seen me riding Bluebell, my nephew has decided the cob is not so bad after all. Unfortunately his new attitude toward his horse will mean that I shall probably end up driving a dogcart, which may be better than Bluebell at that," he joked.

He joined Amanda where she was patting Nancy's nose and began stroking the horse along with her. Their hands brushed, separated, touched again—both of them conscious of each accidental graze.

"Freddie said you are going away again," Amanda said softly.

"Yes, tomorrow. For a few days. My sister-in-law is always happy when Brian and I go off, relieved, I guess, that we are not eating her food and dirtying her sheets. I believe she hopes that we will not come back."

"Where are you going?" Amanda asked. Unlike Lady Woods, she feared that he would take up residence in London again or marry one of the wealthy Antidotes on Ernestine's list.

"Why, Amanda, where else? A place where there is gaming, drinking, and wenching, sweetheart!" he teased.

The wenching in the taunt in which Rance flung her words back at her hurt, but the careless use of the endearment as if she were one of his ladybirds stabbed her heart. Amanda grabbed the saddle and pulled herself onto the horse. "Have a fine time," she snapped. Rance jumped aside as she jerked Nancy's head around and spurred the mare into a sudden gallop. He kept his eyes firmly on her retreating back until she disappeared into the spinney. Only then did he begin his ascent up the hill toward Willowwoods.

Amanda was causing emotions to whirl through his body that he had no right to feel. As she had said on that fateful day when he had foolishly been caught in her father's trap, they dealt well together. Had Daniel Lofton been different, had he not found himself in reduced circumstances, then . . . but he could not let second thoughts sway him. He suspected that his tug-of-war with his conscience was less about the propriety of making advances to her and more about the fear of becoming hopelessly snared. But any permanent association was out of the question. He would not alter his plans, and Amanda Lofton could have no part in them or his future.

When Rance reached the crest of the hill, he stood with his hands folded before him. The thick hedges and dense wooded ridges in the valley were lushly beautiful after the rain. From his vantage point, he followed the course of the swollen brook as it rushed through the meadow, foaming where the water bounded over bottom rocks. Nowhere in all of England was the countryside more beautiful, Rance thought with a catch in his throat.

The time would come, and soon, when the boxing fund would be large enough for him to launch his new life. If all went as planned, odds were that he would never see this country again. A sudden sadness choked him, but he shook off the dismal sensation. Indulging in self-pity sapped a man's power to act effectively.

Rance turned his back on the well-loved landscape and dispassionately watched a squawking rook hop from high branch to high branch on the beech tree, his mind on his changed fortunes.

After Brian convinced Signor Boigotto, a boxing promoter, to arrange a professional match for Rance, his chronic financial worries underwent a complete turnabout. He won his initial fight handily in just two rounds. Impressed with his performance, Boigotto signed Rance on as one of his regulars. Since then he had not lost a single fight. The seed money had grown along with Rance's pugilistic success. He and Brian had put their heads together and bet cannily, doubling, tripling, quadrupling their considerable wagers.

Money had been his prime objective in going into the sport on a professional level, and that priority had not changed. But he had found other satisfactions. The respect his fans bestowed on him was earned, unlike the automatic deference he received by virtue of his birth and title. The adulation of the cheering crowd when he bested an opponent was heady and filled his breast with an unbelievable sense of elation.

Rance reached up and shook a low branch of the beech tree. The rook cawed a raucous scolding at him, but remained lodged on its high perch. Amanda had complained about the name Rook Manor. Did she find the black birds a nuisance? he wondered. One day he would remember to ask her. But with more than a little regret he knew he probably never would, for Amanda would soon belong, irretrievably, to his past. His throat tightened with something akin to pain, for he sensed that his life would lose a great deal of its sparkle and zest when he left her behind forever.

Chapter 8

Amanda drank in the vibrant hues of the flowers in the garden from the top step of the colonnaded porch while she waited for the stable boy to bring Nancy around. The Castleberry cousins and Josie were attending Evan Whitaker's Tuesday afternoon Bible study class, but Amanda had cried off, disingenuously pleading a backlog of chores. In reality she had dispatched her required tasks with celerity and was eager to see if Rance and Brian were home from their most recent journey.

She bent down and scratched the ears of the old spaniel who nudged her knee. Rance's frequent forays to distant towns nagged more and more at her peace of mind. She was afraid that he might be getting desperate for money and be eliminating the Antidotes from Lady Woods's list, one by one, by visiting their homes, looking for the least objectionable female to take as a wife. She dreaded one day hearing from Freddie that Rance had made a declaration.

Would that her parents had spent less time on lessons about dead poets and ancient history and countries she would never visit, and more on casting out lures to catch a man. At least then she would know how to wage a successful campaign to get him to moon over her rather than treating her as a fond sister.

Amanda moved to the edge of the drivepath as Willie came into view leading Nancy. The brown and white dog tottled down the steps after her, although his hunting days were over and running beside a horse no longer appealed to him.

Willie tugged a forelock and held the reins as Amanda pulled herself into the saddle. She clicked the mare into motion. The spaniel watched her for a second before lumbering back up the steps to lie in the sun on the porch.

Amanda dismounted in the high meadow near the sheep, where young lambs frolicked under the ewes' bellies. Rance's baritone and Brian's brogue floated on the spring air from the overlook, bringing an eager smile to Amanda's face.

Having led Nancy through the spinney, Amanda dropped down onto the grass a safe distance from the pugilistic action.

Neither man openly acknowledged her presence, but Brian winked in her general direction as he flicked off a jab.

Brian had likened the sparring to a chess game, yet Amanda could see a marked difference. The relationship was not adversarial; rather, Brian was instructing Rance. Like a teacher he criticized or praised, whichever his pupil's actions warranted.

"Jab, Terry, jab. You missed one," Brian chided critically. Rance rapped Brian's shoulder twice with his fist, sending the Irishman tripping backward. "Better, lad, better," he now encouraged. Rance scored two hits to the body in their next exchange of punches, but Brian parried a shot to his cheek. Both boxers stood nearly immobile in the familiar stance of traditional fisticuffs.

Brian shouted "Time," and Rance dropped his hands to his sides. The Irishman's arm encircled Rance's bare shoulders.

"Don't be afraid to move about, Terry. Some fanciers

don't like that, but Mendoza says that good, quick footwork is essential if you are to gain the advantage," he advised.

Rance rubbed his large hand over the pale hair on his chest. "You're right, Brian. I still need work on my agility. I seem to have the power."

"An' don't I know it," Brian crowed. "After all, haven't you been superb when you've been tested?"

Amanda's curiosity was aroused by the cryptic exchange, but the moment passed as the boxers resumed sparring. She became engrossed in the improved fluid movement, more exciting than the toe-to-toe exchange of classical boxing.

Rance began forcing Brian to carry the fight to him by dancing out of his range. Somewhere from the recesses of Amanda's mind came the term "milling on the retreat," but she could not recall where she had heard the phrase.

The Irishman jabbed at Rance. Rance backed away, and Brian, with his shorter reach, was ineffectual. Brian lowered his guard, and Rance with lightning speed delivered a blow that caught Brian square on his chin, sending the smaller man sprawling in the grass. Amanda gasped and leapt to her feet, dashing to aid the Irishman who for a moment lay flat on his back, unmoving. Then Brian groaned; his dazed eyes opened slowly, and he hunched his shoulders, inching to a sitting position. Amanda knelt beside him, but Rance grabbed her roughly by the shoulders, pulled her upright, and whirled her away from Brian.

"Confound it, Amanda, get out of here!" he ripped up at her. "I won't have you interfering when we are working."

"But you hurt him, Rance," she protested, moving from side to side to get around him as he blocked her path.

"Damn you, woman, get away!"

Amanda's eyes burned with hot anger, and she stood rooted defiantly where he had spun her.

Brian sat slumped over, massaging his jaw, but his lips spread into a giant pleased smile.

"Terry, you'll be the darling of the fancy if you can keep delivering like that. I'm proud of you, lad."

"How do you feel?" Rance asked him, not reassured by Brian's bravado. Amanda strode back to where she had been sitting and sank to the ground.

Brian held his jaw. "I'm ready to quit for today" was his only concession that his pain was greater than he had let on.

Rance threw Brian his shirt and shrugged into his own. He helped Brian on with his coat and stared at his receding back as he set off toward Willowwoods. The Irishman's normally clipped gait was slow.

The leveler had been accidental, but Brian's jaw could easily have been broken, Rance thought, a mountain of guilt burdening his conscience. He should convince Brian that the sparring should be curtailed. It was difficult to pull his punches, for he had surpassed Brian's fighting skills. Defense had become instinctive now that the outcome mattered. But Brian would never agree, since the sparring was necessary to hone Rance's technique to ever-sharper heights.

Rance breathed a resigned sigh and turned toward Amanda, where she sat hugging her legs, her face buried in her skirts. He settled beside her on the grass and lifted her chin, staring into angry, hurt, and misty brown eyes.

"Mandy, you must never interfere again. Do you understand?" His voice was gentle but determined.

"But Brian was hurt," she said stubbornly. "I was trying to help."

"He wouldn't have thanked you, or me for allowing it, if you had coddled him," Rance contended. "Brian would have been humiliated to have you, to have any woman, hovering over him under the circumstances."

"You needn't have sworn at me," she claimed with childish petulance.

Rance's mouth tightened. "If you insist on hanging about where rough play is going on," he said unapologetically, "you will need to plug your ears. A man's language is not always tidy when he is angry."

"Huh? I thought gentlemen curbed themselves in the

presence of a lady. My papa never has used such profanity before me.''

''Maybe he should have,'' Rance retorted. His voice steel, he delivered his ultimatum. ''You listen to me, my dear. Either you get off your high horse and agree to my terms, or I'll take myself and Brian away from here.''

A barb sprang to her tongue, but the serious expression on his face and in his voice smothered her retaliation. He might really go away. She fumed for a moment before surrendering. ''You win. I accept your terms.''

''Good girl,'' he drawled, his antagonism slipping away like quicksilver. He brought her hand quickly to his lips before springing to his feet and yanking her up beside him.

''Come on, minx,'' he said fondly, ignoring her primmed mouth and leading her to the flattened boulder near the beech tree. He spanned her waist with his large hands and boosted her up onto the rock, leaning idly against the gray stone.

''Rance, have you ever heard of 'milling on the retreat'?'' Amanda said, her peevishness forgotten.

''Yes, of course. A journalist critical of Tom Cribb's style invented the expression, I think. As a matter of fact, I was practicing just that when Brian got in the way. How do you know the term?''

Amanda shrugged. ''I have no idea. I must have read it in a newspaper long ago and quite forgotten it until I saw you forcing Brian to attack you. Is Tom Cribb your model?''

''I admire Cribb, but, actually, I favor the style of Daniel Mendoza. We are both slender, but I am considerably taller. Slight as he is, he beat the best boxers in England for the championship, befuddling his opponents with his nimble footwork and scientific boxing. Brian and I attended Mendoza's academy.''

Amanda reached up and ran her fingers over his crisp flaxen strands. ''Your hair is wet,'' she mused.

''Don't do that, Mandy,'' he said quietly, surprised by the disturbing emotions her touch aroused. ''I need to wash my hair under the pump when I return to Willowwoods."

Amanda had expected his hair to be silky like her own, but the blond strands were limp yellow straw. Impishly, she ruffled his hair.

"I told you to stop it, Amanda!" he commanded, grabbing her wrist. Her lips twitched with amusement as she twisted free from him. A strange excitement filled her as she tussled with this tall, handsome man. Disobeying him, she reached her hand toward his head with a small, challenging laugh. He jerked his head away from her outstretched hand and took a step back beyond her reach, a blush rising beneath his tan. A woman running her fingers through his hair had not had this effect on him since he was a raw youth.

Amanda was exhilarated by his discomfort and his determination to elude her hands. She would have leapt from her perch and pursued him had she not at that moment been distracted by a blue bruise beneath his right eye, which she had failed to notice before.

"Seems Brian delivered a leveler of his own," she declared, pointing to the injury.

"Indeed," he muttered wryly, "old Brian can be a formidable opponent," glad to shunt their conversation into a safer direction.

Amanda cocked her head as she viewed the discoloration on his handsome face. "You know, Rance, you don't look anything like Lord Woods or Freddie," she observed.

"Leonard claims that I'm a throwback to a Norse ancestor, but my mother was fair with blue eyes; but I resemble her only slightly."

"Don't you bear a likeness to any of your cousins or uncles on your mother's side of the family?"

"I have none. My last living maternal relative, my great-aunt Agnes, passed away recently."

"Did you look like her?" Amanda asked.

"Good heavens, no! She was a short, plump spinster with hair pulled into a severe coal-black bun," he said. He rubbed his neck. "You know, my mother was exceedingly fond of Aunt Agnes because she took her in when my grandfather died, even though Mama didn't have a shilling to her name. My father had been a widower for a year when he fell in love with my mother."

"Your great-aunt Agnes must have been a kind and loving woman," Amanda surmised. Rance turned around and leaned both palms on the boulder's surface. His blue eyes twinkled merrily.

"She was a cantankerous woman and not great fun to visit when I was small. She had a parlor replete with porcelain statues of shepherds and shepherdesses and lambs and sheep, dogs, foxes, cows, miniature castles, birds of every shape and hue. She followed me about, slapping my hand whenever I reached out for one of her precious possessions."

"Poor little Rance," Amanda mocked, pressing her lips into feigned dolefulness. "What happened to all those knickknacks?"

"Sold at auction. In her will she left the proceeds of the sale of the house and all its furnishings to a home that cares for elderly widows and spinsters without means. You would never have guessed from speaking to her that she had a philanthropic bone. In fact, her acerbic tongue would have led you to believe the opposite."

He moved a little away from the rock and gazed into the valley. Amanda slid from the rock and joined him.

"She left you nothing." She touched the sleeve of his jacket. "That makes you sad?"

He shook his head. "I cannot quarrel with the dispensation of her funds. I am sure her bequest was a godsend to the destitute women forced to rely on the mercy of others, and their need is far greater than mine. But I hoped for some inconsequential memento as a remembrance." His face lit up. "You know, she had a set of four porcelain British soldiers, splendid in red, blue, and gold. One had a drum hung about his neck, and the other three carried rifles in various positions. From the time I was seven or eight, I would sit and stare longingly up at them on a high shelf beyond my reach. At the advanced age of twenty-one, when she left the room, I found the courage to remove them from the shelf and examine them closely. When she returned carrying a tea tray, she berated me for handling them and demanded that I replace them at once before I broke one."

Amanda was touched by his poignancy. She slipped her hand into his and gave a sympathetic squeeze. He looked down at her with a feeble grin. "I considered staying after the funeral and bidding on the soldiers, but I feared seeing the room dismantled would have altered the pleasant memory of the parlor I carry up here," he said, tapping his forehead.

Compassionate tears glittered in Amanda's eyes, for she was touched by his tale. Rance patted her hand and said, "You must think me maudlin?" He had never shared the story with anyone before, not even Brian.

"Oh, no," Amanda protested. "You loved her, and, I would wager, she loved you."

"Yes, I suppose you are right," he said. "As I matured, I recognized that there was affection behind her sharp tongue. I would tease her and hug her and pay her court in an outrageous manner. She would pretend to dislike the tomfoolery, but I could detect small signs of pleasure she could not quite hide. But she would have been embarrassed had I gone soft on her."

Amanda returned to the boulder and hoisted herself up onto the gray rock. Rance resumed his former position, leaning against the huge stone.

Looking not at him but down the hill and across the brook to Lord Woods's green fields, she asked softly, "Will you be attending the assembly next week?"

"No, Brian and I will be going to London about then on business."

He dashed her hopes of waltzing with him, which had been uppermost in her mind. Lady Woods's dreaded Antidote list sprang with near panic into her mind.

"Business?" she questioned.

"Yes, business," he repeated, noting an element of mistrust in her tone. She was a clever young woman. He wondered if she had stumbled onto the truth. He eyed her closely. But her next question demonstrated that whatever she was getting at had nothing to do with pugilism.

"I suppose you shall be attending dances?"

"Dances?" Nothing was further from his intentions. A slow smile stretched his lips. From long experience, he discerned the look of a jealous woman. "Dances, of course. I probably shall look in on one or two balls. I haven't had an opportunity to survey this Season's crop of sweet young things."

"The Season is nothing but a marriage mart where young women are put on display like fillies at Tattersall's. The Season is a degrading, insensitive custom perpetuated by men," Amanda declared hotly.

"Too true," Rance agreed amiably, "but nevertheless the most desirable girls in England are to be found there."

Her brown eyes smoldered, not recognizing that he was enjoying getting a rise from her. He smiled disarmingly.

"I had no idea, Amanda, that you were conversant with the Season."

"You know I'm not. I'd be tossed out on my ear if I dared to step over the threshold of the hallowed portals of Almack's. But poor Josie has had a Season. She's apprised me of the humiliations. But you can chase every milksop of a debutante for all I care, and I hope you catch one. It's just what you deserve!"

He moved in front of her and cupped a hand on each side of her shoulders. She wiggled to shrug him off, but his strong grip would not be dislodged. Her jealousy fanned his male ego, and a clever retort that would have exacerbated her anger sprang to mind. If the spat could have ended with her in his arms, he would have continued. Instead, he gave her an affable, conciliatory grin. "Mandy, I implore you, spare me a lecture on the shortcomings of my class. By now I know them well."

"I knew I could enlighten you if I persisted," she said dryly, but her primmed mouth twisted into a simper. She lifted the watch around her neck and checked the time. "I was due at home ten minutes ago," she said, undisturbed.

He swept her from the boulder in a high arc that set her giggling, his eyes secretly craving her luscious mouth. He set her down and reluctantly removed his hands from her slender waist. Side by side, but a little apart, they strolled toward Nancy, masking deeper feelings by chattering inconsequentially about this and that.

The day before the assembly, as Daniel and Amanda ate their midday meal, Daniel offered to escort Amanda to the dance the following night, but she surprised him. "No, no, Papa. I wouldn't think of it. The Castleberrys are leaving Ainsworth House for home in a few days, so I can forgo this assembly; by the next one, Lady Ainsworth shall be inviting me again."

Amanda winced at the gratitude in her father's eyes, mindful that only Rance's absence, not her own generosity, had reprieved Daniel from the abhorrent duty. She fiddled with her lobster salad and asked as though simply making conversation, "Papa, have you ever attended a mill?"

Daniel bit into his buttered roll. He was puzzled at her sudden interest in pugilism. "I do not find the spectacle of two men pounding each other with their fists, until their faces resemble raw meat and their legs become rubber, much of a sport, but I did attend the second Cribb-Molineaux fight. When Cribb bested the former black slave from America at Thistleton Gap in eleven rounds, he was hailed as the savior of England," he said, an edge of sarcasm to his voice. He was interrupted by Jeffries bringing him a message that his bailiff, had arrived, and Daniel hurried through his meal and excused himself, answering only a few of Amanda's questions.

On Tuesday afternoon Freddie Straughn informed Amanda that his uncle Rance had just returned from London. Lord Woods was in quite a stew, Freddie said, since Rance had an ugly bruise on his lip just below his nose.

"My father suspects that Mr. McGonigal led Uncle Rance into a tavern brawl," the young viscount announced with unconcealed glee. Amanda congratulated herself for repressing a laugh and holding her tongue. Brian was responsible for the injury, but not because he had led Rance astray; the Irishman had delivered another lucky punch. Her benign smile gave the impression she was disinterested in Freddie's gossip, and she successfully hid from the youth the knowledge that she was much in the company of his rascally uncle.

Not knowing the precise hour Rance and Brian would be sparring the following morning, Amanda had arrived at the overlook after the workout had started. The sparring went on much as usual, although Amanda caught a certain urgency in the proceedings, as though the bobbing and weaving and jabbing and punching had taken on a special significance. Finally, after an hour, Rance reached for a linen towel draped over a hawthorn bush and said, "I guess we are as ready as we are going to be."

Amanda sprang to her feet. "Ready for what?" she asked.

"Amanda," he said, puzzled to find her beside him. He gazed at her in bewilderment. His concentration had been complete while he worked out with Brian. For an hour he had blocked out his immediate surroundings, unaware of sky, grass, and apparently Amanda's arrival.

He flung the damp towel onto the grass with needless force. His mouth and eyes were hard and unwelcoming as he buttoned the white cotton shirt.

Brian's averted face had a decidedly strained and distressed appearance as he, too, neatened himself. Brian picked up Rance's discarded towel and pushed it with his own into a leather satchel at his feet, avoiding Amanda's eyes. Her question remained ignored and unanswered.

Hands on hips, Amanda moved in front of Rance and looked up at him with accusing eyes.

"You are hiding something," she said.

"Nonsense." His tone was not convincing. She mistrusted the look in his eyes as he stared over her head into space. "Look, Brian and I have to go," he said curtly.

He took two hesitant steps toward Willowwoods, then stopped.

A wealth of emotions warred in Rance's chest. He spun around and placed his callused palm against Amanda's cheek, certain the guilt consuming him was painted on his face for anyone to see. He ached to pull Amanda into his arms and bruise her delicious lips with punishing kisses. Instead, he grabbed her shoulders roughly and planted a single chaste kiss on her forehead. Although the yen to run made him feel like a coward, he still gave in to his craven itch, for the barrier around his emotions was in real danger of collapsing. He released her so quickly, Amanda staggered back a step. With long strides Rance left her side, leaned over, and scooped up the leather satchel. In a husky voice he said, "I'm going away." Head down, he vanished into the trees.

Feeling curiously forlorn, Amanda turned to Brian, who stood immobile beside her. "Going away? Where?" she cried in sudden panic. Her heart pounded with alarm.

The Irishman paused a small eternity. "We're going to Wye, lass," he said at last, an unsteadiness in his lips.

Amanda's eyes closed for a moment in relief. The racing in her chest abated and her breath slowed.

Wye was a country town not too great a distance away. Coming from Bristol, she had passed through it a year earlier with her father. The town had an inn, she remembered, a number of taverns, and some repectable shops. The side streets had been lined with well-kept cottages.

Brian laid his hand briefly on the sleeve of her blue riding habit. "I need to be going now, Amanda." She failed to notice the slight tremor in his hands.

"What are you going to do in Wye?" Amanda asked,

drawing her brows together. The specter of an eligible heiress with whom Rance could make a good match plunged her into the doldrums even before she heard Brian's reply. He mindlessly scuffed the turf with the toe of his brown boot, bent over, and picked up a stick which he snapped in two for no apparent reason before he said, "We'll be doing some gambling, we will."

"Indeed." His restless manner raised doubts in her mind that he was being completely candid with her, but before she could interrogate him further, he said, "Take care, lass," and began to back away from her with a careless wave.

"Bye, Brian, and you take care too." The infectious grin she tossed him swiped the solemn set of his mouth into a thin smile, but she did not notice that his merry eyes were strangely cheerless.

Amanda walked over to Nancy. She turned, intending to call after Brian, "I will see you when you get back," but he was already gone.

The next afternoon Amanda stood at the bottom of the front steps, waiting for Josie to take her up for a shopping excursion to the village. Her usual thoughts of Rance had brought her to a point where she considered his brotherly kiss of the previous day. She tentatively touched the spot on her forehead. He needed to improve his aim and zero in on her mouth, she thought dryly, and felt a bit low as she wondered if she would ever again arouse a spark of passion in him.

Rance and Brian had certainly acted queer and secretive yesterday, she thought. The two were concealing something from her, and she considered the possibility that there was more to the trip to Wye than gambling.

At that moment the door behind her opened. Daniel, on his way to the stables, came through the door and walked down the steps to stand beside her.

"If you're still interested in pugilism, I just received an edition of *Boxiana* by Pierce Egan. You'll find the book on my desk in the library," he said.

"Thank you, Papa. That was good of you. I'll read from it when I get back from the village." She should have known Daniel would follow up in his typical manner. *Boxiana* must be the last word on pugilism. "Mr. Cauthen has a new shipment of Brussels lace. Josie and I are going to price it," she told him.

He nodded and suggested a fair price for the imported lace. "I wouldn't pay more than that. Ah, here comes Lady Josephine now." He pointed with his walking stick toward the trap coming into view around a bend in the drive. Before turning and shambling off to the stables, he waved to Josie.

Amanda climbed up onto the box, and the girls set off for the village at a modest gait, the horse Chloe's fastest pace.

Josie chattered nonstop, every second phrase being "Evan said . . ." or "Evan did . . ." Just last week, the day after the Castleberry cousins returned home, Mr. Whitaker had come to the point and asked Lord Ainsworth for Josie's hand. After her papa had toasted the happy couple with champagne, Josie confided, she and Evan had strolled in the garden. At first Evan had kissed her quite chastely, but later more passionately "in an interesting way."

Josie gushed, "Oh, Mandy, he was very romantic and most unchurchmanlike. You know what he said? 'I think, Josephine, you and I shall go on very well indeed!' "

Glancing sidelong at Josie's animated face, Amanda wondered enviously if Rance would ever give her an "interesting" kiss. She could never nudge Rance past a comfortable friendship, but he colored her days. The two of them would often trade memories of their childhood and youth. She entertained him with tales of Bristol and her adventures among the doyens of English letters. He reveled in relating his mischievous antics while he grew up at Willowwoods, and she never tired of the anecdotes about his eccentric great-aunt Agnes and would laugh heartily at the old lady's peccadilloes and acid tongue. But Rance never tried to take advantage of her, not from lack of encouragement, she thought wryly, often recalling with deep regret her muffed chance when she had frozen in his arms weeks before.

Josie parked the trap at the mounting block in front of Cauthen's dry goods store. The urchin Horace rushed over to dicker a fee with Josie to hold Chloe, aware that Lady Josephine was not as generous as Miss Lofton. He settled on a less than desirable fare and smirked when Amanda rolled her eyes in sympathy.

Mr. Cauthen offered Amanda the Brussels lace at a shilling below Daniel's suggested price. She purchased the necessary yards to trim a day gown she had commissioned from a local dressmaker.

When the two young women stepped from Cauthen's to the walkway, Josie linked arms with Amanda, and the two fell in step, chattering, as they marched toward the confectioner's to buy a pound of toffee for Lady Ainsworth.

Halfway down the block, Amanda stopped short and stared at the billboard nailed to the ironmonger's door. The advertisement was for a boxing match Saturday morning in the town of Wye. She read through the details below the principals' names, her lips moving silently as she once again perused the notice to reinforce her first reading. A young English pugilist, new to the ring, who in five matches had knocked out each opponent in less than six rounds while he remained virtually unmarked, was being challenged by a mysterious Russian named Vladimir Rostanov, who had won matches in Paris, Rome, and Berlin. Amanda drew in a deep breath as all the pieces fell into place.

Josie prodded Amanda. "Come on, Mandy, that's of no interest to us."

But Amanda's pulse was fluttering erratically. "Josie, that . . . that's Rance," she stammered.

"Whatever do you mean?" Josie scanned the placard. Nowhere did she see Rance's name.

"That fighter Terry Stone, right there," Amanda said, running her finger over and over the printed name. "Josie, that is Terrance Straughn."

Chapter 9

Amanda turned from the poster and walked at a rapid pace toward the confectioner's. Josie trotted to keep up with her. Amanda's answer to each question Josie fired at her eroded her earlier conviction that she was mistaken and Rance and Terry Stone were not one in the same person.

"I can see how you believe Rance is a boxer and that he has taken the name Terry, but couldn't there be other fighters who use that name? Maybe the man on the poster is not Rance. How can you be certain he is to box at Wye?"

Amanda stopped at the door to the candy shop. "Brian told me," she said. "Yesterday I was at one of the sparring sessions I just described to you. Rance behaved rather peculiarly, as if he had something to hide. He disconcerted me a little because he said he was going away. But when I questioned Brian he admitted he and Rance were going to Wye for gaming. Josie, I think because the town is so near, Rance feared I would hear about the fight and discover that he was boxing for money. That was what made him edgy, I'm sure."

Inside the shop Josie purchased Lady Ainsworth's toffee,

and she and Amanda walked back to the trap. By then Josie was positive Amanda was right, and Terry Stone was indeed Rance Straughn.

"I'm going to see Rance fight," Amanda declared with determination when she and Josie climbed into the trap.

"Mandy, you can't," Josie insisted, holding the horse in check with the reins. "Nice women do not attend pugilistic events."

"Oh, Josie, you can be so stuffy," Amanda shot back.

"Would Mr. Lofton allow you to go to a mill?" Josie asked, ignoring the criticism.

"Of course not! He doesn't even approve of fisticuffs. I have a plan, but I need help." Amanda's implied request sent a quiver of foreboding through Josie's small body.

"Oh, no!" She shook her head repeatedly and set the horse in motion. "Evan Whitaker would break our engagement if I disgraced myself. I am not going to any mill, Amanda Lofton, you can be very sure."

"Don't be a goose, Josephine. You would just be in the way. Besides, no one will know I'm a woman. I intend disguising myself as a man."

Josie wagged her blond curls, convinced her friend had lost her wits, but Amanda's resolve had firmed to where she would listen to no arguments. Her brain churned with possible subterfuges that would ring true and keep her father in the dark. As Josie drove past the livery stable, Amanda perused the building. The trap was a few yards past the entrance when Amanda touched Josie's arm. "Turn around and go back to Gibson's," she said.

"The livery?" Amanda nodded. She ignored Josie's "Why?"

Josie turned the small trap easily in the wide road and pulled up before the wooden building. Amanda hopped down and disappeared into the dark, cavernous barn. Josie tapped her foot impatiently for a full ten minutes before Amanda reemerged, followed by a stable boy carrying a man's saddle.

"Put it behind the seat, Matthew," she ordered the

young man. He did her bidding and smiled broadly when she handed him a tuppence.

Josie's mouth formed into a stubborn line. The saddle was the perfect size for Amanda's mare, Nancy. Her heart grew heavy. This time Amanda was not blowing smoke. She intended to follow Rance Straughn to Wye.

"Josie, stop over there near that stand of trees," Amanda said when the two had traveled nearly to Rook Manor in silence.

Josie reined in the docile horse, edged the trap off the road, and parked beside the miniature forest of beech, elm, and oaks Amanda indicated.

"I want you to call for me in the morning, Josie, at nine o'clock, in your trap, and bring me here."

"Here? The woods?" Josie waved nervous hands toward the trees beside the road.

Amanda nodded. "That is all the assistance I require. You need not fear Mr. Whitaker's disapprobation, for you shall be involved hardly at all."

Josie played with the reins in her hands. No matter how Amanda rationalized her entanglement, Josie would be looked on as an accomplice in this mad scheme even if her part was small. Just being aware Amanda was attending the fight made her a confederate. If only she were talented in the art of persuasion, she might be able to dissuade Amanda; but Josie had no illusions about herself. She was mediocre, at best, in winning people over to her point of view, and no match for someone as strong-minded as Amanda.

"You had best put me into the picture, Mandy. What do you intend to do?" Josie asked, her voice fraught with resignation, her blue eyes miserable. Her one hope was that she would discover a flaw in Amanda's plan that would make it impossible for her to carry out her scheme.

Amanda's eyes, in stark contrast to her friend's, sparkled brilliantly with anticipation. Her voice was nearly joyous as she explained. "Riding Nancy, I can be in Wye by two or three o'clock tomorrow, stay the night at the inn, and go to the mill at eleven o'clock Saturday morning. The fight shouldn't last long, maybe an hour. Each round, you see, Josie, ends when a fighter is knocked off his feet. According to the notice at the ironmonger's, Rance won in six rounds or less. He must be very good indeed, or by now he would have a crooked nose and a bruised body, to say nothing of missing teeth. Rance, or Terry Stone as he apparently calls himself, will make short work of Vladimir Rostanov. I can leave right after the mill and be back at Rook Manor by late afternoon."

"The saddle?" Josie asked, pointing to the floor of the trap in back of her.

"I will hide it here among the trees until morning and switch saddles then."

Josie had to admire Amanda's ingenuity when she detailed the rest of her plan, but that did not keep a hard lump from forming in Josie's stomach.

Amanda stashed the saddle well off the road and climbed back into the trap.

"Amanda, don't do this," Josie begged. "Your reputation will be in shreds if this gets out. A woman, not only traveling alone, but disguised as a man! Wye is not such a distance that someone from the village won't attend the mill."

"I have thought of that, Josephine, but people often see what they expect to see. No one is going to examine me closely, looking for Amanda Lofton in a person he believes to be a young man. Besides, all attention will be on the pugilists; I shall just be one of the crowd."

Josie clicked Chloe into motion. The horse's hooves clip-clopped on the hard dirt, the only sound as Josie remained cocooned with dark expectations. Beside her, Amanda honed her enterprise, studying the plan for flaws.

When Josie stopped the trap before the brick steps of Rook Manor, she made one more weak plea. "Amanda, please change your mind. At least think it over."

Josie's entreaty had no effect. "Josephine, don't fail me," Amanda said. "I want to see Rance fight above all things. If you are truly my friend, you will be here at nine tomorrow."

"You are being terribly unfair," Josie murmured.

Amanda patted her hand. "I know. I can't help myself; I want this too badly. Josie, I'm counting on you."

Daniel questioned, but not too closely, Amanda's concocted story that she was to accompany Josie on an overnight visit to Josie's maiden aunt. Satisfied with her answers, he gave his consent.

The next morning Amanda secreted Nancy in the grove where she and Josie had stopped the previous day and walked back to the Rook Manor stables.

"Jones," she pretended to the head groom, "Nancy threw a shoe near Ainsworth House, and she's being reshod at Lord Ainsworth's forge."

"When should I fetch her, miss?" the man asked.

"You needn't bother. I'm going on an overnight visit with the Castleberrys to Lady Josephine's aunt. I'll bring her back with me when I return tomorrow." Amanda was a little ashamed at how easily the lie tripped off her tongue. Jones simply nodded in a lifelong habit of obeying an employer's directives without question.

In the attic Amanda found a paisley tapestry valise that could be affixed handily onto the saddle. She pilfered Daniel's wide-brimmed fishing hat from the hall closet. The clothes box with cast-off garments for the poor yielded an old pair of Daniel's breeches.

Mary, Amanda's abigail, was offended when her mistress insisted on packing her own bag. "I'm careful, Miss Amanda. You can surely trust me to do a simple chore," the maid protested.

Amanda dismissed her, ignoring Mary's ruffled feelings for the time being, but vowing to make things right with the country girl. For now she could not let the maid be privy to the items that would be stored in the bag.

Behind her locked door, Amanda changed into a plum-colored traveling dress and a pair of gray shoes. The matching pelisse and her plum velvet bonnet, adorned with gray feathers, were laid out on the bed with a gray beaded reticule. She tossed her silver-backed brush and matching comb, along with her toiletries, into the bottom of the bag. Over them she placed her neatly folded undergarments, stockings, a batiste nightdress, a robe, a pair of blue slippers, and a blue muslin day gown. The breeches she had altered after a fashion and her own casual jacket topped these items, leaving scant room for her riding boots and her father's hat. She tamped down the contents of the valise to make everything fit, stretched the brown leather straps to just meet, and buckled the bulging bag.

Amanda had not dared to admit to herself that Josie might not come. Her stomach fluttered when the lower hall clock chimed nine. After five additional intense minutes, the trap appeared around the curve in the carriageway.

Jeffries carried the valise to the vehicle and placed it on the floor behind the seat. Amanda hurried after him, for she was eager to be gone. When she stopped in the library and bent to kiss her unsuspecting father, she experienced a strong twinge of remorse at deceiving him and fled from the room before she gave herself away.

Josie pulled the trap up to the stand of trees, and Amanda hopped down and lifted the overstuffed valise from behind the box. Nancy whinnied from a short distance in the woods at the sound of Amanda's voice as she thanked Josie. But Josie clambered from the light carriage and dropped nimbly to the ground beside Amanda.

"You cannot change your garments without help," she said. "And how will you fasten such a mass of hair and shove it beneath a hat?"

Amanda squeezed her petite friend's arm affectionately. "Josie, you're a gem."

Josie wrinkled her nose at Amanda and proceeded to tie Chloe to a bush before following Amanda into the shelter of the trees, where Nancy, already wearing the man's saddle, was tethered.

With Josie's assistance, Amanda was soon into her breeches, shirt, coat, and boots. The plum traveling dress, pelisse, and velvet bonnet along with the gray shoes were crammed into the valise. Amanda opened the beaded reticule, removed a few coins, deposited them into her coat pocket, and pushed the gray purse with her remaining funds down toward the bottom of the traveling bag. She sat cross-legged on the ground while Josie, kneeling beside her, used half a box of hairpins to fasten Amanda's long brown hair flat against her skull, then pulled Daniel's hat down almost to Amanda's eyebrows, completing the disguise. Amanda jammed the box of pins into the valise, refastened the strap, and affixed the bag to the saddle.

She led Nancy out to the road, where Josie climbed back onto the box of the trap. Amanda mounted the horse. The unfamiliar saddle was hard between her legs. At least a sidesaddle supported the cushioned bottom of her anatomy. She wondered for a fleeting second why she had envied male riders. She leaned over to Josie and touched cheeks with her.

"I shan't sleep tonight, Amanda Lofton, and shall spend a nerve-racking two days," Josie said, but immediately reached out an imploring hand and wailed, "Oh, Mandy, don't go. It's not too late to change your mind. You can tell your papa that our trip to my aunt's was canceled."

Amanda leaned from the saddle and patted Josie's shoulder reassuringly, uttered a few soothing words, circled Nancy away from the light carriage, and headed the horse toward the road that led to Wye.

"Be careful, Mandy!" Josie shouted. Amanda waved without turning around. Watching Amanda's receding back, Josie trembled with a strong premonition of disaster.

A layer of gray dust clung to Amanda's clothes, and her mouth was dry as she approached Wye. She had come to within three miles, when ahead of her she spied a drudge horse plodding before a ramshackle wagon. Some inner warning caused Amanda to approach the rundown vehicle cautiously.

A burly man in a threadbare coat with several days growth of beard outlining a sullen mouth handled the reins. Beside him on the box sat a slatternly, gaunt male. Sprawled in the wagon bed were four ruffians, two, apparently asleep, their hats shading their faces. The other two passed a gin bottle between them and to the driver and his companion. Their vulgar jesting carried back to Amanda over the rumble of the iron wheels. The liberal use of cant in their broad accents disguised some of the meaning from her, but a familiarity with the coarse lexicon of the Bristol wharfmen had imbued her vocabulary with a few select words that were not the vernacular of polite society. One or two of these, coming from the wagon, set her teeth on edge.

Finally impatient with the slow pace, she decided on evasive action and trotted Nancy into the adjacent field, in sight of but well away from the wagon. The bruiser's interested eyes followed her progress. He nudged his thin companion and pointed to Amanda.

In the distance at the edge of the field Amanda noticed a line of willows. She kicked Nancy into a gallop and made for the brook she suspected was hidden by the wispy green leaves. She smiled her satisfaction when she reined in beside a shallow stream that was shaded invitingly from the sun. The willows on each side of the stream met overhead to form a canopy.

Amanda dismounted and rubbed the numbness in the seat of her breeches with a newfound sympathy for male riders. The horse, smelling the water, walked down the sloping embankment and drank from a pool that had been trapped in a basin of rocks.

Amanda tugged off her father's hat. She yearned to release the confined hair and scratch her scalp, but she resisted, for she would never be able to repile the mass atop her head as skillfully as Josie had done.

She splashed a hand in the cold, fresh runnel. Without a second thought she pulled off her boots and stockings. Reaching her toes into the stream, she wiggled them in the refreshing water. The cool sensation ran up her spine right to the top of her constrained hair.

Amanda removed her jacket and tossed the garment onto the jumble of footwear. She unbuttoned the top button of her white lawn shirt and shoved her poorly amended breeches above her knees.

The brook flowed on either side of a flat rock that protruded from the middle of the shallow gully. She waded the few steps through the water and climbed onto the rock and sat with her arms about her bare legs, her head resting on her knees. Nancy was contentedly munching the meadow grass. The shimmering sunlight, filtering through the screen of leaves far above Amanda's head, had a hypnotic effect on her. Only the faint gurgle of the brook and the cadence of the chirping insects broke the sweet monotony.

As usual, Rance ruled her thoughts. The manner in which he had said he was going away had unsettled her for several moments back there on the overlook the other day. But the public notice advertising the mill made everything clear. She had been so absorbed with getting Rance to fall in love with her that she had been blinded to the obvious signs that he and Brian were involved in serious sparring and not in recreational boxing. She should have guessed long ago what Brian and Rance were up to and that their frequent trips were to boxing matches. Her jealousy and fear had obscured the obvious—that Rance had become a professional fighter. She had needlessly worried, thinking he was either pursuing the women on Lady Woods's infamous list or dreading that she would hear from Freddie that Rance had moved back to London.

Rance had gone to great pains to keep secret the true purpose of the sparring. Her sleepy eyes crinkled in amusement. When she next saw him, the fight with the Russian opponent would be over. Already she was forming in her mind the words with which she would tease him when she verbally reenacted the fight for him. What fun it would be to twit him with a precise account of the match. Amanda hugged her knees more closely to her. Her eyelids drooped.

A clatter of wagon wheels in the near distance brought her out of a light doze, and a nervous tremor of impending danger shot through her body. She sat erect on the rock and peered from her shelter into the field where grasshoppers were rising, stirred up by the wheels of the one-horse wagon coming toward her at a slow pace. She slid from her perch and splashed through the water to the bank of the stream where her shedded garments lay.

Mud clung to the bottoms of her feet. She hastily reached her legs back down into the pool where she had first tested the water and swished her feet about, rubbing them dry on the inside of her jacket. Her heart began to thump when the wagon was close enough for her to recognize the drudge horse, burly driver, and his lean partner. She hastily buttoned her shirt and pulled on her stockings with trembling hands. She grabbed Daniel's hat and tugged it down over her pinned hair, thankful that she had not undone Josie's meticulous coif. She had one foot booted and was working on the second when the wagon pulled up a scant yard from where she wallowed on the ground.

Amanda hustled to her feet, still tugging at her left boot, and hopped on one foot in the direction where Nancy cropped at the grass. The burly man wrapped the reins to keep the wagon horse in check, jumped to the ground, and set himself between Amanda and her mare, drunkenly rocking on his heels. Amanda stepped back, recoiling from his breath, which reeked of gin.

"Gotta a stone in your stampers?" he asked without preamble, staring at the expensive boot she had just wiggled onto her foot.

"No," she stammered, then a quick "Yes" when she realized it was easier to dissemble than to go into a lengthy futile explanation that would serve no purpose. She scooped up her jacket from the ground and tugged on the garment, the lining damp from having been used as an emergency towel.

The big man swept his beady eyes larcenously over Amanda's coat. Although many sizes too small for him, it would nevertheless fetch a good price from the used-clothes merchant, or could be traded for a replacement for his own frayed coat with its greasy lapels. The remainder of the cove's expensive rig out would get him a respectable set of duds, he thought.

With bloodshot eyes he studied Nancy. The horse, if it could be sold before a Redbreast clapped him on the shoulder, could keep a man in gin for a lifetime. If, as was likely, he would have to turn the mare loose, the saddle and the rest of the tack would fetch a tidy sum even if he had to split the take six ways.

Amanda was taking deep breaths to staunch her terror. Her eyes darted toward the wagon. Loud snores came from the four occupants who were tumbled haphazardly in the wagon's bed. From his seat on the box, the bruiser's partner grinned at her, baring his rotted teeth.

"You gotta proper highbred there, ain'tcha?" the scarecow indicated with a toss of his head toward Amanda's horse. She inclined her head in affirmation. Horror tales warred in her brain with wild schemes of escape. She could make a dash for Nancy, but if the bruiser caught her . . . no, she must not think of that.

The wraith sprang down from the wagon and joined his friend. Now, two of them were between her and the mare. She could not risk a move. She forced herself to calm down. As long as the brutes were talking, she might yet have a chance.

"You a gentry cove?" the new arrival asked.

"I beg your pardon?" Amanda kept her voice low and masculine.

"What do you be, huh? A lord? Lord who?" He doffed

a soiled black hat and scratched his tangled gray hair, which had not seen a comb in recent weeks.

"Lofton, my name is Lofton," Amanda mumbled once she discerned he was asking her name. She could not reach Nancy without stepping around the bruiser.

"Lord Laughter! Ain't that a name, Mr. Mooney?" he snickered, ambling drunkenly a few steps nearer his partner.

"You going to the mill?" the bruiser asked, ignoring his partner. Amanda merely nodded, for her throat was now constricted with fear, as her situation seemed ever more hopeless. Highwaymen were known to steal their victims' clothes. Her fate would be worse than being robbed if she had to shed her male garments. An involuntary shudder raced through her body.

Mooney turned and reached out a hand to stroke Nancy's neck, but the horse shook him off and reared, sending the bruiser tottering backward.

"Whoa, Nancy," Amanda cried instinctively, and the mare settled down at her command. Mooney snatched the reins and held fast to the animal.

"Whatta you think, Spees? You wanna referee a mill between Lord Laughter and me for this prad," he joked, but his tone was ugly, not jovial.

"No, no, sir," Amanda protested. "I could never engage in fisticuffs with you. I am no pugilist!"

"Hee-hee." Spees giggled in a near falsetto. "Ain't that pretty flash Lord Laughter talks, Mr. Mooney?"

"Shut up, Spees," Mooney commanded nastily. "That mare cost hundreds of guineas, unless I miss my guess. Since you ain't likely to beat me in a mill, if you was to grease my fists, we could part all right and tight. You got a lot of mint sauce?"

Amanda looked blank. "Sovereigns, pounds, shillings," he clarified. Her hand went to the coins she had placed in her coat pocket. The quick move did not escape Mooney. He squinted lustfully.

"Empty his lordship's pockets, Spees," he ordered, "while I check this fancy valise."

As Spees reached for her, Amanda's palms shot out with a powerful thrust and smacked the emaciated man with both hands in his puny chest. He tumbled backward and slid down the embankment into the bed of the stream. His short boots stuck fast into a patch of soft mud.

Amanda leapt past Mooney and ran with all the speed she could muster along the brook's embankment and away from her menacers. The bruiser, afraid he would lose the horse if he dropped the reins and pursued his quarry, held tight to the horse's bobbing head. Mooney bellowed to arouse his drunken cohorts in the wagon from their stupor, while he fought to control the horse. Spees was working furiously to extricate his shoes from the mud.

Amanda realized no one was in pursuit of her. She stopped a good distance from her adversaries, panting hard, half from running and half from fear. The men in the wagon, she saw, were rubbing sleep from their eyes as they climbed listlessly from the vehicle.

Mooney's rallying cries to his drunken friends agitated Nancy further. The mare bucked and tore the leading reins from the bruiser's hands, for despite his strength he could not control the frenzied horse.

Amanda placed two fingers into her mouth and whistled shrilly. The brutes froze into ice statues at the unexpected sound. Nancy knocked Mooney to the ground and galloped to her mistress. The bruiser unleashed a tirade at his hapless partners while Amanda leapt onto the mare's back and rode away.

In her elation at having escaped, Amanda continued unthinking for several miles before she became aware she was riding in the wrong direction. She stopped and took stock of the country around her. In the distance beside a stand of trees was a farmhouse. She made for the building and found a sympathetic farmer's wife, who treated her to a tin cup of cool water in exchange for welcome conversation and pointed the smart "young man" in the direction of the road to Wye.

After a number of false twists and turns within the town itself, Amanda happened onto the main street with its various businesses, including three well-patronized taverns, and the Wayside Inn. On the side street beside the inn she located a livery stable and eased Nancy into the yard, which was dominated by an ancient oak tree. She dismounted and called for a groom, but the premises appeared to be deserted.

Her heart lurched when her nemesis appeared from around the corner of the building, a smug grin on his evil face. "If it ain't Lord Laughter, who gave us the slip. Come see, Spees," he called into the air, but kept his eyes fixed on Amanda. The grinning skeleton shuffled into sight, his footwear coated with dried mud.

Amanda's foot slipped into the stirrup, but Mooney leapt across the yard and pulled her, squealing, to the ground.

He clapped a filthy hand over her lips. "Shut your mouth," he warned menacingly, "or I'll knock you senseless. You understand?"

After she nodded her assent, he flung her at Spees, who grabbed her arm, holding her fast.

Mooney fastened the mare securely to an iron hitching post.

"Now let's see if Lord Laughter hid his blunt in the lady's bag," he sneered, lifting the valise from the saddle.

Amanda's eyes darted around for help. Where was the groom? She pushed down her panic. This was ridiculous. She was in the center of a town. Not a block from there she had seen pedestrians on the sidewalk. Her boot came forcefully down on Spees's foot. The thin man howled and released her arm. Mooney, startled into inaction, stood mesmerized as Amanda grabbed her valise and ran toward the street to summon help.

Spooked by the commotion, Nancy reared and her hooves resounded against the metal post. Mooney flung his arms over his head, for he was a whisper away from the horses' thrashing legs. Spees grabbed a whip from the box of a carriage that was parked nearby. The mare shrieked as the leather thongs bit into her flesh.

"No!" Amanda screamed, and rushed back into the yard at the abused beast's pitiful cry. She grabbed Spees's raised arm to stop the flogging, but he shoved her to the ground. "Stop it! Stop it!" she cried, her heart breaking at the man's cruelty to the innocent animal. "I'll give you all my money," she wailed, flinging the valise at Mooney, "but leave her alone!

Spees dropped the whip at Mooney's command, and Amanda jumped to her feet and calmed the frightened mare, who had never until that day known a moment of mistreatment.

"All right! Where's your blunt?" Mooney barked. She pointed to the valise. Tears streamed from her eyes as she nestled her face against the mare's red coat. Spees kneeled before the bag under the oak tree where Amanda had dropped the valise and proceeded to undo the straps.

"What's this?" he asked with a bewildered frown, holding up a pair of women's gray shoes, which he tossed aside on the cobbles. He drew out the plum velvet bonnet and dangled the headgear by its strings for Mooney's perusal. He shook out the plum traveling gown, and, still on his knees, held up the dress before his frail chest. Mooney grabbed Amanda's arm and turned her toward him. He brought his face right up to hers, peering at her. He snatched the hat off her head and pulled out several of the pins, loosing long tendrils of brown hair.

"Well, well," he croaked with a knowing leer. Amanda backed away, but he gripped her arm in a viselike grip and fumbled at her breasts. Amanda squirmed, her eyes widened with indignation at the humiliating grope. She kicked hard with her boot and caught him a glancing blow off his shin.

"Ow." He heaped a stream of vile invectives on her, wrapped both arms about her waist, and raised her feet off the ground. Amanda kicked and flailed at him without inflicting damage. "I'll soon be taming you, you little hell-cat," he cackled. "You ain't had a real man before, I wager." Tears of rage sprang to Amanda's eyes.

Spees stopped ransacking to stare at Amanda with wonder. Shaking his head, he continued his quest for money in Amanda's valise. He had just flung a pelisse and her blue dress onto the cobblestones, when his grimy hands paused in their frantic rummaging. A figure above him blocked out the sun. His head whipped around. Amanda's heart soared at the sight of the intruder.

"Release her, Mooney. Terry Stone won't be pleased you're manhandling his cousin," warned the man in an Irish brogue.

Chapter 10

"Cousin?" Mooney sneered, spitting on the cobblestones. "More like a doxey," he muttered, releasing Amanda, who flung herself into Brian's arms, burying her head against his shoulder.

"Watch your tongue, man. I said cousin, and cousin it is," Brian warned, easing Amanda aside to enable him, should it be necessary, to reach a small French pistol secreted in his inside pocket.

"Let's cut line and go," Spees mumbled to Mooney. The skinny ruffian was an innate coward who had spent the greater part of his life hanging on to the coattails of bullies, not plunging in when the odds were weighted against him. But Mooney, who was the bully and, therefore, of a different breed, brushed his crony aside.

"I ain't gonna pitch you no bouncers," Mooney said to Brian. "I planned to squeeze a borde or two out of this cousin," he snickered, "when I took her for that Lord Laughter she masqueraded as. But I ain't so cork-brained that I'd take on Terry Stone." His treacherous eyes narrowed. "But you can't blame a poor man for cutting a sham to put a bit of silver in his pocket."

"You'll have to find your shillings elsewhere, Mooney." Brian held his ground. "We won't be bringing the law down on you for trying to rob her, but you best find a place to sleep off the Blue Ruin before you get into real trouble."

Mooney glared at Brian, unwilling to depart without some reward for his larcenous efforts.

"Now, I'd like to, Mr. McGonigal, but four coves is sleeping in my wagon," he announced with bogus civility.

"All right, Mooney, I've been low on blunt myself. Here," Brian offered, reaching into his pocket, "a half-borde for each of you."

Both men's hands shot out at the same time. Brian slapped a sixpence in each dirty palm, and the two would-be thieves ambled off, grumbling at the paltry sum.

"How could you do that?" Amanda stepped away from her protector, her expressive brown eyes resentful.

"An' what would you have had me do, lass?" he asked mildly.

"Call the constable, of course, and have them arrested. But give them money?" Her voice raised a pitch on the huffy query.

"Had I sent you for the constable, you would have found me knocked senseless, or worse, when you returned. I have a pistol, I do. But thank the good Lord I didn't need to make use of it, for I would surely have been detained and questioned and greatly overset Terry just before the fight and to no purpose."

Brian lifted Amanda's sulky face with a finger under her chin, took a handkerchief from his pocket, and wiped her eyes and face. "The money, lass, I trust, will keep me from having to protect me back for a time. You don't wish to see me sent to me maker yet, do you now?"

Amanda shook her head, but she milked her pique as she scooped up Daniel's hat and replaced it on her head. She tucked the loose strands of hair beneath the crown.

"How did you know I was here?" she asked, curiosity overcoming her prickliness.

"I heard you squabbling with the pair of them from inside, where I was negotiating for a hackney for tomorrow. I thought me ears had deceived me when I recognized your voice. Glory be, I still couldn't believe it was you, even when me eyes couldn't deny it. How do you come to be here?"

Amanda recited how she had enlisted Josie, misled her father, and outwitted Mooney and Spees successfully at the stream but reencountered them in the yard with unfortunate results.

"Ah, no one uses this door much. 'Tis the back of the stables," Brian explained. "The entrance is on the other side."

"I didn't realize." Amanda moved to her horse's side and traced the cruel welts left by the whip with a gentle hand.

"The cuts are just on the surface of her skin, lass. The brute did not damage her seriously," Brian observed, coming up behind her. His mind was on mitigating the havoc her unexpected appearance would cause in Terry. If she indicted Mooney and Spees in her colorfully outspoken manner, Terry would be compelled to rush out and avenge her honor.

"Uh, Amanda," he began, placing his hands on her shoulders and turning her to face him. "Don't be telling Terry what happened with Spees and Mooney," he pleaded. "Just seeing you again will be upsetting him enough. He could lose the fight if he involves himself in your troubles. You do understand me, lass, don't you?"

"Oh, I don't expect to see Rance face-to-face, just from a distance when he fights," she said. "I'll hire a room for the night and be gone after the mill tomorrow. He need never know I was here."

"It's not so simple. There's not a bed to be had in town."

"Oh, dear, that does pose a problem. Perhaps you and Rance would let me bed down on the floor of your room," she suggested with a frivolous titter.

"I don't think either of us would care to compromise

you in that manner. In any case, it won't be necessary . . . Lord Laughter, was it?" Brian jested.

"Isn't that the silliest thing!" Amanda giggled.

"You'll move in with Maggie . . . for the night," Brian said.

"Maggie is with you? Did she come just for the fight too?"

"No, not exactly. Maggie gave notice at the household where she was in service. She is with me now for good." Explaining no further, he untied Nancy from the post and led the mare into the stable to arrange for her stall, feed, and attention to her superficial wounds. While he was gone, Amanda picked up her scattered belongings from the cobblestones, refolded the garments, and repacked her valise.

Within minutes Brian returned from making the arrangements and picked up Amanda's bag. She fell in step beside him as they entered the street that led to the inn. In the lobby he guided her toward the stairs.

A dapper gentleman lounging in a chair, a cigar smoking in his manicured hand, glanced up from his newspaper.

"Hey, McGonigal," he called across the room, "can I safely wager a respectable sum on Stone to knock the Russian out?"

"Indeed you can," Brian answered, ushering Amanda up the narrow stairway. On the second floor he stopped before a door, rapped once, and called out, "It's me, Brian."

A bolt inside scraped and the door opened. Rance filled the doorway, his white shirt undone at the throat, tan breeches tucked into a pair of brown riding boots. Amanda's heart squeezed into the funny little twist, but the smile died on her face as his eyes flashed with anger.

He rounded on Brian. "What the devil is she doing here?"

"Amanda's here for the fight," Brian said. "I ran into her while she was stabling her mare at the livery." He stepped past the tall fighter with Amanda following. Rance closed the door to the hall, where a curious guest peered at him from the corridor.

"She doesn't have a room," Brian said evenly. "I'll convince Maggie to take her in, and I'll rack up here with you."

"Oh, no, you won't! Back home she goes! There's a coach leaving soon." Rance's eyes noted the time on a bedside clock. "Damn," he blared, "it left ten minutes ago. Now I'll have to take her back myself!"

Amanda glared at him. Her ire was raised because he had ignored her and had spoken to Brian as though she were a backward child incapable of handling her own affairs.

"You are not my parent to order me to return home. I'll find my own accommodations." She reached for the valise, where Brian had set it on a chair by the door.

Rance grabbed her wrist and wrested the bag from her. "You're not going anywhere until I resolve what's to be done with you. Gad! Does that chuckleheaded father of yours have so little sense he would allow you to travel to a mill without a male escort."

"Mr. Lofton doesn't know she's here, lad," Brian interjected. "Amanda smoked him with a Banbury tale about accompanying Lady Josephine on an overnight trip to visit a maiden aunt."

"Lud, Brian, you didn't rashly go all softhearted and let slip about the mill when I left the two of you together the other day?"

"Don't let your brain get addled over this, Terry," Brian warned. "Amanda saw a notice of the mill on a placard in the village. She put it together for herself."

"Papa knows nothing," Amanda said. "He would never have permitted me to come. I rode Nancy early this morning and pretended she had cast a shoe, but actually left her tethered in a little grove near the main road. The grooms at Rook Manor think she's safe at Ainsworth House being attended to and that I'll bring her home tomorrow when I return from my journey with the Castleberrys."

"Lady Josephine aided her. She helped Amanda change into her disguise in the woods," Brian added. "The lass rode all the way here masquerading as a lad."

Rance slouched down into a chair and stretched his long legs before him. Amanda and Brian waited, watching him. He closed his eyes and tilted his head toward the ceiling. After a moment he looked at Brian and spoke with measured calmness.

"I wouldn't be fit for the mill tomorrow if I drove Amanda home tonight. I guess there's nothing to be done but to have her sleep with Maggie. I'm sorry, Brian, I know you've had only the one night with Maggie."

"She will raise a fuss, but I'll bring her around," Brian promised, his hand on the doorknob. "An' haven't Maggie and me the rest of our lives together?" He shrugged philosophically.

When he was gone, Amanda sat on the bed facing Rance. She smoothed the blue bedcover without purpose, waiting for him to speak.

"Damme, Amanda, you are a top-drawer widgeon to undertake such a dangerous journey," Rance scolded. "Before a fight, the worst scum in the land are on the road. Cutthroats and footpads who seek an easy mark to waylay and rob. Even were you a young man traveling alone, you would not be safe, especially without a weapon."

"I can look after myself. I am not a child, Rance," she insisted.

"A child would have the sense to be frightened," Rance rebutted with a sneer.

Amanda burned to prove her worth by relating how she had outwitted Mooney and Spees at the brook. Unfortunately the humiliating encounter at the stable with the ruffians canceled out the heroic escape, but, in any case, she had promised Brian to remain mum.

"Surely a young man is safer than a woman on the road," she said, defending her disguise. "It seemed quite sensible to me, but perhaps I should have taken one of Papa's guns," she conceded.

"Had you, you would, no doubt, have ended up shooting yourself."

His open mockery touched a nerve, and she opened her mouth to retaliate, but recalled Brian's admonition about upsetting Rance before the fight and stopped herself. Their eyes dueled, however, neither giving ground. She had an insane inclination to plop herself into his lap and run her fingers through his crisp, corn-colored hair and watch him squirm as he had that day on the overlook. He had no right to be so handsome.

"Would that you hadn't involved little Josie," he mused, bringing her back to earth. Amanda's mouth primmed with envy at the affectionate tone in which he spoke Josie's name.

Unable to erase the jealous heat from her voice, she responded, "Josie's part was small. I don't believe Mr. Whitaker is such a fribble that he would reprove her."

"No?" Rance took issue. "I'm not so certain. He's a serious young man who chose the church for principle, not expediency . . . his justification, no doubt, for throwing you over," he twitted.

"I wasn't his to throw over!" she shot back. "Evan Whitaker may have fancied himself besotted with me, but I never shared his feelings or gave him any encouragement."

"Be that as it may. Whitaker will not marry a woman who is tainted with scandal direct or indirect. Josie is your bosom bow. You would not want to be the instrument of her unhappiness by causing the curate to break their engagement?"

"No, of course not. Josie need never reveal her part." Rance cared more about Josie's welfare than her own. Life was unfair. If a woman loved a man, he should love her back.

Amanda rose from the bed and wandered about the room to blunt her irritation. She chided herself for being mean-spirited. It was natural for Rance to be concerned about his longtime friend. But why couldn't he regard her welfare in the same light as he did Josie's and heap the same kind words on her instead of deriding her?

She paused before the oak dresser on which personal grooming aids were laid out neatly. With idle curiosity she picked up a water jug with a picture of the bare-chested fighters Molineaux and Cribb in the classic boxing pose of raised fists. She turned the silver-luster pitcher around to the opposite side and studied the portrait of a curly-haired Tom Cribb, resplendent in formal attire. The legend below read: World's Champion 1811.

"Is this yours?" Amanda asked, holding the jug aloft.

"Yes, I hardly think the inn could afford to supply their rooms with Staffordshire wares," he jeered. She made a face at him in retaliation for the snideness.

His lidded eyes watched her handle his ivory comb and silver-backed brushes, replace them on the dresser, and pick up the silver knife he used to pare his nails. Two days ago he had held her and kissed her brow, and, not trusting himself, had hastened off before he disclosed too much and left Brian to offer the shrouded responses to her questions. All the guilt he had felt then came rushing back into him. Many a mistress whom he had cared little for had been treated with more consideration than Amanda when he had presented them with their congé. Yet Amanda was the one woman who had crept into his heart, and he had treated her ill.

He would hire a carriage and drive her safely home the following day. For too long he had consigned the truth to some sheltered place in his brain where it would not obtrude on his conscience. She deserved no less than a completely forthright confession. Moreover, her misguided adventure could easily come to light. He would remain at Willowwoods as long as she needed his support and protection.

Amanda replaced the sharp knife and faced Rance.

"I'm going to the fight, Rance," she said, her hands on her hips, ready to do battle with him.

"I know." He surprised her with his prompt submission.

His acid tone had disappeared. "You'll go to the fight with Maggie, but not in those clothes. Such hoydenish attire is a license for disrespect from even the most honorable of gentlemen. Where did you get those breeches?"

Amanda held her jacket open and revealed the two unsightly tucks she had taken on each side of the garment to snatch in the waist. "They are Papa's," she said with a small smile.

Rance grimaced. "Do you have female attire in your bag?"

Amanda nodded. "A day gown and a traveling dress."

"Good. Tomorrow, after the mill, I shall see you home and stand by while you confess your exploits to Mr. Lofton."

Amanda caught her lower lip between her teeth. "That's necessary, is it?" she asked, knowing the answer.

"You lied to him."

Amanda winced at his candor. "I suppose, I knew from the start a confession was inevitable, but you needn't accompany me."

"I owe Mr. Lofton an explanation."

Amanda shrugged. "If it's your choice, but I can do better with Papa alone. You will only inflame him."

"A hazard I must face. You see, I have an obligation to confess my culpability, for I knew I was in the wrong."

A sardonic smile touched his lips at her dismayed expression.

"I could easily have put quit to the sparring sessions on the overlook and trained elsewhere." His voice softened noticeably. "I am no flat, Mandy. I knew Mr. Lofton would never approve of his daughter observing half-naked men boxing, even given his permissiveness. You wouldn't be here today, my dear, if I had acted responsibly."

"Then I am thankful you, too, can be a chub," she said with an impudent smile, "for I would not have missed the sparring between you and Brian, nor the fight tomorrow, for all the king's gold."

The door flung open just then, and Brian's "It's settled" blotted out Rance's ironic response.

"Amanda will share the bed with Maggie," Brian announced cheerfully, beckoning to Amanda while picking up her bag.

She stopped at the door and turned back to Rance with an impish grin. "Wouldn't it have been a lark, Rance, if Brian hadn't found me and when next we met at the overlook I would have amazed you with a detailed description of your mill?"

Brian pulled the door to, hiding from her the guilty flush that spread over Rance's cheeks at her words.

Brian stepped aside while Amanda preceded him into Maggie's room through the door he held open for her. "This is Amanda," he proclaimed as he set down her valise on a chair. Amanda's smile faded.

Maggie might have been Brian's sister with the same red hair, green eyes, and freckled nose. But whereas Brian's face was genial, hers was sullen. His mouth turned up; hers curved downward.

"Maggie." Amanda acknowledged the dour woman.

Maggie merely grunted with unmasked dislike.

Artificially hearty, Brian said, "Now, I'll be leaving the two of you to become acquainted."

At the door he drew Maggie to him and murmured a few private words to her. In return, she whispered in his ear. Amanda averted her eyes as Brian kissed Maggie full on the lips. With no real evidence she decided Brian was in love with Maggie but the plump little Irishwoman was only fond of him.

Maggie shoved a bundle of neatly folded male garments that had been piled on top of a chest of drawers into Brian's arms before she pushed him through the door.

Crossing the room without glancing at Amanda, she lowered herself into an easy chair. She lifted a man's white cotton shirt from a sewing basket and began stitching along the seam of a sleeve.

Amanda cleared her throat. "Would it be all right if I poured myself a glass of water?" She stood like a compliant child in her dusty garments waiting for permission to alleviate the thirst she had relegated to the back of her mind since arriving at the stables.

"Suit yourself," Maggie said without raising her head from her sewing. She glanced surreptitiously at Amanda, watched her pour water from the decanter, drink half of the liquid in one huge gulp, and sip the rest until she emptied the glass.

Uncharitably, she wanted Amanda to suffer for intruding on her and Brian.

Amanda glanced around at her surroundings. She noticed a wall rack with empty pegs. She began to unpack the valise with the object of hanging up her dresses.

"You'll be needin' to freshen up and such," Maggie muttered, putting aside her mending and deciding to be civil.

She saw to Amanda's immediate needs with the air of a martyr, but Amanda pretended not to notice and forced herself to be courteous for Brian's sake. She removed her toiletries from her valise and set about restoring herself to her usual decorousness. The Irishwoman resumed her sewing and continued to monitor Amanda's movements with covert glances.

Seated in front of a vanity, Amanda removed the countless hairpins Josie had woven into her hair and brushed the brown tresses back into a controlled neatness. Satisfied with her handiwork, she got up and lifted her blue gown from the valise.

"Oh, it's wrinkled beyond being fit to wear," she moaned aloud. She turned to the Irishwoman. "Maggie, can I send for someone who will see that my dress is pressed?"

"Ring the bell on the wall there," Maggie directed.

When the maid knocked, Maggie motioned for Amanda

to secrete herself behind the door, for she was still attired in breeches.

"What a grand gown, missus," the maid complemented as she removed the dress from Maggie's outstretched hands. "The cloth is so fine." She fingered the cotton appreciatively. "Now, don't you fear I'll scorch the cloth, missus, I use a flat iron expertly."

Maggie slammed the door after pressing the coins Amanda had given her into the maid's hand.

"She'll be wondering, no doubt, where the likes of me came upon quality apparel," Maggie jeered. "Probably the tart will decide I stole it."

"Maggie," Amanda implored, having had her fill of the Irishwoman's continuing animosity. "Brian and I are good friends. Can't you and I be likewise?"

Maggie fixed a vinegary sneer on Amanda. "I'm not in need of any friends like you. From Brian's own mouth I know you are a spoiled English girl with a rich father who buys you needlessly expensive gifts that cost what could feed a whole Irish village. For some reason, Brian delights in you," she railed, "but I have no use for any of you English!"

Amanda's hackles rose. "What about Rance? He's English." She pointed out, her eyes sparks of flint.

"Terry is a near saint and as good a friend as a body would want," Maggie proclaimed, "but there are no more like him in this cursed country. It'll be a sad parting for Brian after tomorrow's fight."

"What do you mean?" Amanda perked up at this information.

"This will be Terry's final mill. Brian and Terry will have the money they need to start a new life. Brian and me'll be going home to Ireland, where he'll buy a cottage for us with a bit of land where he can raise horses, far from his dad's place," her voice died, aware she was revealing more than she intended. She sat down and lifted her sewing basket into her lap. She moistened the end of a length of thread between her lips, threaded a darning needle, and began mending a black stocking.

Amanda sat in a companion chair, separated from the Irishwoman by an end table. She noticed the gold band that gleamed brightly on Maggie's finger. The surly woman perceived Amanda's interest.

"Yes, missy, Brian married me yesterday," she crowed, fluttering her beringed left hand in the air in front of Amanda's face.

"I wish you happy," Amanda mumbled halfheartedly. Maggie jabbed the needle into the heel of Brian's black stocking, a maliciously smug smile on her homely face.

Amanda spent a miserable hour of enforced silence before dinner was served in an adjacent antechamber. Four places had been set with serviceable white plates and cups and tin knives and forks at a wooden table. The sideboard held three covered dishes of food, a teapot, a decanter of port, and a basket of black bread. A servant had delivered the items to the small dining room minutes before. The faint rumble of passing vehicles drifted up from the street below through the curtainless casement window as the party gathered to dine.

Maggie's red tresses flew in a hundred directions, but Brian seemed oblivious of the untidy hair and dowdy navy worsted gown she wore. He pressed his bride's hand to his lips, whispered an endearment, and smiled sweetly at the acerbic woman.

Rance kissed Amanda's hand and admired her figure, which showed to advantage in the form-fitted blue dress. His hand touched her flawless cheek with a brief tender stroke.

Amanda glowed in light of Rance's gallantry. Their eyes locked with mutual admiration and affection. His warm looks were satisfactorily unbrotherly.

She helped Maggie transfer the unexceptional dinner

from the sideboard to the table while the men discussed the strategies for the next day's fight.

To break the silence between Maggie and herself as the meal progressed, Amanda directed some quite ordinary remarks to the Irishwoman, hoping to precipitate a polite if uninspired exchange, but Maggie paid more attention to the overdone beef, the burnt potatoes, and runny pudding than to her. Amanda toyed with the unappetizing supper and pushed the food around on her plate between miniature bites, unaware she was being observed until Brian spoke to her.

"What's wrong, Amanda, is the food not up to the standards of the Rook Manor cook?" he teased. She smiled wanly at the negative attention. Rance smirked, but Maggie glared at her.

"It's fine," she dissembled, uncomfortable to have her appetite the focus of the dinner conversation. "I guess I am not particularly hungry. Who is this Signor Boigotto you keep mentioning?"

"Boigotto is the promoter who arranges my matches. I've been fortunate until now, for I have bested all my opponents quite handily," Rance said. "However, I know nothing of the Russian Rostanov. He hasn't had any bouts in England as yet. But the odds favor me heavily."

"That sounds promising," Amanda observed.

"Not really," Brian explained, "because we've been making good money by betting on Terry, which was advantageous when he was an unknown. But, alas, his reputation has grown since the first mill, and the odds are a whopping ten to one in Terry's favor."

"I see." Mathematics was not the alien, mind-boggling subject to Amanda it was to most women of her day, and she understood as the odds on Terry Stone increased, their profits on any fight would be diminished.

"I've been thinking we should forget wagering on this fight," Rance admitted. "Luck's been with me, but it may not be prudent to risk two hundred quid for a possible return of twenty pounds."

"You'll win," Brian said, mashing a crusty potato with his fork.

Rance speared a second piece of beef with his fork and removed the slice from the platter to his plate, sawing through the tough meat heedlessly. "No doubt." He winked at Maggie. "Still, Brian, let's just go for the lucrative purse. It's enough of a risk."

"Aye, we'll do as you say," Brian agreed easily. He chewed and swallowed the piece of potato before noting conversationally, "Schofield, bless his soul, for all his willingness, still doesn't grasp the value of intelligent boxing."

"Schofield?" Amanda questioned.

"He's our new bottleholder," Rance said. "Our former second left us after our last fight. Young Schofield is no older than you, with a plethora of enthusiasm, but he knows only brawling, not using one's head. But it hardly matters who acts as bottleholder, Brian, I'd rather you gave me all the advice anyway."

"Sure an' Terry's right, you know," Maggie seconded, polishing her plate clean with a piece of bread. "You're to be credited, Brian, for training Terry. Whoever seconds alongside you is of no consequence. An' wasn't it you who single-handedly developed the famous lightning punch that's made the difference in every mill?" Maggie said, chewing her final morsel of bread noisily.

"Now, am I not a lucky man to have such a loyal wife?" Brian laughed, a touch of embarrassment evident in his brogue. "I'm not the one in the ring, me darlin'; our fate is in Terry's hands."

Rance reached out and patted Maggie's hand. "You're right, Maggie. Without Brian I would never have been successful." She bobbed her head with satisfaction at his admission, but turned with the others toward the window at the commotion from the street below.

Rance rose and pushed the casement window open. He glanced back at Brian with a wide grin. "It's Cribb!"

Brian hurried to join him, Maggie and Amanda at his heels. Rance grabbed Amanda around the waist. "Look there, Mandy, the man in the brown checkered coat." He pointed out Tom Cribb surrounded by admiring fans in the street below, which was illuminated by torchbearers. Amanda stretched her neck to see the famous champion who had upheld the honor of England against the American Molineux.

Chants of "Tom! Tom Cribb!" drifted up to them. Amanda beamed, catching the excitement that raced through Rance's body pressed close against her. Brian held Maggie before him and peered down to the street over her head.

"Tom!" Brian shouted. Tom Cribb was a smallish man with a heavily muscled chest and shoulders and huge forearms, obvious even through his coat. He lifted a straight-nosed, pleasant face toward the man calling his name from above.

"Ha, Brian! Good luck, Terry!" he hollered back.

"Thanks, Tom," Rance called down. The fancy swept Tom Cribb out of sight into the door to the taproom of the inn. A few stragglers called, "Terry" and "Give 'im your lightning punch." They waved to Rance, and he, Amanda, Brian, and Maggie waved back. Amanda felt joyously elated.

The streets emptied, and Rance pulled the window closed. As they reseated themselves around the oak table, they vied with one another, talking excitedly about Cribb and the crowd and the reaction to Terry Stone. Rance poured a glass of port for each of them, including the women, and he toasted Tom Cribb, and Brian toasted Rance, and the little dinner turned into an impromptu celebration. Rance grinned at Amanda frequently. More than just genuine affection trembled in the air between them. Amanda could not remember a night when she had been happier.

"Come, Mandy, let's go for a walk," Rance said after the celebratory fervor had slackened to a pleasant glow. The unexpected invitation and the idea that Rance wanted to be alone with her set Amanda's heart singing.

"I'll get a wrap," she said. When she returned to the dining parlor, Rance placed a guiding hand on the small of her back and moved her toward the door. Out in the hall he turned toward the rear of the building. A staircase at the end of the corridor led down to a door that opened onto a residential street. Just as Amanda and Rance stepped outside, the full moon swam clear of a great cloud and patterned the village cottages with interesting shadows.

Amanda linked her arm through Rance's and felt the sinewy strength of his arm beneath the fine broadcloth of his coat. A shiver that had nothing to do with the outside temperature slid up her spine when she came in contact with his hard, masculine body.

"It is such a lovely evening for a walk," she said, her speech slightly tremulous.

"Yes," he agreed in a deep, calm voice. "I was certain you would enjoy a stroll on such a fine night. But, I must confess, I was thinking more of giving Maggie and Brian some deserved time to themselves."

Amanda experienced a twinge of regret that Rance had not wanted to be alone with her after all, but was actually concerned with the privacy of the newlyweds. But she pushed the discontent aside. She was not going to let one minor miscalculation on her part taint her bliss or spoil these private moments with him.

Candlelight flickered in the uncurtained windows of the houses that extended almost to the moon-bleached sidewalk. Before them in the distance a tall church spire was silhouetted against the night sky.

"We'll go as far as the church," Rance said. Amanda nodded. Her secret trip to Wye was turning into an unqualified success. Rance had done an about-face since his initial flare-up when she had first appeared at his hotel room door with Brian. Every bit of his criticism had fallen away and been replaced by an affectionately indulgent mien. All in all things were humming along famously, she thought, except for one worry that every so often triggered an inner alarm. She did not want Rance to accompany her to Rook

Manor after the mill and speak to her father. She had doubts about the wisdom of allowing him to exacerbate Daniel's wrath. Her mission to secure him for her husband would not be furthered by Rance being once again assailed by her father's bitter tongue. Moreover, she had this irrational premonition that if Rance and her father came to verbal blows, her dreams would permanently collapse, never, ever, to be realized.

"You know, Rance, I have been thinking," Amanda said.

"Thinking, have you? Before acting? How novel."

"Oh, dear, you are going to rip up at me again for coming here, aren't you?"

Rance chuckled. "Not at all, my dear. I am not in a combative mood tonight. I'll save that for tomorrow."

The church loomed in front of them. Moonlight poured over the stone façade and illuminated the tall cross on the steeple.

"It's much larger than St. Catherine's," Amanda said, impressed by the beautiful church's size.

"Yes, but, then, Wye has a population at least five or six times as great as our village."

With a hand beneath her elbow, Rance turned Amanda back toward the inn. He slid his hand down her sleeve and tightened it over hers. She smiled up at him. The moonlight did attractive things to her face, he thought.

He recalled her stiff, unyielding body when she rebuffed his attempt to kiss her weeks before. Time had softened the humiliating scene in his mind. He could even find some humor in having made a cake of himself.

My dear little innocent, he thought with affection. His urge to kiss her was as strong as ever. But he could see no reward in clinging to hopeless desires. Experience had taught him that brooding availed him nothing.

"What were you going to say, Mandy, before I interrupted you?" he asked to push the sense of loss from his heart.

"Oh, yes, that. I question the wisdom of your accompanying me to Rook Manor to face Papa. Won't the servants be curious as to why you are with me? One of them might listen at the door when we confess to Papa and spread harmful gossip about us."

Rance shrugged complacently. "Probably, but let's not speak of that thorny future now." He changed the subject abruptly. "Look how the moonlight runs like quicksilver through the clouds."

Not fooled by his obvious diversion, Amanda glanced apathetically into the sky where Rance pointed. He was not going to be persuaded to let her go home alone and, furthermore, he did not even care to discuss the matter.

Amanda reluctantly gave in to his wishes, for she could not bring herself to start an argument with him and ruin this perfect night. She pulled herself closer to him. Her love surfaced to warm her as the need to be near him became intense. Now that Rance had some funds, he would soon be leaving Willowwoods. Suddenly the realization frightened her. If only he would stay at his brother's estate until she could make him love her.

Without thinking, she spoke her fears aloud. "I wish you could remain with Lord Woods forever."

Rance put a gentle hand on Amanda's shoulder.

"My dear, Willowwoods is no longer my home. Although Leonard is family and will always make me welcome as a visitor, I cannot live with him permanently."

"I know you can't," she admitted. "It was foolish of me to say that." Why, she wondered, did these unsettling doubts still keep popping into her head, resurrecting the insecurities she was sure she had put to rest? "I suppose you will take rooms in London now that you have enriched your purse."

They resumed walking. She took his silence for assent.

After a while Amanda said, "You deserve credit for making money through your own efforts, Rance, and not depending on Lord Woods's generosity. It took courage to take up a venture which were it widely known would bring disapproval from your peers."

They paused as one before a house to listen to the merry tune some unseen occupant played on the piano.

"Not total disapproval," Rance said, picking up the conversation as they moved on down the street. "Polite society understands and applauds a gambler who ends up ahead of the game. That I am paid to box, I fear, that will not sit well with the beau monde."

"Your peers are a passel of wrong thinkers," Amanda said with spirit. "Being compensated monetarily for a boxing match is like an actor earning money for performing on the stage. You receive a legitimate payment for your services. Papa says there is no dishonor in working for an honest wage."

"Does he? But the greater part of our income, Brian's and mine, comes from the wagers. Mr. Lofton once accused me of never earning a farthing except by the turn of a card. I'm sure in his eyes, and he's right you know, there is not a whit of difference between betting on cards and gambling on a fight."

"Oh, but there is in your case." Amanda's voice rose with righteous enthusiasm. "You controlled the outcome. You did not bet on an unknown entity. I saw how you toiled to reach perfection as a boxer. You honed your skills and relied on your talent each time you made a wager."

"Dear little Amanda, how did you acquire such misplaced faith in me?" he asked with a faint smile.

Amanda laughed. "I'm not little, Rance. You have me mixed up with Josie."

"Oh, no, I could never mistake you for Josie Castleberry. Our Josie is proper and prim and would never run off to a mill."

Amanda sprang from his side. "Don't you like me even a little?"

Rance was too taken aback for a moment to do anything but stare at her. The doubt crowded in her eyes gave him pause. He longed to pull her into his arms and kiss away the anxiety. Instead, he took a step toward her and let a finger trail down her neck until his hand rested on her shoulder. "I am fond of you, Amanda, you know that."

When he had left her behind on the overlook two days earlier, he had forced his heart into a safe place behind high walls. Now she was coming close to breaching the walls and subverting his plans. Tomorrow, when he drove her back to Rook Manor, he would set her straight.

Amanda sensed he fought some kind of private battle that was detrimental to her dreams. She frantically hoped he would lose.

The door to a whitewashed cottage was thrust ajar and a path of light cut through the darkness. The figure of a man stepped out into the deep shadows of the porch. From behind him a large, nondescript dog hurtled itself off the stoop and jumped repeatedly against the wooden gate where Amanda and Rance stood, barking ferociously at the invaders.

"Get back here, Scratch," the man called. "Stop that noise, you beggar you. Want to wake the whole neighborhood?"

Not sorry for the interruption that cut short the need to further placate Amanda, Rance hurried her from the dog's sphere. They laughed simultaneously when the barking stopped.

"Old Scratch set my heart beating out of control for a minute there," Amanda gasped, her breath coming in short, shallow bursts. "I guess you are not afraid of barking dogs."

Rance held up one hand in midair and caused it to visibly tremble. "Only ones that are preparing to attack me," he said with a wink. The small talk continued in the same vein until they reached the inn.

Maggie opened the door to Rance's knock. "Brian's gone to bed," she said in her abrupt manner. She turned back into the room.

Rance reached for Amanda's hand and threaded his fingers with hers. He lifted the back of her hand to his lips.

"Sleep well, Mandy," he said with a sweet softness that made her tingle.

Inside the room Amanda leaned against the closed door for a minute, a dreamy expression on her face.

While she prepared for bed, she basked in the remembered warmth of Rance's attentions. "Fond" was not exactly the degree of love for which she cared to settle. She wanted more. Much more. But "fond" was getting close, she thought optimistically.

Clothed in her fine batiste nightdress, Amanda faced the bed. Maggie sat in her usual chair, swathed in an old flannel robe, drinking a glass of port. Her petulance was once again evident.

Resenting the Irishwoman's sour countenance which intruded on her happiness, Amanda brittlely broke the constrained silence. "Which side?"

"Brian sleeps on the left; you might as well take that," Maggie groused to remind Amanda once again she was Brian's usurper.

Amanda slid beneath the coarse sheets and tugged the quilt to her chin. She rose up on one elbow. "Maggie," she said, "I wish you and Brian could be together. I'm truly sorry for separating you, but it was Brian's idea for me to share your room, not mine. Can't we call a truce? After all, I will be gone tomorrow."

"Good thing too," Maggie grumbled, not giving an inch. Amanda sighed, curled up on the unfamiliar mattress, and within seconds was fast asleep.

Chapter 11

Early the next morning Brian stormed into the dining room, his face red with anger, his breathing hard, as if he had sprinted for a considerable distance.

"What the devil's wrong with you, Brian?" Rance asked, stirring sugar into the coffee Amanda had just finished pouring for him. "You look positively livid. Have the odds shot even higher?" He removed the spoon from the coffee cup, picked up a knife, sliced into the butter, and began spreading it on a piece of toast.

Amanda filled her own cup and Maggie's, set down the coffeepot, and moved into her chair across from the Irishwoman.

Brian quivered with rage. "Boigotto has double-dealt us!" he sputtered. The two women exchanged puzzled glances.

"What are you saying?" Rance probed, the buttered knife poised in the air.

Brian trembled visibly. Amanda and Maggie stared at him with obvious concern in their eyes, for he was not a man given over to unwarranted anger.

He seized the top of the chair and scraped it back from

the table and sat down. "Your opponent is no Russian!" he thundered, bringing his fist down on the table with a fearful thud. Amanda steadied her bouncing coffee cup, the hot liquid lurching to the brim.

"He's a Cornish quarry worker. A giant of a man, nearly your height, but burly and strong as Goliath, I hear!" He reached for the brandy decanter on the sideboard behind his chair, filled a tumbler, and downed the fiery spirit in one gulp.

Rance laid the knife and the partially buttered toast onto his plate and shoved the dish away from him. "Calm down, Brian, and tell me where you heard this." His voice was controlled, but as he ran a hand over his mouth, an unpleasant image of an opponent more formidable than he had ever faced loomed before him.

Brian drew in his breath to compose himself. "I went to check the odds, as I said I would, and met Schofield downstairs. The lad told me last night he was drinking with two of Boigotto's men at the Red Swan. They weren't aware Schofield was now working for us." He paused to let the significance of what he said sink in. "We haven't given the lad enough credit for his intelligence; he was canny, and didn't give himself away. A couple of pitchers of ale loosed the henchmen's tongues and set them talking free." Brian's voice dampened. "There's no doubt, lad, Rostanov is a ringer, for Boigotto has wagered his own money heavily against you."

Rance shook his head in momentary disbelief. Amanda gasped and Maggie's hand flew to her throat. No one spoke for a full minute.

Then Rance, his lips set in a hard line, asked, "Anything else?"

Brian inclined his head. His voice lowered to a chary, embarrassed hush. "According to them, you never knocked anyone out, not a blessed one of the levelers you threw ever did damage. Your opponents faked the knockouts."

Brian paused for his friend's reaction to the startling

revelation. Rance's troubled eyes narrowed. "Go on," he urged.

"Boigotto's lackeys boasted their boss would be covered in guineas by the end of today from collecting his wagers against you. We would be dispensed with, you beaten to a pulp by Rostanov, and Mooney and Spees would take care of me, making sure I wasn't in a position to cry rope on Boigotto."

Maggie gasped in horror. "Nooo . . ." She drew out the single syllable. "We should leave for home at once, this morning, and forget the fight," she wailed.

Her outburst checked Brian as he realized he had frightened her. He ran a soothing hand up and down the sleeve of her brown country gown. "Aw, love, 'twas but the ale talking. Besides, forewarned is forearmed. I can take care of meself, I can. They shan't get the better of me."

Amanda had paled at Brian's disclosure. "It's my fault," she confessed in an undertone.

"No, lass, no!" Brian assured her, wishing he had had the presence of mind to clear the women from the room before speaking. "Your clash with them has nought to do with this."

"What are you talking about?" Rance asked. "What does Amanda have to do with those ruffians?"

"She ran into Mooney and Spees behind the livery stable when she went to stable the mare. You know those two, Terry. They tried to extort a few shillings from her, but I intervened. That has nought to do with this," he repeated.

Amanda flopped a spoon back and forth in her cold oatmeal, her countenance guilt-ridden. Her eyes met Brian's; he silently pleaded with her to hold her tongue. She acquiesced with a barely perceptible nod that was not missed by Rance. His mouth worked, certain Brian and Amanda were hiding the truth, but he backed off. "No matter what the reason, Maggie is right. It's best if you leave for the coast and book passage for Ireland today."

"An' what of you?" Brian asked suspiciously.

"I'm going to fight," he acknowledged.

"Don't be putting your life in danger, Terry, Maggie implored. "The money will be a pittance if you lose. But Brian and I must go, for I won't be a widow when I've hardly been a bride."

"Of course you must leave," Rance agreed. "Brian's safety must come first. Schofield can second me well enough."

Brian had listened to the exchange between his wife and his friend with growing indignation. When he finally erupted, his brogue was a high squeal.

"Have your brains turned to mush, then, Terry? An' you, Maggie, in heaven's sweet name, would you have me disgrace meself by deserting the one friend who has made our happiness possible? Terry and me started this together, and we'll see it through together. I will have no more from either of you. Pour me a cup of coffee, woman, and fill me plate from the sideboard."

Maggie's shoulders heaved in a spurt of anger, but she forced back a retort that could be like poison from a long habit. Instead, she obeyed him, reached for the pewter coffeepot and filled his cup, rose, and piled his plate with kidneys and eggs from the dishes on the sideboard, then set the breakfast before him. She breathed deeply and pressed Brian's shoulder in a conciliatory gesture. He reached back and patted her hand.

"So much for lightning punches!" Rance scoffed at his own expense, but his self-derogation only enhanced their gloom.

Amanda played with the salt cellar on the table. Brian devoured his food with a vengeance, and a tight-lipped Maggie studied her folded hands. Rance rocked on the two back legs of his chair, arranging and rearranging Brian's disclosures in his mind.

Suddenly he righted himself, banging the front legs of the chair with a crash onto the wooden floor. "Damn! No, it can't be!" he swore as three pairs of startled, baffled eyes fixed on him.

"What?" Brian asked, his fork poised above the lukewarm scrambled eggs and greasy kidneys on his plate.

"I am not so addlepated that I cannot tell the difference between a solid hit and a man shamming a knockdown. Look, Brian, if Boigotto paid *you* to throw a match, would you confess to him you were knocked out legitimately?" he asked Brian.

"I'd be a real cod's head if I did," the Irishman admitted, "for he'd surely not pay me."

Rance continued eagerly. "We both believe in scientific boxing. Are we ready to dismiss Mendoza's methods that we have practiced religiously as a hum? Was the training all in vain? I don't think so," he answered his own questions. "I won those fights fairly. Granted, the opponents Boigotto chose were not first rate, but that does not prove I cannot win against a more skilled fighter. I dispensed with them in record times. A redoubtable adversary might give me a more challenging scrap, but nowhere is it written that I can't win."

His eyes darted around the table. The skeptical faces reformed as his words took hold. Brian bobbed his head in agreement, and Amanda smiled with new hope. Only Maggie's face showed a lingering doubt.

"I concede, Boigotto has set me up for today's fight," Rance continued. "My previous wins have caused me to be an overwhelming favorite. But we have benefited from his scheme as well, for we earned sizable sums from the wagers and purses. All in all we have done splendidly."

"You know," Amanda said, the thought having teased her mind for a spell, "the odds could change, Rance, if we let it be known here and there that Rostanov is a ringer."

Rance took a sip of coffee and smiled appreciatively. "You do have an inventive mind, my dear. The odds on me, no doubt, would drop, but I don't think we'll chance wagering. I can see no sense in pushing our luck. Better to protect the money Brian and I have amassed to date. It will keep us afloat for a long while and will go far to making a start in bettering ourselves."

"Not wagering is sensible," Maggie agreed. "Risking your and Brian's savings now would be foolhardy, but why won't you walk away from this fight altogether, Terry?"

Rance worried his lip with his teeth for a moment before speaking. "Maggie, the fancy have packed the town, and they are entitled to the mill that was promised them. I intend fighting Rostanov with all I have. I won't lie down and die, although, I admit," he said with an impish smile, "it might be the more prudent course."

Brian grinned. "Well said, lad!" Amanda nodded, her eyes shining with pride in Rance.

Maggie conceded, "As Brian said, he's come this far, he'll see it through to the end. 'Tis only fair."

Amanda sat on the backless stool and inspected her face in the mirror of the vanity. Did her love for Rance show in her face? Josie's countenance lit up whenever Evan Whitaker came into the room. She touched her cheek. Her face looked the same, but the new happiness in her heart was undeniable since Rance had begun treating her like a desirable woman to whom he was attracted.

At a knock on the door, she called, "Come in, it's open," expecting the maid to be delivering the freshly ironed traveling dress and pelisse she had sent down an hour before to be pressed. Her smile quickened as Rance strode into the room.

"Maggie isn't here, Rance. She's gone to the chemist for some headache powders. I think I've quite undone her," Amanda quipped. Rance came up the room, leaned against the bureau near the vanity, his arm resting on the top of the chest, and grinned at Amanda.

"I met Maggie downstairs; it's you I want to speak with," he acknowledged. His smile at her quip melted into a serious mien.

Amanda looked at him expectantly. He seemed impressively tall standing above her.

"Mandy, I don't want you to go to the mill."

"Why?" she demanded in a raised voice.

"My dear, it's not going to be as it was at Rook Manor when Brian and I were sparring. Fisticuffs is a brutal sport."

"You did not object before," she protested. "From the beginning you promised I could attend the fight. What's different now?"

"A great deal." He stepped away from the bureau and held out his hands in supplication. "I expected this mill to be like the others," he said. "I would survive unscathed and my opponent would be knocked down . . . with my famous lightning punch." His lopsided grin mocked the phrase that had become a battle cry with his proselytes among the fancy. "This is going to be very different, Amanda."

Daniel had described fighters with faces like raw meat and legs like rubber. That could happen to Rance. But she could not wait there during the fight, alone in this room, not aware of what was happening to him. Even watching him being whipped by the fake Russian was preferable to imagining the horrors.

"No, Rance, I must go. I couldn't bear being here alone, not knowing." Rance would have given a great deal to spare her, but he could understand her reasoning. At least the fight should cure her of any dewy-eyed notions she had that a mill is romantic. He shrugged his submission. Any further entreating would be futile and destined him to coming off second best anyway.

Amanda picked up her brush and began needlessly neatening her hair. Rance moved to stand directly behind her. He rested his hands lightly on her shoulders and watched her image in the mirror. How could he have ever believed that she was not beautiful? She was a stunner. He could think of no woman of his acquaintance who was lovelier than Amanda.

She glanced at him over her shoulder with a mischievous smirk. "I think we still ought to put out the truth about Rostanov. Imagine the money Boigotto would lose when the odds plummeted."

"Nice idea, my dear, but, I daresay, Boigotto had firm wagers down days ago," he drawled lazily, his mind far from thoughts of Signor Boigotto as his scanned down her trim figure.

Rance ran a sensuous tongue over his lips. Amanda was lifting a blue silk ribbon toward her hair when her brown eyes met his in the mirror. Her breath came faster, matching his own as she caught his handsome reflection observing her.

"Your hair is soft . . . like silk," he murmured, fingering a lock of her warm brown tresses.

Their eyes tangled for several moments in the glass. She dropped the ribbon and closed her eyes against the ardor that surged in the nether regions of her body. Her love for him overwhelmed her. His nearness unloosed a wild hunger that cried for him to master her untested sensuality.

Rance's hands tightened possessively on her rounded shoulders. His vow to leave her untouched was crumbling rapidly. He hadn't intended this when he came through the door, but now he was unable to hold himself in check. He defended himself without conviction. *I'm a man, not a saint.*

His blue eyes caressed the mirror image of her luminous face and paused at her parted lips. His gaze wandered over her long neck and loitered at the rise and fall of her rounded breasts, framed by the square neckline of her blue dress. The desire that coursed through him was not so different from the passion he had experienced before when making love to other women, but there was a perceptively subtle difference to which he could not yet put a name. All he knew was she touched something in the core of his being that no woman had touched before.

He did not stop to examine this nebulous sensation. He cupped her shoulders, lifted her from the chair, turned her to face him, and lost himself in her sultry brown eyes.

Amanda's arms encircled his neck while his arms enfolded her waist, eagerly gathering her to him. At first he played with her mouth with teasing kisses, but then, greedily, carried one kiss deeper and deeper, urged on by her zealous response. Finally, he lifted his lips from hers, went back for a less intense kiss once, then again, before he nuzzled the hair at the top of her head with his mouth and asked in a strangled voice, "Who taught you to kiss like that?"

"You just did," she parried, looking up at him with a tender smile. "More than you can say," she mocked softly.

Rance held her away from him and grinned. "How do you know I'm not a natural?"

She chuckled at his sally. Their foreheads touched.

"Now, tell me, love, what is the big secret between you and Brian?" he asked in a quiet voice, catching her off guard.

She moved a step back. "I don't know what you mean," she said, casting her eyes downward at the soiled carpet at her feet.

"What really happened with Mooney and Spees?"

"I can't . . . I promised Brian," she declared.

"Brian can be an old lady, Mandy. Did Mooney hurt you?" His voice was gentle so as not to alarm her, but he wasn't certain how he would react to the full disclosure he meant to have.

"On my way to Wye, he and Spees followed me to a secluded brook where I had stopped to rest." She spilled the details almost with relief, finally summing up. "They tried to steal Nancy and rob me of my funds, but I outwitted them by pushing Spees into the stream and running a distance away and whistling for Nancy before they could reach me. But when I came to the livery here in town, they were there at the back of the stables."

Her face began to show her remembered pain. "Oh, Rance, those two were awful. Spees started beating Nancy with a whip!"

"The craven cur," Rance muttered, clenching his fists.

"I had to make him stop, so instead of running for assistance, I hurled my valise containing the money at him. Well, when Mooney saw the women's garments Spees pulled from my bag, he peered at my face and . . . fumbled over my person . . . until Brian came and made him stop." Her voice dwindled to a hush. Rance closed his eyes and pressed his fingers to his forehead to subdue his rage.

"Thank God," he whispered, "for Brian's intervention. Damme, Amanda, I shudder to think what would have happened to you had you not eluded them at the brook." He slammed his fist into his cupped hand. "I'll settle with those two after the fight."

"No," Amanda pleaded, "let it go, Rance. Should you be injured because of me, I couldn't stand knowing my foolish behavior caused you harm. Promise me you won't confront them!"

"All right, Mandy. Don't fret," he enfolded her protectively into his strong arms. She nestled her head against his chest while he stroked her back.

Rance looked up expectantly when the door burst open, but he held Amanda tightly against him, her back to the door. She heard the "Oooh" and recognized the single stunned note as Maggie's voice.

Amanda moved free of Rance's embrace, but he encircled her waist, keeping her beside him as he raised an inquiring brow to the Irishwoman.

"Brian asked me to fetch you. He said he wants to talk over a few details with you. Schofield is waiting with him in your room."

Rance acknowledged her message with a nod. "Maggie, listen, be sure you stay in the gig when you get to the grounds where the mill is being held. You'll have a better view perched above the crowd. Let Amanda borrow a cloak to cover her dress and an old bonnet to shield her face; otherwise, she'll draw attention, for the crowd will expect a woman dressed in her finery to be peeping from her coach window to see the fight, not conspicuously in sight in an open carriage."

"I'll find something," Maggie promised. "You take care now, Terry. Don't you be taking unnecessary chances with that oaf."

"No fear of that, Maggie," he assured her.

He bent down and kissed Amanda on the cheek. "Wish me *bonne chance,* love," he murmured.

"Oh, I do, Rance! I do!"

He gave her a quick hug and moved to the door.

Maggie clutched his arm with a rough show of affection. "Luck, Terry," she uttered.

Rance winked at her and was gone.

The cloak fit Amanda in all particulars except length, for she was nearly a head taller than Maggie. The Irishwoman threaded a needle to repair a four-inch rent along one seam over Amanda's vigorous protest that she did not mind the tear. But Maggie waved her off with a harried expression, even after Amanda, seating herself in the companion easy chair, volunteered to sew the rip herself.

"You best not take Terry too seriously," Maggie advised unexpectedly after sewing a few stitches into the threadbare black garment.

Amanda's mouth pursed as she lowered the two-day-old London newspaper Rance had left in the room earlier that morning and which she had just taken up to read.

"I've put up with a lot from you, Maggie, but this is the outside of enough," Amanda informed her through all but gritted teeth. She refolded the newspaper and set it on the table.

"How dare you presume to counsel me on my relationship with Rance?"

Maggie did not miss a stitch, nor was she perturbed by Amanda's acid tone. She completed the repair, broke the thread with her teeth, shook out the coarse cotton cloak, and handed the garment across the end table to Amanda.

"How old are you? Seventeen? Eighteen? A green girl," Maggie claimed. "You are in for a shattered heart, you know."

"I suggest you keep your opinions to yourself, *Mrs.*

McGonigal." Amanda emphasized the name as though it were a malediction. "You don't even love Brian!"

Maggie's eyes sparked. Amanda's own eyes boldly dared her to contradict the allegation.

Maggie removed her sewing basket from her lap and placed the wickerware on the floor beside her chair. She sat up and said softly, "You are right, you know, Amanda."

Amanda gawked at her, jarred as much by Maggie's addressing her by name and her dulcet tone as by her blatant admission.

"Brian first proposed when he was eighteen and I was sixteen. But I wanted a passionate love. Brian was too ordinary. I turned him down. But when I buried my husband two years ago, Brian began courting me again . . . pestering me to marry him." She noticed Amanda's astonishment. "Oh, Brian didn't tell you I had been married before, I see. Yes, I was wed to a brute for ten miserable years. Me own father was a drunkard who needed no excuse to beat me mama. You would think I would have had better sense than to marry a man who was a replica of me dad, wouldn't you? But I was an eejit, that much in love at the time. My former husband was stabbed in a tavern brawl before he had a chance to kill me in one of his drunken rages."

She turned her rough red hands this way and that in nervous contemplation. "By then I knew Brian's worth, but his father threatened to disown him if he married me," she revealed. "Brian's not gentry, but his dad has money and fancies himself better than he is."

She picked up the sewing basket again and began untangling the spools of thread whose ends had intertwined.

"I ran off to England to find a position in a household. The money's better here. I wanted to put distance between me and Brian, but he came after me, even though Mr. McGonigal issued his final ultimatum that if Brian left Ireland, he would no longer consider him his son. I did everything I could to discourage Brian. As the Holy Mother is my witness, I married him only because I care that much for his happiness." Maggie unraveled the final snarled spool and slid the basket to the floor again. "His dad had scratched him out of his will in favor of young Davy, Brian's brother. What could I gain by refusing Brian any longer, except to leave him miserable. I tell you this to let you know that I married Brian for his sake, not mine."

Amanda smoothed the wrinkles unfruitfully from the cloak in her lap. Brian was decent—sweet—good. How could Maggie not love him?

Maggie's thoughts paralleled Amanda's as she reproached herself. "I should love him. No man deserves it more. But how do I force my heart?" She angrily dashed a tear from her cheek, her voice hardening. "Never, never will Brian know that I have no more than affection for him, but God willing, someday I might love him as I should."

Amanda fiddled with the frayed ribbons at the neck of the cloak while Maggie twisted her gold wedding band round and round her plump finger. The silence between the two women after the heart-rendering confession was awkward. Having learned Maggie's background, Amanda was even more bewildered that the Brian she knew could be in love with this unlovable woman.

Maggie broke the silence. "I don't caution you about Terry from spite," she said, "though the Lord knows it isn't out of fondness for you either. But some men, even those as good as Terry, who have received favors from a multitude of females, can be careless with women. What you take seriously could be a mere flirtation to him."

"It doesn't signify," Amanda said with an impatient wave of her hand. "When he is back at Willowwoods, at his brother Leonard's, we'll sort things out."

Maggie removed the cloak from Amanda's lap and hung the garment on a hook near the door. She stood, arms akimbo, in the center of the room. "I wasn't going to tell you," Maggie confessed, "but I can see he hasn't been right with you. Terry is going to America."

"America?" Amanda's voice rose. A sinking sensation

traveled quickly from her throat into the pit of her stomach.

"His boxing money will buy passage on a ship and set him up in a new life. America has all sorts of opportunities for a lad with Terry's brains. He wanted Brian and me to go too, but we said no, for how could we leave Ireland?"

Amanda froze, stunned. All the confidences she had shared with Rance, and he had never even hinted he was going to America. She ached from his betrayal. Had she not come to Wye, she would never have seen him again. She would have ridden to the overlook day after day, searching for him, until one day Josie or someone would have said, "Have you heard? Rance is settled in America." She was too stupefied to shed tears. But his innocent kiss the last time they had met back on the overlook, and his "I'm going away" now made perfect sense. Rance had been kissing her good-bye for good. Forever!

Maggie opened the gold filigree watch, Brian's wedding gift, pinned to her gray kersey gown. "We need to get ready. If we don't leave soon, all the good places to see the mill will be taken."

Maggie could think of nothing to say to comfort Amanda. She knew there was no balm for a bruised heart. You just went on living until time cured you. The girl was young. There would be other Terrys in her life.

Amanda walked in a daze to the livery stable, Maggie's cloak flung over her back. An old black bonnet of the Irishwoman's covered her brown curls. *Rance is going to America! To America!* repeated itself like a mantra in her brain. An ocean would separate them, and she would never see him again.

Before Amanda was once again aware of her surroundings, she was climbing up beside Maggie onto the box of the hired gig Maggie would drive to the field where the mill was being held.

Chapter 12

Over the gently rolling countryside, rustics and townfolk bustled from all directions, pushing through hedgerows and fording streams to make their way to the meadow where the fight was to be held a mile from the town. Rabbits flushed from the brush scurried here and there before the sportive throng, which was imbued with a festive excitement.

The road from Wye was jammed with vehicles, while the trail across the meadow from the main road to the ridge overlooking the ring was a creeping, snail-paced line of carts, gigs, wagons, and carriages.

Maggie positioned the hired gig on a grassy rise with a clear view of the boxing ring.

Taverners, bakers, farmers, ironmongers, harlots, lords, schoolmasters, the rich, and the poor intermingled and jockeyed for advantageous positions to view the pugilistic contest. By eleven o'clock, spectatators had packed themselves against the ropes of the ring and fanned outward and upward to the rise where the chaises, gigs, and carts were parked.

Gray clouds overlay the dreary sky. Neither fighter would

be blinded by the sun, and rain by all indications, if it came at all, would hold off until late afternoon or evening. Perfect conditions for a mill.

Amanda wrapped the black cloak close around her against the chill and adjusted the black bonnet over her long hair. She examined with interest the large roped-off area empty of the participants. Rance had explained that the three-foot square in the center of the ring was the scratch mark where the fighters would face off. After a boxer was knocked down, the umpire stopped the fight and both men came up to scratch with their toes against the line. Only then did the official give the signal for the boxers to resume fighting.

A prolonged cheer and a singsong chant of "Ter-ree, Ter-ree" from a group of young dandies pierced the cool summer morning, heralding Rance's appearance. A moment later he vaulted the ropes into the ring. Brian and Schofield, less dramatically, separated the barriers and stepped in after him. Their arms were crammed with towels, water bottles, and ointments and plasters to soothe and patch the bruises and cuts, the inevitable aftermath of a brutal fight.

Rance raised one arm in a salute to his fans, who erupted into another jubilant shout. The smart young fighter known for his lightning punch had a growing cadre of fans, who were already anticipating the privilege of joining the popular boxer for a victory drink after the fight.

Maggie nudged Amanda, diverting her attention from the ring, and pointed to Mooney and Spees approaching the gig. The two men stopped on Amanda's side of the carriage. She reached across Maggie and slipped the buggy whip from its holder.

"No need to arm yourself, Lord Laughter," Mooney snarled. "I had my fumble in the stable yard. You're too skinny a wench for me. Now, McGongigal's doxy here has some meat a man can grab on to."

Incensed by his coarse ridicule, Amanda with practiced skill flicked the whip a scant inch above Mooney's head. He reflexively cringed, and Spees stumbled backward, nearly losing his footing. Mooney's evil face darkened ominously. He rushed the carriage and snatched at Amanda's leg. She snapped the whip. The thongs bit into the knuckles of his right hand.

"Damn you to hell, you whore," he sputtered, but he backed off, clutching his hand. The blood seeping from the stinging abrasion infuriated him. "You'll pay for that! You ain't gonna be so high and mighty when the Russian thrashes Terry Stone. Then he won't stand 'tween you and me. And you, Mrs. McGonigal, will be a widder soon. Let's see who'll keep me from using you as I see fit then!"

"Off with you before I have you hauled before the magistrate," Amanda snapped with false bravado, for his threats had sent an involuntary chill along her backbone. She lifted the whip, but Maggie reached over, wrested it from her hand, and replaced it in the holder.

"Enough," she mumbled sullenly to Amanda.

"Terry's going to win," Amanda taunted, blind to Maggie's posture.

Spees sneered. "Not likely with the umpires having been paid off by Boigotto."

"Stubble it, you cork-brained idiot!" Mooney lashed at him. "You want someone to rumble the whole havey-cavey business!"

He peered around furtively to see if any of the nearby spectators had heard, but the crowd's eyes were glued to the ring. While Amanda had fenced with Mooney, Rostanov had entered the arena with Signor Boigotto. The spectators gawked at the monster's enormous biceps, bull neck, massive chest, and hamlike hands. Rance was an inch taller, but a slender reed beside Rostanov.

Disgruntled groans sprang from the majority of the fancy who had bet on Terry Stone. The hubbub increased to an uproar. Most of the crowd had come to witness Terry Stone's lightning punch. Many had wagered on the number of rounds it would take for the young fighter to dispose of his opponent. Only a few true gamblers had bet against

Terry Stone, hoping to cash in big on an upset. The monster added a new facet to the fight.

His appearance spawned a swarm of activity from the bookmakers. Odds against Terry Stone were hawked, and takers were plentiful as some of the fancy began to hedge their bets.

A satisfied smile sketched Signor Boigotto's lips as he turned from the fighters, and flanked by his bodyguards slipped through the ropes and clambered up the hill to his chaise.

Butterfies batted their wings in Amanda's stomach as she and Maggie turned their eyes on the ring and saw the behemoth beside Rance for the first time.

"Spees said the umpires are in Boigotto's pay," Amanda reminded Maggie as Mooney and Spees blended into the crowd. "Shouldn't we warn Rance or Brian that not only is Rostanov a ringer, but the fight itself is fixed."

"There's naught we can do now. The mill is about to begin." Maggie's eyes ran over the tightly packed spectators. "Neither of us could make our way through this crowd even if we was to try."

Amanda was irked at Maggie's defeatist attitude, but when she herself scanned the crowd, she had to admit the Irishwoman was right.

She ran her tongue over her teeth as she watched the instructions being given to the fighters in the ring. Rance would have to employ every trick of scientific boxing to outmaneuver Rostanov. He had a powerful punch, but would it be strong enough to knock out the giant? Even in a fair fight Rance was at a disadvantage, but with the umpires against him, he would surely lose. She couldn't just sit there and watch it happen.

"I could send him a note," she said aloud.

"What do you propose to do? Conjure up an inkpot and quill?" Maggie jeered.

Amanda dug in her reticule and pulled out a miniature paper tablet with a tiny drawing pencil attached to the top by a silver cord. Daniel had brought the curiosity back with him from a trip to Paris.

Maggie watched with dumbfounded interest as Amanda, using her knee as a desk, wrote "Boigotto has bribed the umpires, A.L." on a small paper square. She held up a shilling toward a small boy in the crowd who appeared to be a likely messenger. The child reached up for the coin and scrap of paper and nodded as she leaned from the box and gave him instructions.

The two women followed the boy's blond head with their eyes as he wormed his way through the crowd. Eellike, he found cracks between solid-packed bodies. He was clouted and cursed, but did not falter, for the generous wage compensated for the minor hassles he was forced to endure. He reached the perimeter of the ring, edged along the ropes until he was opposite Brian, and delivered his message with an outstretched hand.

Brian unfolded the scrap of paper, read it, and stared up toward the ridge. Amanda waved and received an answering nod.

At that moment the fight began, and Amanda riveted her eyes on the familiar movement of Rance milling on the retreat. Rostanov lumbered clumsily after him, obviously lacking skills in footwork. The giant threw a punch toward Rance's head, but a quick evasive move by the young fighter left the hit short.

Rance's reach exceeded the larger man's. He hit Rostanov with a glancing blow on his shoulder and bobbed back and forth, avoiding the giant's ineffective jabs for several minutes. But then Rostanov dashed forward and smashed his fist into Rance's stomach below the belt.

Rance grabbed his midsection and crumbled to the ground. The crowd booed and hissed at the low blow. An unwritten law among boxers precluded hitting below the belt, and although the foul was not written into the rules, umpires routinely reprimanded the perpetrator of the unsportsmanlike conduct. To the crowd's displeasure, the umpires did nothing.

Brian and Schofield jumped into the ring and assisted Rance to his feet. Rance had thirty seconds to rise and resume boxing. Schofield ran a towel over the fighter's face while Brian whispered Amanda's message in his ear. Rance gave Brian a dazed, uncomprehending look and moved sluggishly to the scratch line, where Rostanov already stood.

The umpire gave the signal for the boxers to resume fighting.

Almost immediately Rance dropped to one knee from another of Rostanov's low blows. He regained his feet before his seconds reached him, but Rostanov slammed his huge body full force into him without coming up to scratch, knocking Rance flat onto his back. Rance's dandy supporters booed at the official foul and hooted and screeched until all the fair-minded of the crowd flared up at the umpires and took up the cry.

Amanda's stomach twisted into knots. Maggie's face paled.

Brian's warning about the crooked umpires rang in Rance's mind as he staggered to the scratch mark, his breathing labored.

Rance recovered his breath during the next round as he and Rostanov circled each other. With his second wind Rance resumed his spirited movements, dancing out of Rostanov's reach. But with an ungraceful lunge the Cornishman got under Rance's guard and delivered a blow that opened a cut below Rance's left eye. In a volley of exchanged punches, Rostanov bruised Rance's left cheek while Rance punished the Cornishman's upper body with three solid blows.

Rostanov twice deliberately tripped Rance, who went down, but without injury. The fifth round began without Rance having scored a single knockdown, but Rostanov had not escaped unscathed. Besides the body blows, he had a bruise on the side of his head and a darkened eye. The bruiser seemed indifferent to the hits and plowed toward Rance with abandon. Rance's stance was cool and confident but not cocky. The giant was an awkward boxer, but his massive size commanded respect and caution.

For several minutes Rance managed to avoid his opponent by circling and retreating, waiting patiently for an opening. Then, unbelievably, Rostanov dropped his hands as though they were too heavy for him to keep aloft. He barreled in toward Rance, and Rance shot out with the left punch for which he was celebrated. Rostanov's monstrous bulk struck the ground.

Wild cheers erupted over the hillside. Rostanov's seconds dashed cold water onto his bewildered face and prodded him to rise. Boigotto stood up in his chaise, a worried expression on his dark face. Watches were pulled from pockets and a countdown began. When the count reached thirty, the fancy roared "Terry!" in one thunderous voice. Amanda hugged Maggie happily.

Suddenly those nearest the fighters, who could see best, and the people in the vehicles on the rise with a clear view of the ring, began to moan. Rostanov was on his feet, facing Rance at the scratch mark. The umpires were signaling for the fight to continue. Brian, his face red with outrage, shook his fist at the umpires. Those who had bet on Terry Stone were booing loudly while Rostanov's few supporters heaved a sigh of relief at the long count. No one paid heed, but Boigotto slipped away.

Rance's left eye was swollen and his midsection ached from the potent blows to his stomach. When he had hit Rostanov with his lightning punch, he had cracked the skin of three of his knuckles. He rubbed his hands against his breeches to wipe off the blood, praying his left eye would remain open, even a slit, for with impaired vision, his chances of delivering a leveler would be seriously diminished.

As the fighters broke from their mark, Rostanov seized Rance below the waist and the two men fell down in a tangle and wrestled on the ground. The winded giant, gasping for breath, pinned Rance with his enormous body and pummeled him with a tattoo of severe blows to his chest and face. Rance covered his head with his hands, at the same time shouting through his bruised fingers for the umpires to remove his adversary.

"Foul! Foul!" was coming from all directions, for taking down an opponent by tackling and hitting a man when he was down were forbidden.

Amanda clapped her hands over her mouth, and Maggie wailed, "No! No!" Brian tried to get through the ropes, but the spectators were rocking on them while clamoring angrily for fair play. The bribed umpires feared the angry mob more than they did Boigotto. Reluctantly, they freed Rance from Rostanov.

Brian worked ointment into Rance's bruises and stemmed the bleeding from the scrapes on his knuckles while Schofield poured water down his throat. Rance's torso was a mass of scarlet marks, but his eyes shone with a ferocity Brian had never witnessed in his friend before. Rance shoved his seconds aside and stood firmly on his mark.

Rostanov showed fear for the first time, for his wind was gone; he was exhausted. Terry Stone, who should have been put away by now, was still on his feet and looked extremely dangerous. Rostanov backed away, but Rance was on the offensive. He rapped his opponent's shoulders with three hard blows. Rostanov slipped to both knees, but was helped up immediately by his seconds. When the match resumed, Rostanov shot some feeble jabs at Rance's body, but Rance maneuvered skillfully and avoided them. The giant, spent, moved without even a semblance of finesse.

The crowd quieted, waiting for the kill. Amanda's tongue flicked over her lips, moistening them, and the knots in her stomach began to untie themselves. She clutched Maggie's hand.

Rostanov dropped his massive hands. Rance's fist shot through the air, connecting with the monster's jaw, and left an imprint of his own blood from his bruised knuckles on the giant's chin. Rostanov thudded to the ground, a dead weight, his open eyes staring unseeing toward the gray sky. The umpire dared not elongate the thirty-second count again, although he could have counted twice thirty and the pseudo-Russian would have remained prone. The umpire nearest Rance reluctantly lifted the winner's arm in victory. The fields thundered with the roar of the crowd. No one could doubt that the fancy had been partisan to Terry Stone. Brian leapt into the ring. Rance lifted him into the air in a bear hug. Amanda and Maggie danced a perilous jig on the box of the gig.

Amanda made to leap from the carriage and go to Rance to congratulate him, but Maggie held her back. "He wouldn't like that, missy. Ladies don't do that sort of thing."

Amanda watched the fancy surround him.

"There are ladies down there," she said.

Maggie made a sound somewhere between disgust and amusement. "Women, maybe. Those are lightskirts, not ladies, my girl, offering Terry their favors, hoping to earn some of the shillings in his purse."

Rance seemed to bask in the adulation. Some gaudily attired females vied for his attention and grabbed at his arms. A buxom blonde in a garish red dress planted herself in Rance's path, impeding his progress through the crowd. Stretching up on tiptoe, she tugged down his battered face and kissed him boldly on the lips. Jealousy washed over Amanda when Rance tossed his head back and laughed lustily at the words she had whispered to him.

Grim-faced, Amanda easily followed his progress, a lady-bird on each arm, through the adoring crowd, for his blond head towered above everyone else's. It was only when Maggie turned the horses toward town that Amanda lost sight of him.

The dull ache that had been brought on by Maggie's disclosure that Rance was going to America had temporarily been relegated to the back of Amanda's mind. She had been concerned with Rance's performance in the ring. Now the hurt flowed back into her consciousness again.

A few moments earlier she had been intensely proud of him, had thrilled with his supporters among the fancy when he had knocked out Rostanov, and had reveled in his victory. But now the specter of the terrible void that would be caused by his emigrating to the New World reared within her again. That morning Rance had kissed her in Josie's "interesting way." She had been present to cheer him to his most challenging triumph. She should be top-of-the-trees. Yet she felt bereft. Could it have been only yesterday when she was a carefree girl, waving farewell carelessly to Josie? In a single day Rance had turned her into a disillusioned woman.

Men lifted their tall beavers to Amanda and Maggie and cleared a path for them when they entered the inn after turning in the horse and rig at the livery stable. A man in a gray slouched cap handed Maggie an envelope tied with a thin black ribbon as she and Amanda passed through the crowded lobby thick with cigar smoke.

"Missus, give this to your husband," he said. "It's Terry Stone's purse from the prizefight."

Before Maggie could reply, he was swallowed by the crowd.

"What the devil!" she exclaimed. "Why didn't the lout deliver it to Brian or Terry?" She craned her neck to look for the messenger, but he was nowhere in sight.

Twenty minutes later Brian burst into the bedroom and tossed his hat into the air with a celebratory whoop, ignoring where the beaver landed on the wooden floor. He hurled Maggie off her feet and spun her around crazily before setting her down again with a quick kiss on the mouth.

"He did it, Mag! I could burst with pride!"

Smelling faintly of brandy, he grabbed Amanda about tne waist and hugged her more genteely. But Amanda was in no mood for a celebration. She had made up her mind to leave for home on the first available coach after she arranged for Nancy to be delivered by the livery to Rook Manor. Whether Rance escorted her or not mattered little to her. In fact, she would prefer that he did not, but first she would confront him with his deceit, for she wanted to hear his explanation for his untenable duplicity.

"Where is Rance?" she asked Brian after stepping away from his encircling arm.

"Ah, well, Amanda girl, everyone of the fancy wants to buy the lad a drink, you know. Gad! But he deserves it! Tom Cribb was at the mill. He's downstairs with Terry right now. Terry could be the next champion of England!"

Maggie's lips tightened. "An' I'm hoping you don't have plans along that line."

Brian dropped down onto the bed, stretched out flat, and adjusted a pillow behind his head. "No, love," he lamented, "unfortunately Terry's still set on going to Amer—" He stopped short and glanced guiltily at Amanda.

"It's all right, Brian. I know," Amanda said quietly.

"An' glad I am he's told you, Mandy," he replied as relief flooded his honest face.

"He didn't," Maggie interjected. "I did. The girl is that besotted, and you would allow her to go on believing she had a chance with him," she said crossly.

Brian stared at his shoes, shamefaced, and wiggled his foot against the faded bedspread. He sat erect and swung his legs to the floor, an apology to Amanda on his lips, but he was kept from his good intention when Maggie cried, "Oh, where's me head!" She handed Brian the envelope that she had laid on the table when she and Amanda had returned from the fight. "A man pushed this into me hands when I came through the lobby. He said it's the purse for the fight."

Brian untied the ribbon of the brown envelope and lifted the flap. He pulled out the notes and counted them. Ten pounds. He peered into the packet, ran his finger along the interior surfaces, turned the envelope upside down, and shook it vigorously.

"Where's the rest?" he wondered aloud. "The winning purse is a hundred, not a piddling ten pounds! Boigotto has cheated us!" He leapt up from the bed and paced up and down, the two women's faces fastened on him.

"I'm going to see Boigotto. Tell Terry where I am when he comes up," he instructed in a tense voice. He scooped up his hat from the floor near the chest of drawers where it had landed.

"Brian, wait for Terry," Maggie implored, but he had already dashed out the door and was racing down the hall, oblivious of her pleas.

Within five minutes Brian was standing before the store Signor Boigotto had rented to use as an office while in town for the fight. Banging on the front door, he shouted Boigotto's name, but there was no answering voice. He perked his ears for any faint sound and jiggled the doorknob forcefully against the stillness. Growing increasingly agitated, he walked around to an alley that ran along the side of the building, cupped his hands around his face, and peered through a grimy windowpane into the dark, empty room.

Noises coming from the yard in the back of the building sent him scurrying down the alley to investigate. He turned the corner sharply into the backyard and nearly collided with Mooney, who was standing beside his wagon loaded with decent furniture. Brian pulled up short and backed up. He knew immediately that he had stumbled onto a robbery in progress.

"Gentlemen"—he raised his hat in a futile bluff—"I'm looking for Signor Boigotto. Have either of you, by chance, seen him?"

Brian glanced up at Spees arranging a table in the bed of the wagon. Mooney circled Brian and cut him off from the alley, placing the Irishman between him and Spees. Mooney's cruel mouth curled into a sinister smile. Spees jumped down from the wagon, giggling menacingly. Brian searched frantically in his pocket for his revolver, but he had left the weapon in the drawer in Terry's room before he left for the mill.

"We trapped us an Irish rat, Spees," Mooney gloated. Spees bared his teeth wickedly.

Brian made a futile dash for the alley, but Mooney snatched his arm and tumbled the Irishman to the ground. Brian rolled and hunched to avoid the savage kicks from two pairs of booted feet. He grabbed Mooney's shoe and twisted the brute's ankle, sending him toppling backward to the ground. Mooney swore and leapt to his feet. Brian lurched for Spees's foot, but the skinny man jumped back agilely. As Brian braced himself to sit up, Spees ground his boot into Brian's hand.

The excruciating pain shot through his body, and he screamed. The sound, harsh in the quiet yard, triggered a realization that his sole hope of remaining alive depended on attracting help from a passerby on the street beyond the building.

Mooney and Spees were momentarily taken aback when Brian let out a series of ear-piercing shrieks.

"Shut your face," Mooney ordered through clenched teeth, and clasped his hand on Brian's mouth. But the Irishman yanked his head from side to side to avoid being stifled and continued his caterwauling. Mooney raised his foot and delivered a brutal kick to Brian's head. Brian screeched in unfeigned agony, his hands flying to cover the crown of his head. Mercifully the excruciating pain lasted but a split second before the nausea rose in his throat and his brain spun toward oblivion. The last thing he heard, coming from it seemed a great distance, was Terry shouting "Down here!" before everything went black.

Rance unlocked the door of his room and stepped aside for Amanda to enter. They had just left Brian, asleep from the laudanum the doctor had given him. The surgeon found no broken bones in Brian's hand. The painful bruises over the Irishman's body and head, the medical man assured his overwrought wife, would mend after an extended convalescence.

Maggie banished Rance and Amanda from the sickroom, pleading with Rance to allow her husband to rest.

Before Brian lapsed into the drug-induced sleep, Rance consoled the mangled Irishman who still anguished over the loss of the prize money. "Forget about Boigotto, Brian. He's on his way to the coast by now to book passage for Italy. Look, we at least got a share. Poor Rostanov, or whatever his name is, was left with nothing."

Mooney and Spees had been locked up for burglary. With their long record of arrests, the two felons would be deported to Australia, Rance assured Brian.

Amanda packed her bag in a slapdash manner before Maggie ejected them. Rance now placed the valise on his bed and reached for her. She wiggled from his grasp and stood at a distance.

"What's wrong?" he asked. "You smell the brandy? I'm not foxed."

"Just when did you plan on informing me you were going to America?" she said.

Rance ran a nervous hand over his mouth. "Ah, so that's it. I intended to tell you when I drove you home."

"And if I hadn't come to the fight?"

He studied the window, the bed, and her face. "I would have written to you."

"Uh," came from Amanda as an aspirated sound of disdain, disgust, and disbelief at his inadequate answer.

"I thought it was best that way," he added.

"For whom, Rance? You?" she accused.

Rance crossed his arms over his chest. "Look, Mandy, I'm hungry," he said. "Let's go downstairs and get a meal. Afterward I'll hire a chaise and drive you home. We'll talk then, I promise."

Amanda's mouth puckered as she considered his request.

"All right," she agreed, and scanned the purple and

black bruises around his eye and the cut on his lip. She stilled the hand that had instinctively reached up to sympathetically soothe his hurt. He deserved no pity from her. Instead, she said, sounding too harsh, "You know your face looks horrible. The patrons in the dining room will be gawping at you."

He stroked the puffiness below his eye gingerly and smiled. "The fancy will expect me to appear bruised and battered. It's a badge of honor," he drawled. She rolled her eyes to the ceiling at the male foolishness.

"Oh, wait, Rance." Amanda stopped his progress toward the door with a hand on his arm. "Could you give me a moment? I'd better change into my traveling dress before we eat. My gown was pressed this morning, and if I leave it in the valise, it will wrinkle beyond wearing."

Rance nodded and motioned to a screen behind which she could change.

Amanda had fastened the last diminutive pearl button on the high-necked plum gown and emerged from behind the screen in her stocking feet, dangling one gray leather shoe in each hand, when several sharp, insistent knocks sent Rance to open the door. Daniel Lofton's tall, rigid frame blocked out the hall. His fevered eyes and bitter mouth soundlessly denounced the man before him.

Chapter 13

"Papa!" Amanda cried. "How . . ."

Daniel Lofton brushed past Rance, who shut the door and leaned heavily against it. He opened his mouth to explain the scene that to a casual observer must appear to be the culmination of a seduction, but Daniel's lugubrious voice overrode him.

"I've come to see you home, Amanda." His dispirited countenance flushed as he took in her indecent stocking feet peeking from beneath the fine gown, and her shoes swinging in her hands.

"I sent the stable boy around this morning to bring Nancy back from Ainsworth House, but his lordship's grooms knew nothing of the horse coming up lame. I had the humiliation of having to go myself and question Lord Ainsworth. I think you can guess the outcome. Lady Josephine tearfully confessed your whereabouts." The strained, stiff speech had been rehearsed for hours, but pained him anew. Amanda's actions had damaged the trust he had vested in her since her mother's death.

"I'll join you in a moment, Papa; I just need to put my shoes on," Amanda said. The magnitude of her duplicity was brought home by his lowered countenance. She sat on a ladderback chair and slipped both shoes on her feet, buttoning one with trembling fingers.

The thunder that had been building in Daniel's breast since his mortifying interview with Lord Ainsworth burst forth. He turned on the man he believed had despoiled his innocent daughter.

"You have exacted your revenge, Straughn. I took your measure for the bounder and cad you are when you came sniffing after her at Rock Manor. Are you satisfied, now that you have ruined her?"

"Fustian, Lofton," Rance said, "you do Amanda an injustice. She's as chaste as when she left home. I am not completely innocent, but not as you suppose. I fostered her interest in pugilism, which brought her here to see me box, so in that regard I am guilty, but I have not violated her."

"You liar!" Daniel exploded, his emotions leading his reason. Amanda gasped and Rance's back stiffened at the slur.

"You think to weasel out of your responsibilities. What kind of a fool do you take me for? No man brings a woman to his room in an inn except for one purpose!"

"No, Papa, no!" Amanda denied. "He didn't touch . . . he didn't do that! I spent the night with Brian McGonigal's wife, Maggie. I've been in this room for only a few minutes. Brian was set upon . . . had an accident this morning, and just before you came, I was changing into my traveling clothes . . . behind the screen."

Rance's bruised fists clasped and unclasped, his inflamed eyes fixed on Daniel, who leaned on his gold-headed cane with a near-demented expression on his handsome face.

"What's your game, Straughn? Money?" His voice grew wily. "You never did want to marry her, did you? Why burden yourself with a wife whose family carries the stigma of trade. How much easier to lure her into a dalliance, which compromises her just enough for blackmail. All right, Straughn, what's your price for keeping silent?"

Rance visibly ground his teeth, balling his fists, barely controlling himself from hitting Daniel. "You have impungned my honor, Lofton. Name your weapons," he challenged with youthful melodrama.

"No, Rance, no!" Amanda shuddered. "Please, Papa, apologize! Rance was taking me home this afternoon. He wanted to tell you everything. Papa, listen! Say you are sorry!" Amanda jumped up and ran to him, tugging at his unyielding arm.

Daniel shrugged her off, his brown eyes, so like his daughter's when peaceful, were maddened with rage. "You surprise me, Straughn! I had heard that your kind would never deign to call out a social inferior," he sneered.

"I'll make an exception in your case."

Amanda's appalled gasp at the blatant insult drew Rance's black stare. "Rance," she whispered, "please. He is not himself."

She moved to face Daniel, a barrier between her father and the man she loved. "Papa, I know I did wrong, but if Josie revealed all to you, you must realize Rance never encouraged me. He believed he had left me behind forever. I was the one who followed him, because I wanted to see the mill beyond all things."

"You know, Amanda, two days ago I would have believed anything you told me. Today I know you are capable of lying to me."

The stinging rebuke caused her eyes to brim, but she could not dispute the justice of his claim. Her offense *was* unpardonable. "Papa, I'm sorry I hurt you. I know I shouldn't have misled you . . . been untruthful. I was wrong, but don't blame Rance. He is innocent."

Rance led Amanda to the chair she had occupied before. "That's enough, Mandy. I can speak for myself." His hand rested protectively on her shoulder. He softly reissued his challenge. "If you're certain I'm guilty, Lofton, name your weapons and avenge your daughter's honor."

Daniel glared at him, but his choler was being supplanted with a fervid relief that his daughter's virtue remained intact. He tapped his cane with a staccato beat on the wooden floor. Having acknowledged his error to himself did not immediately soften his attitude toward the other two occupants of the chamber, but his next words signaled his impending change of heart.

"Get your things together, daughter," he muttered in a tacit truce. "We are going home."

Amanda jumped up to kiss his cheeks, but he waved her off. "Fasten your shoe," he growled, but the acrimonious atmosphere of the room had lightened.

While Amanda buttoned her fashionable footwear, Rance approached Daniel. "Lofton, hear me out, please," he begged as the older man scowled and made to turn his back. Daniel paused and listened. "Amanda can be ruined for life by this episode. I have seen women brought down by cruel gossip for far less, never to recover. The tattlemongers will make much of the fact she remained in the same establishment with me last night. Regardless of the circumstances, the denizens of society will believe the worst."

Without malice, Daniel said, "You should have sent her home yesterday."

Rance shrugged in resignation. "It just wasn't possible. Amanda can go into the reasons with you later. Listen to me. I have known the Castleberrys all my life. Lord Ainsworth will be discreet, but that does not insure Amanda's misstep will not come to the fore."

The contusions beneath his ruffled shirt ached. His head throbbed. He should have accepted the powders the doctor who treated Brian had offered him, but he had been afraid he would be impaired while he drove Amanda home if he drugged himself. He nudged his discomfort aside and concentrated on what must be said—must be offered. His code of honor required he make the gesture, even if Lofton consigned him to perdition.

"I know you are against a union between Amanda and me," he said. Daniel's eyes narrowed in expectation of a proposal. The scamp is not going to sneak in the back door and get his hands on my money, he decided. But Rance's offer gave him pause.

"Would you reconsider if I willingly sign a marriage contract, however tight you want to make it, which would keep Amanda's money out of my hands?"

Daniel rubbed his chin and pondered. Amanda and Straughn had been close, for all the rhetoric to the contrary that had passed that day. Straughn was granting him a position of supremacy, where he could dictate the allocation of Amanda's dowry and oversee the young aristocrat's expenditures. Under those conditions, why not give Amanda what she obviously desired? Without consulting her, he nodded his head in silent assent.

Rance broke into his most charming smile that not even his battered face could undermine. Neither he nor Daniel noticed Amanda's hardened eyes.

"The gossip will be quelled when Amanda and I announce our betrothal," Rance said. "We may be a nine days' wonder, but society easily forgives indiscretions when the parties are brought to the altar." He smiled at Amanda. "It seems, my dear, we are to be wed."

"No, Rance." She shook her head. "I won't marry you. I have no intention of entering into a loveless marriage to save my reputation. Never!"

Amanda's vehement rejection jolted Rance. Appalled, he stepped away from her, a more emotional separation than a physical one.

"You don't mean that, Mandy," he tried again.

"I most certainly do. Such a union would be loathsome to me."

Her strong words and the admission she expected theirs to be a loveless marriage cut surprisingly deep. His blue eyes darkened with anger and disappointment. "I abide by your decision, then. Far be it from me to subject you to an odious marriage," he said in a clipped, brittle tone.

Daniel rubbed his arthritic knee distractedly. In spite of her forceful rejection, Daniel was certain Amanda cared for Straughn. The desire for her happiness crept into his bones.

"Amanda, don't be rash. You have been accepted by Lord and Lady Ainsworth and made a mark in society at the assembly. Do you wish to throw away all your new friendships? Married to Mr. Straughn, you would have an entry into the best houses."

"No, I shan't accept him simply to gain a hand up in society! A few months ago, Papa, you would not even let Rance call on me!" she cried in confusion.

Daniel sighed. "I was wrong to do that. But neither shall I force you into a marriage against your will over this misadventure. I thought you wanted . . ." His voice trailed off. Perhaps he had miscalculated and Amanda's interest was in Straughn's pugilistic abilities and had nothing to do with romance. Theirs may have been that rarity, a strong platonic friendship between a man and woman. Straughn had offered; she had rejected him.

"There it is, then." Daniel closed the matter. "We have a long drive, child. We best be started."

"Papa, I want to speak to Rance alone, please," Amanda said. "I shall meet you in front of the inn in fewer than ten minutes, I promise."

Daniel acquiesced with a nod and shambled to the door, leaning on his cane. Almost as an afterthought, he tossed over his shoulder, "Your servant, Straughn."

Rance bowed, "Mr. Lofton," to Daniel's black-coated back.

Amanda began fastening the straps on her valise with trembling hands. "You know, Rance," she said, unable to control the rising misery that tightened her throat, "to give up all your dreams of America over one kiss and settle for a lifetime shackled in a marriage you do not desire is the height of stupidity. You would have spent the rest of your days regretting your wasted opportunity." And blaming me, she thought but did not add.

Rance studied her. He would miss their verbal sparring

about the frailties of the gentry. Her lovely face was always a page of expressive emotions he never tired of deciphering.

An unbidden tear formed in the corner of Amanda's eye, and she brushed at it with an abrupt sweep of one hand. Rance, moved by her sadness, hastened to her side and grasped her shoulders. Reading her face, he discerned her wretchedness.

"Oh, Mandy," he drawled huskily, running a thumb gently down her cheek, outlining the trail of the tear.

"Stop it, Rance!" she cried, and slapped his hand away, genuine anger flashing across her tear-stained face.

Rance's mouth tightened. He stepped from her side, showed her his back, and stared from the casement window into the street below, where Nancy was tied to the rear of a smart phaeton. The saddle Amanda told him she had bought at Gibson's was stashed in the back.

Daniel Lofton was perched on the box, a reminder to Rance that he should be congratulating himself for successfully appeasing an irate father. He had made the honorable gesture, offering marriage of his own volition, and had escaped without having to make the supreme sacrifice. He could not think of a single contemporary who would not felicitate him on his good fortune at dodging a forced proposal. He could pursue his ambitions without encumbrance. Then why was he not at peace?

Amanda puffed out her plum velvet bonnet that had been crushed in the carpetbag and fluffed up the gray feathers with her fingers. Using Rance's shaving mirror, she adjusted the hat on her head, slipped into her pelisse, shrugged into her gloves, and picked up the valise from the bed.

"I won't knock on Maggie's door in case Brian is asleep. Will you say adieu for me?" she asked Rance's back. He nodded curtly but continued to stare through the window.

She turned the doorknob gingerly. "Godspeed, love," she whispered too low for him to hear, and slipped noiselessly into the hall. He heard the faint click of the door closing and turned toward it, his back to the window.

"Damn," he cursed at the empty room. "Damn!" he repeated, shouting at the ceiling, dragging out the oath. He slammed his fist into his palm, breaking open the thin skin that had begun to heal over his battered knuckles, oozing blood onto his hand.

Amanda sat beside Daniel on the box of the phaeton, buried in her own dark thoughts. The pain she felt, knowing she would never see Rance again, was comparable in her mind to experiencing the death of a loved one.

Neither she nor Daniel had spoken since leaving the inn twenty minutes before. To her left she saw across the fields the willow trees surrounding the hidden brook where Mooney and Spees had accosted her. She said nothing to Daniel about the incident, fearing to resurrect his waning wrath.

He cleared his throat. "The Blue Duck is but another mile or so ahead. We can refresh ourselves there. It's a decent enough place."

Not responding to his suggestion, Amanda confessed without preamble, "I do love him, Papa."

"Amanda! Then why on earth . . . ?"

"He doesn't love me. Oh, he's fond enough, but I want him to be so sure, so very sure that he cannot go on without me. Do you see?"

"I see he's a fool not to love you," Daniel said.

"I think so too," she agreed poignantly.

By mutual unspoken agreement, father and daughter set aside that conversation for the remainder of the journey.

The evening after Daniel brought Amanda home from Wye, a groom from Ainsworth House delivered a letter to Amanda from Josie. She read the missive in the library, perched on the arm of Daniel's favorite leather chair, where he was seated.

Amanda handed the vellum paper to her father. "Lady Ainsworth has forbidden Josie to speak to me."

"I'm sorry," he murmured, enfolding her hand in his and lifting it to his lips.

She patted his arm. "Don't fret, Papa. I shall survive."

When she left him to retire, he crumbled the letter in his fist. He had counted on Josie to restore Amanda's former vivacity. He smoothed out the paper and laboriously deciphered the cramped handwriting.

Half the letter was devoted to Lady Ainsworth's decree that forbade Josie contact with Amanda, and her ladyship's reasons for the mandate. But Josie's last lines offered hope that the forced estrangement would one day be rectified.

Daniel read, "I shall miss you frightfully, Mandy, but Evan is kinder than Mama. I know I shall be able to bring him around, and you can visit us after our nuptials, for I have good news. Dr. Canfield is retiring in November, leaving the living at St. Catherine's vacant. Evan has been offered the place there and accepted!!! I have not been meek, Amanda, in defending you. I have argued with Mama and been sent to my room for my impertinence as though I were still in the nursery. You would have been proud of me. Unfortunately, I have not prevailed. Your friend forever, Lady Josephine Castleberry."

Daniel refolded the letter and set it aside. Being separated from her bosom bow and confidante would further lower Amanda's spirits, to say nothing of putting an end to her social life, which hitherto had revolved around Ainsworth House.

Daniel reached for the decanter of brandy beside his chair and filled the bottom of his snifter. He inhaled the vapors and sipped the brandy slowly, his thoughts returning to the Castleberrys. He could approach Lord Ainsworth and clarify the situation, assuring him that while Amanda behaved unwisely, she and Straughn had not . . . Damn! How would he ever be able to get out the words?

He could not forget the prim, censorious lips of her ladyship when Josie revealed that Amanda had run off to

Wye to see Straughn fight, nor Lord Ainsworth's quizzical eyebrow and blundering speech. "I had no idea Miss Lofton was fast!" The humiliating scene was burned in Daniel's brain. He would not grovel before those priggish aristocrats! Not even for Amanda!

His eyes roamed over the shelves with his priceless book collection. Rook Manor was perfect in every detail. He had fallen in love with the run-down house, recognizing its potential, the first moment he had set eyes on it. He had renewed the property, which had been abandoned when the owner had died leaving no heirs, to its former magnificence. The bucolic life suited Amanda, who like himself was an inveterate equestrian. When Lady Ainsworth had readily accepted her as Josie's friend, all reservations that leaving Bristol had been the right decision had melted away. Now the doubts were surfacing again.

The brandy was mellowing him. He should propose to the pretty little widow and build a fine home for them in Bristol among his own kind of people. Amanda could use a mother figure to keep her from blundering into social transgressions. His daughter might even be guided by the right person into reconsidering one of the young Bristol men who had favored her and whom she had rejected when she was too young to know her mind.

He inspected the fine furniture about the room, the cherry-paneled walls, and the Turner landscape above the fireplace in this room he loved so well, and had second thoughts. How did the adage go? "Act in haste and repent in leisure?" He would reflect on his options but do nothing for a month or two, he decided, and drained his glass.

Chapter 14

Daniel rode his gray stallion over his fields, ostensibly estimating the sacks of corn he would garner from his land, but his mind was very much occupied with thoughts of Amanda. After two full months there were no visible signs she missed Rance Straughn. Romantic novels would have one believe unrequited love ended in heroines withering away from a beleaguered heart. But his daughter had courage and a strong spirit. Straughn was gone, and she had curbed her outer emotions nicely. Daniel did not, however, delude himself that she no longer had secret yearnings for the young aristocrat.

But her days were productive. She kept the household and estate ledgers under his direction in the office next to the kitchen. Whenever he and his bailiff discussed estate matters in the small room, she sat in and listened carefully, asking sensible questions. The housekeeper was in her pocket, and the other servants all but worshipped her.

Daniel rode beside the brook that defined his property. The stream gurgled pleasantly. Amanda was an asset to him in his dealings with his tenants too. Her congeniality endeared her to them when she accompanied him while he listened to their concerns and small discontents.

Daniel urged the horse up the green hillside toward the high meadow where the sheep were pastured. On the overlook he stopped and looked around. The beech leaves shimmered in the sunlight, and nature had strewn blue wildflowers artistically over the grassy slope. This was the spot where Amanda had watched the sparring between Straughn and his Irish friend. At first he had been amused when she showed him an essay she had written about pugilism, but on reading the vivid, perceptive work a second and third time, he decided to contact a publisher he met when his wife had been steeped in the literary world. The man could direct him to an editor who might consider the piece, for the writing was of a professional quality and publication of the article would give Amanda a lift. He prided himself on not being as narrow-minded as many of his contemporaries were where a woman's capabilities were concerned. His daughter had not been raised with any constraints on her brain. He would encourage Amanda in her latest endeavor. Besides, the scribblings would keep her too occupied to yearn for the Honorable Terrance Straughn.

He reached the stables, patted the horse affectionately, and handed the reins to the groom. Pleased with what he saw as Amanda's excellent adjustment, he had given up the notion of moving to Bristol. He smiled secretively, but he had *not* given up the idea of wedding the little widow one day.

Amanda, encouraged by her father's praise for her article, decided on using the nom de plume Terry Stone, since the public would never accept a piece on boxing from a female writer. She was certain there would be some among the fancy who would recall the brave young fighter with the lightning punch who had carried the name and would wonder if he was the author.

Her fond reminiscences of Rance were bearable and bright during the daytime when she sat under the beech tree on the overlook or rode along the brook in the warm sunshine. She would ford the stream onto Lord Woods's land and peer back toward the rise, and imagine the bobbing and weaving of two bare-chested figures on the hilltop, silhouetted against the summer sky. The memory was a cherished keepsake that warmed her heart.

But at night, with her head on her pillow, images of Rance would cause waves of hopelessness. Once she had fantasized that a sporting paper containing her essay on pugilism had found its way to America, and Rance had identified her from the pseudonym as the writer and remembered her with affection. But a beauteous American had intruded, spoiling the cheery dream, as Amanda imagined the voluptuous woman laughing with Rance at the silly English girl who had followed him to Wye to see him box, and her heart had ached unbearably from the longing that came from still wanting him.

On a mild day, as the calendar drifted from summer into fall, Amanda put on a pale lavender muslin gown and tied a straw bonnet decorated with purple and yellow pansies over her brown curls and drove her curricle to the village to buy a few necessities for Daniel at Peterson's sundries. She parked in front of the shop and negotiated with Horace and Joshua for the usual ha'penny each to watch Lucie and Lizzie, which the urchins knew would grow to a full penny when Miss Lofton paid the shot.

Within the store she selected the brand of shaving soap Daniel had requested and six blades for his razor, and placed the items on the counter. After Mr. Peterson marked the purchases in his green ledger and wrapped them in brown paper, she gathered up the package and walked to the curricle. She had placed one foot on the step of the carriage, when she heard a familiar female voice call her name from the direction of the milliner's shop.

She turned to see Josie remove her arm from Evan Whitaker's and hurry toward her, smiling, while the grim-faced cleric trailed in his fiancée's wake.

"Oh, Amanda," Josie gushed, "it is so good to see you." She grasped Amanda's arms, and standing on tiptoe touched cheeks with her in their usual manner.

"This is a surprise, Josephine," Amanda greeted her with formal cordiality. "Mr. Whitaker." She nodded perfunctorily to the curate, her manner cool, for she could see the disapproval on his long face.

"Evan, leave us alone for a few minutes, please," Josie requested.

The curate's thin lips pursed. "Josephine, I don't think your mother would—"

"Please, Evan, don't scold," she interrupted him. "I must have a private word with Amanda." Amanda's eyebrow rose at Josie's forceful dismissal of her swain.

Mr. Whitaker hesitated and stared beetle-browed at Amanda for a moment, but moved off toward his carriage parked before the ironmonger's without further verbal protest. He had never fully forgiven Amanda for spurning him, even though he knew she was unsuitable for a man of his temperament and profession, while Josie was his ideal, a malleable female whom, more often than not, he could bend to his will.

"My, my Josie, I never thought to see you resist your fiancé with such spirit," Amanda teased, an edge to her tone. "Aren't you afraid Evan will tattle to your mama?"

Josie's bow mouth quivered. "Don't fun me, Mandy. I really did try to get Mama to let me visit you, but I haven't the strength or self-assertiveness to keep up a prolonged battle. And as far as Evan is concerned, I know you find him dull and boring and too proper, but, Mandy, I love him, and I would die if I lost him."

"Oh, Josie, don't turn into a weeping pot on me," Amanda chided gently, seeing tears begin to brighten Josie's blue eyes. "I'm glad to see you being a bit more of a dragon with Evan. And look how nicely he obeyed you." She chuckled. "I understand about your mama too," she added in a supportive tone. "You cannot go against your parent, nor would I urge you to."

"Oh, Mandy, I'm so glad you forgive me," she cried, touching the sleeve of Amanda's elegantly simple dress.

"Of course I do, but as happy as I am to see you, perhaps it would be wiser if you obeyed your mama. I see Evan is glaring at us." She was ashamed for hurting Josie, who had been a stalwart ally. Without her aid Amanda would never have seen Rance fight, but she could see no profit in stretching out the small talk. She and Josie would never be blithesome bosom bows again. Lucky Josie was to wed the man she loved, while, she herself had lost Rance irretrievably. Amanda knew her sudden misplaced bitterness toward her blameless friend was unreasonable, but she could not help herself.

Josie, unaware Amanda had put a period to their old relationship, said, "Evan acts the bear at times when he doesn't get his way, but he can be terribly sweet too."

"Yes, I'm sure," Amanda was forced to comment. "But I must go now, Josie, and there is no point in alienating your beloved over me." She smiled and hugged Josie, the intimate touch washing some of her unwarranted ill will aside.

When Amanda stepped toward the curricule, Josie reached out her hand to forestall her friend.

"Mandy, are you still in love . . . well, interested in, Rance Straughn?" she asked in a hushed voice.

A fresh rush of resentment surged through Amanda. "Idle curiosity, Josephine," she drawled, "or do you have a more devious reason for your inquiry? If you mean to inform me he is in America, I already know."

Josie's blue eyes grew large, and she blurted out, "But he isn't!"

Amanda sucked in her breath. "No? Where is he, then?"

"Rance has been visiting with his brother Lord Woods for the past week. We, Evan and I and Mama and Papa, were invited to Willowwoods for dinner last evening. Rance was there."

Amanda's knees weakened, and she clutched the side of the curricle. "He's been here for a week?" Amanda repeated.

Josie nodded. "In a private moment I asked him if he had called on you. 'No,' he said. 'When are you and Evan getting married, little one?' Just like that, Amanda. He changed the subject that abruptly."

"How is he?" Amanda's heart raced. Rance here! She felt faint.

"Quite well, in fact, top-of-the-trees. He's splendidly attired and has a magnificent blood stallion, Freddie told me. No one said, but I think he's gambling again."

Eager to escape, Amanda bent down and touched cheeks with Josie, mumbled appropriate words mechanically, tossed pennies to Horace and Joshua, and drove off in a daze. Josie covered her mouth with her gloved hand and stared after Amanda. "He still has her heart," she whispered with pity. "Poor Amanda."

At the outskirts of the village, Amanda pulled up under an oak tree by the side of the road. She waited for her breathlessness to subside, and her pounding heart to beat more normally. Her life had begun to have meaning for the first time in months. Even the nightly gnawing pain had diminished to a tolerable wistfulness. Now he was there to tear up her heart again. Belligerently, she clicked the horses into motion.

Amanda tracked down Daniel in his small office immediately after crossing the threshold of the house. He looked up from the estimate he had been going over for remodeling the carriage house into her stricken face as she bent over his desk.

"What is it, child?" he asked, alarmed.

"He's back," she threw at him.

"Straughn?" he uttered. "Did you meet him in the village?"

"Not him, but Josie. She dined with Rance and his family at Willowwoods last night. He's been here for a week."

Neither spoke for a few seconds as rapid glances passed between them.

Daniel steepled his fingers against his mouth. "Would you like to see him?" he asked. The longing in Amanda's brown eyes belied her negligent shrug.

Just that morning Daniel had decided to invite a few of Amanda's female friends from Bristol, along with three or four eligible bachelors, for a weekend as a surprise for her at the end of the month. He had been certain the time was right. Now he was glad he had not tendered the invitations.

"He has been here a week, Papa, so it would appear he is not eager to see me," Amanda said wryly, belatedly forming a verbal response to Daniel's query. "However, if he remains at Willowwoods, within such a narrow sphere, we are bound to meet sometime."

The inevitable happened four days later. Nancy was behaving fractiously after an encounter with a barking village dog and wanted her head. Having left the mongrel behind, Amanda guided the prancing mare onto the open road that led to Rook Manor. She leaned over the horse's neck, purring into her twitching ear to quiet her and regain full control. Unnoticed, a tall rider on a black stallion entered the road from a shortcut to Willowwoods several yards in front of her. Rance's breath quickened at the vision in a dashing blue velvet riding habit, a saucy russet hat with a pert peacock-blue feather topping her warm brown curls, pacifying the familiar horse. When he rode up to her and their eyes met, Amanda, who had anticipated coming across Rance at every turn for days, was taken by surprise. All the clever speeches she had prepared and rehearsed ad infinitum fled from her brain.

"Rance!" was all that came to her.

"Amanda." He grinned at her, his voice so familiar yet somehow strange after the intervening months. A small scar at the edge of his lip was the sole legacy of the infamous mill.

She regained her composure. "You have traded in Bluebell, I see." She admired the blood stallion with her eyes, but teased, "What a shame. I always felt the cob gave you a certain panache."

"Bluebell fitted my quixotic period. I fear, my life has taken a more practical turn. I have had to give up tilting at windmills. Kelly-too belongs to the sober gentleman I've become, not the brawler." The animosity that had marked their months-ago parting had fallen away without a trace.

"I never saw anything but a gentleman," she maintained. The serious tone hung uncomfortably in the air. Amanda forced a jolly note into her question; "You named the horse Kelly the second?"

"No, too, t-o-o," he spelled. "I suppose I was trying for something poetic or whimsical or maybe just plain silly," he confessed. His engaging grin warmed her. Just being close to him was more wonderful than she would ever have believed. If only he would dismount and hold up his arms for her to slide from Nancy's back into them. Her image of being pulled forcefully against his slim, hard body for a deep, seductive kiss made her blush as if she had voiced her passionate cravings aloud.

"You didn't go to America after all." She said the obvious to deflect her hunger for him.

"No, I went to Ireland for a while. Brian bought his dream farm with a cottage that Maggie adores. There was much to do: buying equipment and furnishing the house, hiring the hands and selecting prime horses to stock the farm. The barn was fairly sound but needed a bit of patching here and there. I helped where I could. Brian and I put in a kitchen garden for Maggie ourselves."

"Farmer Straughn! Now, there's a picture!" Amanda chuckled, her eyes shiny with glee.

"Do you dare deride a loyal subject who follows in George's footsteps?" he parried with mock indignation.

"Touché, my good man, I had quite forgotten his majesty's penchant for agriculture." She fairly bubbled. Rance's mere presence had rejuvenated her.

"Brian and Maggie are happy, then?" she asked.

"Indeed! Brian's over the moon, in fact, for Maggie is increasing."

"How wonderful!" she cried.

"He struts about like a game fowl, he's that full of himself." He parodied an Irishman's lilting brogue.

"He'll make a fine father, he will," she entered into the play, pronouncing the word "faither," as Brian would.

"Maggie's the same though. She rags at the hired woman for every real and imagined carelessness, forgetting she herself was once a servant."

"She must have been glad to see the last of me," Amanda guessed without resentment.

"You're right, Mandy," Rance conceded. "She's jealous of you, I'm afraid. It rankles her that Brian is too fond of you, at least in her eyes."

Almost in concert, each of them leaned over their horse's necks and patted their animals as though requiring a respite to calm the emotions the other had unleashed.

Amanda spoke first. "Why didn't you sail to America, Rance?" She asked the question that was uppermost in her mind since Josie had jolted her with the news Rance was at Willowwoods.

"Heavens, Amanda, America is too wild for a peaceable man like me!"

"Don't fun, Rance."

"How can you accuse me of gammoning you? I am terrified of Indians," he pretended with a dry chuckle.

"Hogwash, you are not hen-hearted. But I shan't press, since you choose not to own up." He did not dispute her. Any further entreating on her part to discover the reason the trip to America was aborted would fall on deaf ears.

"Isn't there an assembly tomorrow?" The words had passed his lips before the futility of the question struck him. He could not trust himself to dance with her.

"I don't go anymore, so I don't pay attention," she replied.

His head snapped up. "Gad, Mandy," he said, mildly berating, "you haven't locked yourself up because you fear rumor-mongering about us?"

Amanda found his supposition droll and smiled. "Rance, you have me pining away in the manner of some romantic consumptive in a novel. I'm not such a fribble. I keep quite busy, believe me. I work with my father on estate business and do some writing, among other things."

"Then why do you no longer attend the assemblies?" he persisted. "I can assure you, no gossip about us exists. Ernestine would have been picking at me unmercifully if she had even a hint you and I were involved in a contretemps. Amazingly, she and Leonard do not even know about the mill in Wye. Apparently there are no fisticuff fanciers among their intimates."

"I don't fear gossip exactly, although, I admit, I do not relish the prospect of Lady Ainsworth giving me the cut direct at the dance. I'm so wont to being seen in her company, our neighbors could not help but remark should the Castleberrys shun me. You see, her ladyship has forbidden Josie my company, Rance. I am no longer received at Ainsworth House."

"What?" he thundered. "Damme, Amanda, that's not to be borne! Her ladyship was to dinner at Willowwoods not a week ago and treated me with deference, and I, silently grateful to her for not divulging you came to me at the mill in Wye. I did not dream, my dear, she had treated you so shabbily."

What hypocrisy! Rance thought. As a member of the aristocracy, his public brawling in the guise of a boxing match was bad *ton* and on a par with a gentle female witnessing the mill. Amanda's guilt was no greater than his own. If Lady Ainsworth pardoned him, she should acquit Amanda as well.

The stallion sensed his rider's distress, thrust his fine head into the air, and rattled his traces. Rance calmed the horse and crossed his hands, resting them on the pommel.

"I shall put an end to that woman's sanctimony, Amanda. Be at the dance tomorrow. Lady Ainsworth will not dare to rebuff you if I approach her with you on my arm."

A warm glow filled her because he cared enough to

support her, but she found flaws in his plan. "Rance, Lady Ainsworth cannot easily be turned from a course she believes she is justified in pursuing. She may be affronted by our presumptuousness and reveal the truth in a fit of pique. At least, presently, only a handful of people are aware of my escapade. If we confront her, we may precipitate a widespread scandal that does not now exist."

But his sea-blue eyes were intractable, his mouth set in a determined line. "I won't allow this to go on, Amanda," Rance said. "Promise me you shall be at the assembly. I can assure you Lady Ainsworth will not risk a rift between her family and mine by alienating me. You did nothing to warrant her harsh treatment. Josie's involvement was minor, and Whitaker stood by her. Where's the harm? I want your word, Mandy," he said, leaning toward her. A faint odor of sandalwood soap reeled her senses.

"I can't give it, Rance," she balked. "I could never agree without consulting my father about the wisdom of what you propose."

She put up her hand to ward off any further arguments as he opened his mouth to protest.

"All right, Amanda." He gave in. "I shan't press further, but I will be at the assembly, looking for you." Her nod would have to suffice as a sign she might let him help her. He should be about his business, but he found he was reluctant to leave her.

"Did you say you were doing writing? Perhaps one of those essays on contemporary life we once talked about."

Amanda's lips quirked with pleasure that he remembered. Eager to share her accomplishment with him, she said, "Yes, Papa is planning to offer a boxing piece of mine inspired by you to a publisher friend. I hope a magazine will use the essay in their sports section. You shan't be displeased if I should use the sobriquet Terry Stone, since I must assume the persona of a male writer?"

"Displeased? Never! I am honored, Mandy," Rance assured her.

"It isn't at all certain the piece will be well received, but

I am encouraged, for Papa is a severe critic and does not give praise lightly. Maybe this Terry Stone will be a winner in the literary world as the other was in the ring."

Her zeal, glittering smile, and unforgettable brown eyes reaffirmed the appealing image he had carried with him these months. He wanted to snatch her from the saddle and wrap her in his arms, taste her lips. The sudden desire roughened his voice. "You will allow me a peek at the masterpiece before Mr. Lofton sends it off, I hope."

"If you really want to read it," she murmured, unexpectedly shy.

"Indeed I do. Very much." He had been witless to have talked himself into believing he could be near her and remain uninvolved. Inevitably the day would come when he would lose control, gather her into his arms, and recklessly make love to her. He must remove to London before he did something wild.

Rance lifted his gold pocket watch by the chain and snapped open the lid embossed with a stag's head. "I have an appointment with a solicitor in ten minutes."

"Dear me," Amanda quipped, "has one of your flirts sued you for breach of promise?"

"Can't be that. I've proposed to only one woman, but she found me wanting," he said, immediately repenting the careless remark which would open wounds for both of them that were impossible to heal anytime soon.

Amanda's heart turned over at his sad smile and the reference to the proposal she had occasionally, during periods of abject loneliness, lamented rejecting.

"The horses are getting restive," she declared. "Bye now, Rance," she said abruptly, and urged Nancy toward Rook Manor with a careless wave.

"Tomorrow night, Mandy. We will settle with Lady Ainsworth, I promise," Rance called after her. She fluttered her hand at him just before she broke into a sprightly canter, but there was no commitment in the wave.

Chapter 15

"No, Amanda, I won't have it," Daniel insisted. "If young Straughn wants to call here, I am willing, but to deliberately provoke Lady Ainsworth could unleash her tongue. Your name and his have not been linked adversely to date. Her ladyship has the power to do just that." He elevated his leg onto an inadequately small lady's footstool. His shoe completely covered the fancy embroidery. He leaned back into the upholstered chair, arms crossed.

Birch logs crackled in the drawing room fireplace, which cast a warm, mellow glow in the gathering dusk.

"Rance believes there is little danger of Lady Ainsworth snubbing me," Amanda informed him.

"Little?" Daniel repeated. "Unless Straughn can guarantee no danger, because he has already approached her and has her word, I cannot agree for you to attend the dance. *Little* is not good enough. As a wagering man, he should be aware of the difference between little and a sure thing."

Amanda nestled into the cushions of the yellow damask sofa. She pleated and folded and refolded a handkerchief. Lady Ainsworth was not a vindictive woman, but Papa had a point. Josie's mother might be nudged into a rash reprisal if Rance forced an unwanted reconciliation.

"I cannot condone a rude confrontation," Daniel persisted at her silence. "Time may be a wiser healer. Lady Ainsworth has been genuinely fond of you. She may yet come around on her own."

Amanda nodded, acknowledging the soundness of his argument, but she had learned from her encounter with Rance just how deeply she still cared for him. He may not share her love, but neither was he indifferent to her, or he would not have volunteered to champion her with Lady Ainsworth. After the agony she had suffered when she believed she had lost him forever to America, she could no longer deceive herself that a casual friendship with him was worse than never seeing him at all. Rance would be at the dance tomorrow night, waiting for her. Reason enough for her to be there.

"Rance is a gentleman and would never be rude to Lady Ainsworth, and her ladyship is not the sort to create a scene in a public ballroom," Amanda pointed out.

Daniel's long fingers rubbed his arthritic knee absentmindedly. The defect in raising a child by persuasion and example instead of coercion and punishment was that sooner or later she became an astute logician equal to one's self.

"You want to go," he stated. "You would beard the lion in her den."

"I wouldn't put it so, but I'm not averse to mending fences with the Castleberrys, Papa. All in all, Lady Ainsworth has been good to me. Josie is to marry soon, and that will change things between us. But we can still be good friends. At the dance Rance and I can see how the land lies, and if his idea is feasible, we'll approach Josie's mother. If we detect problems, we can desist."

"I see I have been overruled."

"No, Papa," Amanda disagreed with a faint grin. "I cannot go if you refuse to escort me."

Answering her ingenuous smile with a good-natured but

skeptical shake of his head, he contended, "You know I am not such a despot." She laughed and picked up a book she had been reading earlier in the afternoon.

Daniel rubbed the bridge of his nose between two fingers and stared into the fire. In his mind he echoed the question Amanda had asked Rance earlier; why hadn't Straughn gone to America? Daniel had often thought the young aristocrat would do well in the New World. He had a certain innate authority about him. Whatever business he would have chosen to take up, Daniel decided with grudging admiration, Straughn would have been the one giving the orders.

Mary had fashioned Amanda's hair into a coronet intertwined with gold cord and framed the sides of her face with Grecian curls. The abigail winced at the ambivalent expression on Amanda's face. She had already undone two intricate coiffures and recombed and reworked the soft brown hair into this third style.

"Well, miss?" she asked tentatively. Amanda was normally not difficult to please. But that night she twirled her head to the right and left and studied the skillfully plaited crown and the faultless curls in her vanity mirror with a frown. She lifted the silver-backed hand mirror and caught the reflection of the back of her head in the larger glass.

"I suppose it will have to do," Amanda sighed, ultracritical even of perfection in her present mood.

"I declare, Miss Amanda, I have never seen you fuss so while preparing for an assembly dance. You look just fine. Right pretty, in fact."

"I want to look beautiful, Mary! I must look beautiful!"

"Well, you do, miss," Mary vowed. This was the first assembly her young mistress had attended since her rift with Lady Josephine. She must be anticipating a reunion with her old friend, although Mary was mystified that Miss Amanda should be overly concerned with being beautiful for another woman.

Amanda postured before the cheval glass in the corner of the room, swaying from side to side in a waltz step. Her gold gown had been designed by a French couturier in London and forged from a bolt of Oriental silk that Daniel had imported. The incomparable dress, gold kid slippers, and unique black opal necklace would have been admired by a host of guests at a ball given by the Regent himself. Amanda sought only one man's approval. She gathered up her gold mesh reticule and black velvet pelisse, frowned into the glass once more, and swept from the room. She joined Daniel in the library, where he had been pacing for twenty minutes.

"At last," he said as though he were eager to attend the dance. He wrapped Amanda's pelisse around her shoulders and took his silk hat, white gloves, and gold-headed cane from the hands of Jeffries. Outside, a liveried footman handed Amanda and Daniel up into the waiting carriage with its lamps ablaze. Daniel sat back and silently reflected on the prudence of prodding Lady Ainsworth. He hoped Rance Straughn would be tactful. Amanda, beside him, dreamed only of waltzing with Rance, and had pushed from her mind her specious arguments for attending the assembly.

A contredanse was in progress when Amanda and Daniel entered the ballroom. They each scanned the lines of dancers on the crowded floor and the spectators on the perimeter of the ballroom for Rance.

"He is not here yet," Amanda observed. Daniel nodded and led Amanda to a pair of unoccupied straight-backed chairs set against the wall that were free of either a reticule, scarf, fan, or punch cup that indicated the seat was reserved for someone who had stood up to dance.

Daniel leaned forward in the chair, resting his hands on his cane. Almost immediately the schoolmaster and Geoffrey Samuels came to greet Amanda and Daniel.

"Miss Lofton, good to see you again. It's been a while." Geoffrey nodded to Daniel. "Sir."

"You've been missed, Miss Lofton," the young schoolmaster added. "We feared you might have abandoned us for Bristol, although Lady Josephine mentioned that you had been poorly. I'm glad you've made a fine recovery."

"Thank you for your concern, Mr. Wayne. I'm quite the thing again," she assured him. She blessed Josie for inventing a plausible excuse for her absence and saving her from a barrage of annoying questions.

Amanda accepted an invitation for a country dance with Mr. Wayne after promising Geoffrey the next set.

She urged Daniel to seek a diversion while she danced. "I'll be outside having a smoke, and then I might try the card room," Daniel said. "Send for me if you need me," he added sotto voce before handing her over to Mr. Wayne for a Scottish reel.

The Castleberrys were ensconced in their favorite place beside the Palladian window, Amanda noted as she twirled with the schoolmaster. She saw that Lady Ainsworth had invited Lord and Lady Woods to share the green sofa. Josie's mother appeared to be disclosing some choice bit of gossip behind her ostrich-feather fan to Leonard and Ernestine. Josie and Evan Whitaker were standing close together, conversing with Lord Ainsworth, who sat in the wing chair. No doubt Rance would be asked to join his brother and sister-in-law when he arrived.

Amanda was claimed for each dance as the evening progressed, but her amiable mood was slowly deteriorating, replaced with anguish. Her eyes came away from the entrance to the room time after time without seeing Rance Straughn.

Midway through the evening she rejected Mr. Wayne's invitation to waltz, pleading fatigue, and sat fanning herself as she fixed on the dancers with unseeing eyes. She was furious with Rance. He had probably forgotten his promise and gone off to gamble or drink. Even at that moment he might be in the arms of a piece of muslin while Amanda monitored the entrance assiduously and foolhardily for him. He would have been at the dance by now if he had intended to keep his word. How many disappointments must she suffer at his hands before she came to her senses? She whipped her fan with a vengeance before her angry face.

Unknown to Amanda, her saturnine expression was causing a wave of gossip to sail through the ballroom. Had she not been steeped in frenzied self-pity, she might have observed a woman with pink feathers in her hair, pointing with her fan in her direction. The gossip shielded her face with gloved hands while confiding to her partner, her quizzical eyes bobbing between Amanda and the Castleberrys. Had Amanda's brown eyes leapt from group to group at the end of the waltz, she would have found herself the object of covert attention along with Lady Ainsworth. She was too absorbed in castigating Rance Straughn in her mind for his perfidy and herself for being a nodcock for still willing him to appear.

"Blast Rance!" Amanda whispered under her breath. "How could he entice me to appear here and then desert me while he follows his wanton proclivities." Fortunately the chairs on either side of her were unoccupied, and while her tenacious observers from across the room saw her lips move, they did not hear her oath.

From the corner of her eye Amanda saw Lady Ainsworth and Josie bearing down on her. Her heart leapt into her throat as she realized she was about to be involved in a social coil and it was too late to send for her father. She concluded that Lady Ainsworth, irate that Amanda would dare to attend the assembly without her approval, had decided to ask her to leave.

I'm being evicted, Amanda thought. She remained glued to her chair, watching the grim-faced woman advance, too near already for Amanda to make a graceful exit. Amanda straightened her shoulders in anticipation of the rebuff, but Josie was smiling.

Amanda rose to greet her, and the two friends touched cheeks in their old familiar manner.

Josie whispered, "Mandy, smile, please, and act normal. An *on-dit* about the rift between us is circulating the room.

I have convinced Mama she must invite you to join our party and squelch the unpleasant talk before things get out of hand.''

Lady Ainsworth grasped Amanda's arm. ''I'm prepared to forgive you, Amanda, if you sincerely apologize for your misconduct.''

''Oh, I do, my lady,'' Amanda assured her, ''and, moreover, I am truly, truly sorry for involving Lady Josephine.''

''And you regret having attended that horrible mill?'' Lady Ainsworth asked, scanning her face for any sign of dissembling.

Amanda crossed her fingers behind her back and mustered a full measure of earnestness into her voice. ''Very much so, Lady Ainsworth.'' She dropped her head contritely, acting the penitent to perfection. Josie pressed her lips together and forced back the laugh that was rising into her throat.

Lady Ainsworth tilted Amanda's chin with her chubby finger while Amanda fluttered her eyelids and swallowed in a quite believable performance of suppressing tears, although her eyes remained dry.

''We shall say no more about the deed,'' Lady Ainsworth promised, quite puffed up with her magnanimity. ''Come now, I will present you to Lord and Lady Woods, who are eager to make themselves known to you.'' Amanda knew this was only in Lady Ainsworth's imagination. The Straughns had had better than a year to make Amanda's acquaintance and had not chosen to do so.

The obdurate gossipers sighed with disappointment as Josie and Amanda with linked arms trooped after Lady Ainsworth.

Ernestine, who had hoped to see the merchant's daughter and her disreputable father banished from the assembly forever by Lady Ainsworth, was let down and sulked visibly. Geoffrey and Mr. Wayne glowed when it became apparent the lively Miss Lofton would remain safely in their midst.

When Lady Ainsworth presented Amanda to Lady Woods, Ernestine smiled superciliously and offered the merchant's daughter a limp hand. Her eyes were envious as they scanned the gold Oriental-silk gown. Amanda bobbed a careless superficial curtsy in deference to social custom, flatly uninterested in Rance's sister-in-law.

Lord Woods inspected Amanda through his ruby-studded quizzing glass fastened to a black silk cord. Leonard pronounced Rance a poor stick for not having offered for the merchant's daughter as Leonard had advised him to do. Her smashing figure was shown to advantage in the smart gown, and she was darned attractive. Ernestine boiled as her husband's eyes lagged on the full curve of creamy breasts at the low neckline.

Oblivious of his wife's disapproval, Leonard deliberately prolonged his conversation with Amanda. He ignored his wife's repeated glares. On another night Amanda would have indulged him, but his presence was a reminder Rance had jilted her and left her to deal with Lady Ainsworth on her own. Aware she was committing a social blunder by inquiring about an unmarried man who was not a connection, she was unable to curb her need to know. "Where is Rance this evening?" she blurted out to Lord Woods.

Unnerved by Amanda's indiscreet query, Lady Ainsworth's hand flew to her mouth. Lord Ainsworth, who initially guffawed, hurriedly covered his mouth with his hand at his wife's scathing glance. Josie's heart sank into her shoes, and Evan Whitaker gnashed his uneven teeth. Ernestine's thin eyebrows zoomed up at the social gaffe, reinforcing her sentiments that a merchant's daughter had no business being received in polite society.

Leonard, throughly enchanted with her, appeared to be the only one unaffected by her inquiry into Rance's whereabouts.

"My brother left town on a personal matter this afternoon. I have no idea when he intends to return to us. Rance is rather secretive about his affairs, I'm afraid."

Ernestine lifted her toplofty nose haughtily. "True, Mr. Straughn does not always have the courtesy to confide in us, as Lord Woods has told you, Miss Lofton. Knowing his love of the cards, I imagine he sought out a game where the stakes are more interesting than those he would find here at the assembly." She sniffed audibly. "You seem to be well acquainted with my brother-in-law, Miss Lofton."

Josie, mercifully, cut off Amanda's reply by imploring her fiancé, "Evan, stand up with Amanda. You haven't danced with her in an age."

"Well, yes, yes, of course," Evan replied, nonplused at the abrupt, rather suspect command.

Amanda slid her hand through Evan's crooked arm and allowed him to lead her onto the dance floor for a quadrille.

Josie diverted the attention from Amanda with an innocuous question, and soon the conversation among the party was taking on a normal tone. However, Ernestine made a mental note to grill Leonard later about Rance's association with the forward Miss Lofton and ring a peal over her husband for his liberal attention to the merchant's daughter. Leonard, on the other hand, wondered if Rance had not, after all, secretly taken his advice to propose marriage to Miss Lofton to alleviate his financial burdens. His brother had come into money recently. Could this windfall have relieved him of the necessity to take the drastic step of matrimony with a socially inferior woman, and now Miss Lofton was distraught because he had cried off?

As soon as Amanda and Mr. Whitaker joined a set, the curate voiced a longtime concern brought to the fore by Amanda's behavior. "Miss Lofton . . . Amanda, Josephine is very fond of you, but I worry that you have little regard for conventions. I want her to be happy. It's my primary concern, of course. But as a clergyman, I also have to maintain a certain decorum as does she—"

"Evan," Amanda interrupted, "I shall never entangle Josie in another imbroglio, I promise you. I honor the closeness we had, for she was as dear to me as a birth sister rather than sister in friendship. Believe me, you shall never again have cause to criticize our comradeship."

"I sincerely hope not, Amanda," he said, his voice a whit dubious as the two of them were separated by the steps dictated by the dance. They came back together for an allemande, and for the remainder of the set their conversation was sparse. As Evan escorted her back to the Castleberry party, Amanda spied Daniel at the door of the ballroom. She made her farewells.

"My papa's leg is bothering him this evening," she claimed. "It's best we make an early evening of it."

She hurried to Daniel's side, where he had been watching her cross the dance floor.

"I see you have been reclaimed by the Castleberrys," he applauded.

Amanda's eyes flashed. "He left me to my own devices. I had to face the Castleberrys alone." Pernicious wishes for the disposal of Rance Straughn filled her mind. "Take me home, Papa, please."

"Of course," Daniel said, offering her his arm.

Jeffries was disconcerted by the unaccustomed contentious voices of his master and young mistress as he opened the front door to admit them to the entrance hall.

"I would think you would be perfectly satisfied! After all, 'All's well that end's well,' Amanda," Daniel quoted.

"How can you defend him?" she retorted. "His conduct is insupportable!"

"I am not defending him; far from it, dear child, but he may have had a legitimate reason for not having attended the dance. I am merely cautioning you not to jump to conclusions."

"Humph," Amanda grumbled. "I told you what his sister-in-law said. Gambling is not a legitimate reason. He's just up to his old tricks again. I hate him. He is an insufferable reprobate, and hellfire is too good for him!"

Daniel hobbled into the library after Amanda and closed the door against the curious servant, taking the spirited discussion from Jeffries' ears into private quarters.

"Harsh words, Amanda," Daniel declared, a trifle captious. "Why fuss so about Straughn? You were reunited with Lady Josephine and welcomed back into the bosom of the Castleberry clan. The man's presence was not needed to achieve your ends."

"Really, Papa! It is the outside of enough that you are partisan to him! And against your own daughter too!" Amanda fumed.

"Mandy," he coaxed, reaching out a hand to her. She backed away from him. "I am not siding with Mr. Straughn. If he merely reneged on his promise to be at the assembly for some frivolous reason, indeed that would be unconscionable. But I think he is an honorable man and would not behave in such a rag-mannered way."

"Papa, I do not understand you. You once despised him and held him in small regard. Now you defend him when he has insulted me. I shall not discuss that . . . that knave. I can see you are not my friend tonight. Good night to you, Papa." Amanda, head held high, flounced from the room.

Daniel let her go and sank into his favorite chair. For all his blandishments and attempts to distract her and force her to focus on the positive aspects of the evening, he knew Amanda had not donned her most beautiful gown and spent hours on an elegant coiffure to gain Lady Ainsworth's approbation. Dash it all, Straughn had let her down. Amanda was correct on another score; notwithstanding his denials, he had become a supporter of Straughn's. He had no recollection when the transformation occurred, but, slowly he had decided Amanda's inheritance could fall into worse hands than those of his erstwhile adversary. His belated willingness to sanction a union between the young aristocrat and his daughter would be in vain, he knew, unless Straughn's reason for disappointing Amanda was undeniably meritorious, and she could come to trust him again.

* * *

Rance reined in his horse and sprang from the saddle to the graveled drive in front of the assembly hall. A footman raced to his side, calling "Groom" into the darkness. A stableman, his knit cap pushed back on unruly brown locks, materialized from the shadows and snatched the reins.

He tugged his forelock civilly. "Evenin', Mr. Straughn. You want me to walk 'im? The dance is near over."

"No, Spence. There's an extra shilling in it for you if you rub him down. He's had a hard ride."

Rance leapt onto the portico and burst through the door, nearly upending Squire Samuels, who was waiting just inside for his carriage to be brought around to the drivepath before collecting his family members. Rance murmured an apology and steadied the squire by solidly gripping his plump shoulders. Rance's mud-caked boots and travel-stained clothes drew a snort from the squire.

"I say, Straughn, you ain't properly attired for a dance. I shouldn't go in there if I were you," he warned. "The thing's nearly over. You can wait here. If it's your brother you seek, his lordship has already departed, and . . ." The squire's voice trailed off and his dark brows knit into a mark of disfavor. Mr. Straughn had heedlessly vanished through the doors to the ballroom.

Rance remained at the edge of the dance floor for a matter of seconds and scanned the dancers forming the squares for a quadrille. Some of the depleted company scrutinized his disheveled appearance inquisitively. His own eyes paused in the vicinity where Josie Castleberry stood beside Evan Whitaker in the company of three other couples waiting for the small orchestra to begin playing for the final dance. He made a beeline across the floor, elbowing waiting dancers from his path, and reached Josie's side just as the orchestra began playing.

Josie performed her *chain des dames* with Rance at her heels. "Really, Straughn, this is most irregular," Evan Whitaker protested, but Rance ignored him.

"Josie, was Amanda here tonight?" he asked.

"She left better than a half hour ago," Josie told him without missing a step.

"Thanks, little one," he said, squeezing her arm. Mr. Whitaker gave him a black look more for his affectionate liberties toward Josie than for his interfering with the dance. The clergyman opened his mouth to make an objection, but Rance with long strides was already crossing the floor, where he threw several allemandes into disarray before he marched through the door to the vestibule.

Outside on the portico Rance took a thin cigar a solicitor had given him earlier in the day from his pocket and removed the wrapper. A footman sprang forward with a taper he had ignited from a flambeaux and offered him a light. Rance thanked him. With the glowing cigar in his hand, he strolled in the direction of the stable that temporarily housed his horse and away from the side of the building where the coachmen were lined up to take up their passengers. He leaned against a tree, relishing the mild September night. Only the red glow of the cigar in the darkness revealed his presence.

For the next twenty minutes his peace was shattered by the grinding wheels of the carriages, slamming doors, gruff male voices, and piercing orders shouted by an ostler directing traffic as the assembly patrons left for home. The hall went dark, and the more cacophonous sounds faded away. Finally the last human noises—the chatter of the servants hired for the dance—drifted into the distance when in twos and threes the hirelings walked to their various lodgings in the village. The groom who had stabled Kelly-too approached Rance, an arc of light around him from the lantern he carried.

"The stallion's saddled and ready to go, Mr. Straughn."

"Thanks, Spence. I might just walk him home." He reached in his pocket and by the groom's light counted out the stableman's fee and added the promised shilling. Spence touched his cap and turned to follow his peers down the road. If he had a perfectly healthy horse, he wouldn't act all queer-in-the-attic like Mr. Straughn and walk four miles when he could ride.

Rance flipped away the cigar and breathed in the cool air. Above him a crescent moon hung lazily in a blue-black sky studded with sparkling stars. Everyone was gone, but he was reluctant to move. He did not want to return to Willowwoods yet. The excitement of this day had now worn itself into a euphoria. He thought of the money had won while milling, which he had prudently invested. He had expected to live economically on the proceeds, while keeping alert for any opportunity to increase his investments once he and Leonard had squared his father's accounts. But now . . .

His hand fondled the paper in his pocket, a draft on a London bank which the lawyer had advanced him. The sum was sufficient to wipe out his father's debt. He would turn the draft over to Leonard in the morning.

A frisson of the same exhilaration that had gladdened his heart earlier in the day touched his spine. He removed his pocket watch but could not make out the numbers in the darkness. Today was his twenty-fifth birthday. Tomorrow he would call at Rook Manor, confer with Daniel Lofton, and secure Amanda's forgiveness. He strolled toward the stable with a languid gait to collect his horse and walk the four miles to Willowwoods. He wanted to finalize in his mind the plans he had expeditiously formulated during the last few hours.

Chapter 16

Amanda stepped from the sitting room that adjoined her bedroom onto the balcony and stretched catlike, relishing the unseasonably mild afternoon. She surveyed the garden below and decided the pink roses in their final bloom would make a cheerful arrangement in the jasper vase beside her bed. She would fix a bouquet for her papa and place it in the library as a peace offering. At breakfast Amanda had been pettish, suffering from the lingering ill humor brought on by Rance having failed to appear at the dance after bewitching her into believing her benefaction was uppermost in his mind. It was crushing to have to admit he was capable of cavalierly leaving her to face the whim of Lady Ainsworth alone. Had matters, undirected by Rance, not taken a positive turn, today Amanda could be facing social ruin. And all because of him.

She squinted against the bright sun and shaded her eyes when she caught sight of a black horse and a tall rider appearing around the bend of the drivepath near the road. Her heart fluttered erratically as he cantered closer. Afraid he might look up toward the balcony and catch her watching him, she scurried into the sitting room.

"I won't receive him," she pledged aloud to the empty, sun-filled room. "If he thinks he can turn me up sweet after his shabby treatment, he has another thing coming!"

She moved into the bedroom and, contrarily, reviewed her toilette in the cheval glass, straightening the white Chantilly lace collar of her cherry-red dress nervously, fluffing her brown hair, and pinching her cheeks to rouge them. She would send Rance packing without a word . . . no, first she would set his ears ablaze.

Amanda flung open the door to intercept her Brutus in the hall below before Jeffries came to summon her. When she reached the stairs, the butler was already setting Rance's hat on the hall table and the library door was just closing. She flopped down on the top step of the staircase, frustrated at having been foiled from using the clever, deliciously scathing set-downs that had been popping into her head.

Rance, she decided, was apologizing for last night, and her father, in his present magnanimous transformation, no doubt was readily accepting his harebrained excuse. Her rounded chin was propped on her hands. Her elbows rested on her knees, and her stony eyes were riveted on the library door. Ten minutes later she was still in the same position. He was taking an eternity to make his excuses.

"Much good it will do him," she grumbled to a house cat that passed her on its way to the kitchen for a saucer of milk. "He can crawl on his knees in contrition from here to the village, but I shan't be moved," Amanda vowed with a toss of her head as the cat's raised tail disappeared around the corner.

Jeffries came into view in the hallway beneath her. She craned her neck without success to see into the library, when he opened the door. The butler came out almost immediately and disappeared down the hall, reappearing shortly with a silver tray laden with a decanter of Madeira, two wine goblets, and a plate of cook's best wine biscuits.

When the butler once again left the library, he moved down the hall with purposeful steps. Amanda drummed on her knee with the flat of her hand. Papa may have become gullible where Rance was concerned, but she was not going to be duped again.

Her line of thought came to a halt as Jeffries appeared below her with a sheaf of papers stuffed into a green folder. "Those papers have to do with estate business," Amanda whispered to herself. Why would Papa be discussing Rook Manor with Rance? Only one sensible reason came to mind. Rance was representing Lord Woods concerning a problem along the borders between the two properties. Papa had had a disagreement with the Straughns before about the property lines near the overlook. He and Lord Woods had settled that dispute amicably. Something new must have cropped up.

Amanda felt deflated as she inattentively watched Jeffries return to the servants' wing. Rance hadn't come to apologize at all. If that had been his purpose, he would have come directly to her, not troubled her father. It had been nonsensical for her to believe Rance would call on her father to ask him to intercede. Rance didn't care a fig that he had abandoned her at the dance. He had come as Leonard's lackey to conduct business, not to beg forgiveness. She had been witlessly perched there for better than half an hour, deluding herself that Rance Straughn was sensible to her feelings.

Heartsick, she rose sluggishly from her aerie, intending to creep back to her room, but the library door opened and Rance and Daniel stepped into the hall, exchanging pleasantries with newfound camaraderie. Daniel nudged Rance and inclined his head toward Amanda.

"Come down, daughter," he called genially.

Amanda paused, torn between showing her displeasure by disobeying him and her curiosity. The latter propelled her down the stairs. Amanda's suspicious eyes fastened on Rance's crooked grin. He looked cock-a-hoop.

"Amanda," he acknowledged with twinkling eyes, lifting her rigid hand to his warm lips. Childishly, she snatched her hand away and tucked it behind her back.

Daniel laughed. "We'll have champagne in the drawing room when you return with her, Rance," he said, closing the door to his sanctuary and leaving the young people alone in the hall.

Amanda was perplexed by the enigmatic reference to taking champagne with him . . . after returning from where? No matter how cozy Rance and her father had become, she was determined to make Rance pay for deserting her the previous night.

"Come, love, we're going for a horseback ride," Rance dictated in a tone that brooked no refusal.

"Not now! Not ever!" she hurled at him willfully.

"You won't regret it, sweetheart," he cajoled, retaining his high spirits.

"Don't call me sweetheart," she ordered, and launched into a would-be tirade, but did not get past "You are the most . . ." for he put a finger to her lips.

"Shh, no more now." He engulfed her hand in his and pulled her after him as he strode toward the front door.

Her inability to unhinge his good humor annoyed her. She dug her heels into the marble floor, but her kid slippers slid along without impeding her progress. He chuckled maddeningly at her childish tactic.

"Stop being recalcitrant," he said with a grin.

"I don't have on a riding habit," she protested stubbornly.

"No, need. I'll take you up with me on Kelly," he countered, tugging her down the front steps toward the black horse.

"That's scandalous!" she retorted, prolonging the battle. "A man and woman riding together on one horse! I won't behave so ruinously." But he scooped her up in his arms and deposited her in the saddle, flinging himself up behind her. He locked both arms around her and held her close.

Considering the prize position she found herself in, her wounded ego flagged. "Rance, at least tell me where you are taking me," she said.

"To the overlook. When we arrive there, my sweet, I shall satisfy you in every way." She turned her head to glance back up at him at the suggestive remark. He raised a quizzical brow at her suspicious look.

Amanda leaned back against his hard chest, her mind tumbling quickly through the dearth of possibilities for Rance's secretive behavior. Only one fit the circumstances. He was about to propose. His liberal use of endearments, his carrying her off to a special spot, and his tête-à-tête with her father, which culminated in the offer of champagne, no doubt, to toast the union, were sure signs. Well, she would show him what his high-handed methods would get him! She would refuse him. Her mouth quirked with a happy smile. Refuse him, indeed! What stuff! Amanda wiggled against him in her delight, sending a tinge of desire through his taut body. He tightened his grip on her.

"What did Papa say to you?" she asked, unable to quell her curiosity until she and Rance reached the overlook.

"Let me see. For one, he asked me to call him Daniel."

"Are you serious?" Amanda trilled, her brown eyes like saucers.

"Perfectly."

"What brought that about?"

"I'll tell you in good time. We're almost there."

Rance reined in the stallion next to the beech tree and dismounted. Amanda slid off the horse into his waiting arms. He caught her hard against him and captured her mouth beneath his. His zealous kiss delved and sought, reaching into her very soul, raising a rabid response from her. The dormant yearnings, held so long in check by both of them, exploded in frantic kissing. "My darling, my beautiful Mandy," Rance moaned as his kiss slaked.

"My love, my love," came Amanda's whispered, answering endearment against their tangent lips before the kisses resumed with renewed frenzy. Her hands raked his hair. He caressed her back and brushed her breasts with expert hands, until an inner alarm moved his hands to cup her shoulders. He drew his lips from hers and checked his emotions. His febrile breath induced a husky tone as he forced himself to regain control. "Lud, Mandy, if we go on like this, you'll be bedded before you're a bride." She went limp against his taut body, her breath labored. He gathered her tenderly into his arms and held her for a minute or more as their aggrandized senses and pulsing hearts calmed.

He placed an arm around her shoulders and led her still quivering to the beech tree, noticing irrelevantly that the leaves were yellowing. They sank to the grass, where he settled with his back against the familiar silvery bark with her lounging within the crook of his arm. Drained emotionally, Amanda cuddled against him while he stroked her soft brown hair.

Amanda was the first to break the languid silence. "What business did you have with Papa?"

"I bought some land," he said, deliberately vague, planning to savor the slow unraveling.

"What land?" she asked.

"This," he drawled, sweeping the overlook with his hand.

"The overlook?" Amanda cried, incredulous.

"The overlook, the field down to the river, the spinney and the meadow behind, and a few acres besides. This morning Leonard committed to sell me the fields on the other side of the river up to the trees this side of the village. All you see now, my love, I have contracted to buy. Only . . . Daniel's promise to sell is conditional. The condition being you marry me. Will you?"

"What a lovely proposal!" Amanda scoffed. "Probably hard for you to grasp, Rance, but it falls short of what I have dreamed of all my life."

She and Josie had often practiced ideal proposals. This lowering, devoid-of-romance request from the man she loved insanely, whom she had a moment before allowed to take more liberties with her than she would ever have believed she would grant a man before her nuptials, resembled a business deal more than an offer of marriage.

Rance brushed his lips over her hair, smiled, but admitted to himself he had bungled. A woman had the right to expect gallantry in this situation. He paused and groped for the words to rectify his error. "Do you recall, Amanda, the other day when you asked me why I did not go to America?"

"Yes, you answered with some fustian about Indians."

"And that is, of course, what it was, fustian. I could not go to America because I could not bear to have an ocean between us, sweetheart, for I love you to distraction." But he could not refrain from adding with a chuckle, "Does that satisfy you, or must I grovel?"

Amanda wrinkled her nose at him. "Yes, just a bit," she said, holding a thumb and finger an inch apart.

He raised himself up onto his knees, clasped her hands between his, and with a mock lovesick expression declared, "Amanda, I love you. Will you marry me?"

"Idiot! Yes!" she cried, pushing him back into a seated position and snuggling against him again. "But, Rance, you were at Willowwoods a week before I even knew. Why didn't you come to see me and tell me how you felt?"

The amusement vanished from his eyes. "I couldn't," he reponded with a throatiness. "I was in a dilemma, Mandy. The only funds I had were from the investments I made from what I earned as a pugilist. From that money I felt honor bound to assist Leonard with his obligations to clear our father's debts. Had I gone to America, I would have sent Len money when I prospered. He subsidized me for nearly a year while my father was still alive. I couldn't ignore that, even though had I been aware that Papa was passing on money that was rightly Len's, I never would have accepted it. Nevertheless, I had done so. Making good was leaving me thin in the pocketbook. The most I could have offered you were rented rooms in London and a penurious existence. I couldn't ask you to live far below what you have been accustomed to all your life."

"Had you but told me you loved me, I would have accepted you, darling, whether you had a farthing or not. We needn't have merely endured; we could have lived famously on my money."

Rance nibbled on her ear. "I think we both know that would never have worked, my love. Don't think I didn't turn the problem over endlessly in my mind."

"But, darling, where did you get the funds to buy this land?" Amanda asked, puzzled. Rance shifted her a little away from him as he got up.

"Wait right here," he said. He walked over to the black stallion, unstrapped the fastener on his saddlebag, removed a wooden box, and carried it to Amanda. He lifted the lid and tipped the receptacle toward her. She gasped in delight at the four porcelain British soldiers resting on white satin. A shaft of sunlight spearing through the branches of the beech tree glinted off the troopers' vibrant scarlet coats, blue trousers, and gold epaulets.

"Aunt Agnes!" she squealed. "But how?"

"The solicitor from the village summoned me—it's where I was bound when I met you on Wednesday—and served me with a paper which requested that I appear the following day in Hertfordshire at Michaels and Grafton, my late aunt's business advisers. I told you the old lady was eccentric. She lived by herself with one or two servants in the cottage all those years, while the astute investments her father had made for her grew with the interest reinvested year after year. She lived comfortably, but spent far below what she could have. Aunt Agnes left me a rather stupendous legacy to be presented to me on my twenty-fifth birthday. By the terms of her will, I was not to be told before the red-letter day, which was yesterday. Aunt Agnes, Mandy, has outdone Daniel Lofton in the presentation of birthday gifts!"

Rance had a resurgence of the thanksgiving he had experienced when he had ridden Kelly-too home from Hertfordshire the previous day. "The soldiers were also part of this belated bequest, bless her." The gesture of willing him the porcelain troopers, which had fascinated the boy even when he had grown into the man, had touched him in some indefinable way even more than the magnanimous monetary legacy.

"Rance, how lovely," Amanda said. "That's why you weren't at the dance."

"I had no idea before I left Willowwoods of the natal gift awaiting me. I expected to be back in time for the assembly. But I returned too late to catch you. You had already gone home. Aren't you ashamed for all the black things you called me?" He smirked.

"I never said a word to you!" she defended herself.

"I have a vivid imagination." He laughed. "Now, Mandy, we can build our house right here," Rance said triumphantly.

"On the overlook?" Amanda became excited. "Oh, Rance! It's the perfect spot!" She hugged herself, pulled him to his feet, and danced him around the plateau, outlining happily to him the rooms and the directions each would face. He snatched her to him and with a fatuous grin on his face savored the satisfaction of being the agent of her rapture.

"Do you think Papa will mind if we don't live at Rook Manor?" she asked, solicitous of her father's expectations.

Rance let out a guffaw that echoed through the valley. "No, my love, he won't mind a bit. Your father is a relatively young man. If you have been counting on Rook Manor as an inheritance, Amanda, you may be disappointed, you know. He has his eye on a pretty Bristol widow who is young enough to present Daniel with an heir."

Amanda giggled at the picture of her father cradling a newborn child in his arms. "I do hope he has a son," she said generously. "It's Mrs. Carlyle, isn't it?"

"I believe it is her name. You guessed his intentions toward her, then?"

Amanda inclined her head and smiled. "Papa can be obvious when he thinks he's being circumspect. We don't have to wait until the house is built to marry, do we?"

"I think not!" Rance stated emphatically. "As a matter of fact, Daniel and I have worked it out already." She looked at him, eyebrows raised. Papa and Rance had been busy during the half hour. "Daniel plans to reside in Bristol until our house is completed. He confided to me he wants to rejoin the social whirl there and court his little widow properly. You and I shall occupy Rook Manor after we make our vows and have a wedding trip, of course. You'll have to teach me, for he expects us to run Rook Manor together in his absence."

Rance stood behind Amanda, his arms wrapped around her on the spot that would be their front portico. The lovers surveyed the valley that would greet them each morning of their lives. The scene before them was a Constable painting sprung to life.

"I know how you feel about not wanting to take any of my money, but, darling," Amanda said earnestly, "it is customary for a bride to bring a dowry and certain necessities for a home to a marriage."

"I shan't eschew your money completely, Mandy. I am not such a cork-brain." Rance kept his voice even, but his sea-blue eyes were dancing merrily. "You are free to supply the linens and dishes . . . drapes and carpets . . ." She released herself from his grip, turned to him, hands on her hips, and gazed at him warily. Carpets? she wondered. He continued. "A few dozen chairs, pots and pans, wallpaper, several beds, a case of port wine and French brandy . . ." He no longer fought to maintain a sober countenance, but grinned joyously. Amanda gave him a fierce shove in the chest. He pretended to fall over, snatching her arms and pulling her shrieking down with him onto the ground, where the two tumbled in the grass and giggled like children. "A herd of sheep . . . a sack of flour, a pianoforte, a hall clock . . ." he shouted until he allowed her to pin him down. Rance tugged Amanda to him, his eyes narrowed with renewed desire, but she was the one who silenced his outrageous list with her lips.

ABOUT THE AUTHOR

Alice Holden lives with her family in Green Valley, Arizona. *An Unconventional Miss* is her first Zebra Regency romance. Alice loves to hear from readers, and you may write to her c/o Zebra Books. Please include a self-addressed stamped envelope if you wish a response.